ETERNAL TRACES

Eternal Traces

Shonda Brock

iUniverse, Inc.
Bloomington

Eternal Traces

iUniverse books may be ordered through booksellers or by contacting:

iUniverse
1663 Liberty Drive
Bloomington, IN 47403
www.iuniverse.com
1-800-Authors (1-800-288-4677)

ISBN: 978-1-4620-3637-0 (sc)
ISBN: 978-1-4620-3636-3 (hc)
ISBN: 978-1-4620-3635-6 (ebk)

Library of Congress Control Number: 2011960048

Printed in the United States of America

iUniverse rev. date: 11/15/2011

Dedicate

I dedicate this book to my daughter.
Follow your heart's desires.

Acknowledgement

I would like to thank my family and friends for their continued love and support throughout this massive project. I would not have been able to complete this venture without my husband Carlton's support. *I love you.*

I thank all four of my children Sport, Scooter, Pappy and the Diva for their creative ideas and inspirations. I dare not forget a special shout-out to my personal fan-club/editors mom, Raise and Kelly.

I must give Kelly special thanks for going beyond the call of duty.

Chapter 1

Why is it when death is near, the weather is never good? Nitocris thought to herself. It was so hot that it gave the fear in her mouth a sweet, raw flavor. She was tickled to feel any emotion. It had been a month since she had felt anything other than anger and revenge. She knew it was the end. It was only fitting her body matched her soul; she'd been dead on the inside for nearly four weeks. Nitocris was nothing more than an empty shell of hatred, the same hatred that had blinded her and allowed her to be used as a vessel to kill with no regard or mercy. Little did they know, they were doing Queen Nitocris a favor by putting an end to her physical being.

"Queen Nitocris, pledge your loyalty!" Smenkhkara, the pharaoh, demanded. Nitocris stared, searching his face for any reasonable clue that justified all of the deception. She stared until the sweat dripping down from her forehead stung her eyes. It forced her to blink. She opened her eyes in the direction of her sister, Nefertiti, whose body lay beaten and lifeless on the floor. Defeat began to emerge and take root. Nitocris now realized that the sweet, raw flavor in her mouth was not fear but her own blood. The blood was backing up into her mouth from internal bleeding.

"I will not marry you," she said trying to sustain defiance in her dying voice, "and I will not pledge my loyalty to your kingdom. You have no honor, and you have condemned everything you've touched. You will contend with the Creator for your soul. Upon death, your soul must weigh less than the feather of truth. We both know that you have told too many lies and caused too many deaths. A hundred men could not bear the weight of it. Your soul will never be permitted to enter Heaven. You will never take human form again."

Nitocris felt the blood pooling in her mouth, forcing her to choke on her last words. She refused to give the pharaoh the dignity to hear her cough in pain, so she spit the blood out onto the sandy ground before his feet.

"There will be no alliance with the Nubians. This truth will remain. The only thing I can pledge is that you will die by my hand. I will send you to the Creator to be judged, on my honor." Queen Nitocris saw the pharaoh signal the guard to her left. She heard a *swoosh*—a clean cutting sound and felt a small breeze. It was over; her end had finally come, and she was free from physical form to live again.

Chapter 2

Another rainy day, thought Meryt as she stared out her office window, dreaming of something she couldn't fully remember. Her mind was always taken by foolish thoughts and dreams. The stories were never complete, only fragments of lost memories disappearing like smoke over a small fire that had been recently extinguished. She had had them all her life. Sometimes it was the same dream or a fragment of an image repeating itself over and over, similar to feelings of déjà vu, like walking into a new space knowing she'd been there before. Meryt couldn't remember the exact dream, but she knew it was the same. She felt it in her soul.

Meryt used to believe that her dreams meant something. Perhaps the dreams were a premonition to her future, but what future? Meryt knew the dreams came from an ancient time and nothing seemed to be related to the twentieth century. Her mother thought the stories were a product of an overactive imagination and too much TV. Meryt's mother had plans for her daughter's life, and foolish stories were not a part of it. Meryt's life already had a direction: graduate from college and go to medical school or law school. Those were her two choices, and she was grateful that someone cared enough to give choices.

So medical school it was. She was not bad at it. The truth was, she loved biology and science. In Meryt's senior year of high school, her advanced chemistry teacher, Mr. O, single-handedly caused Meryt to fall in love with science and made it, in his words, "Outstanding." But there were always exceptions to rules, and Meryt's first-year biology professor in college made her question her IQ as well as her reading and comprehension levels. Meryt imagined the professor was sent to derail her from graduation but the professor failed. She could not stop Meryt's yearning for science and the unknown.

Understanding the human psyche was second nature to Meryt. She could look into a stranger's eyes and within a few seconds understand their pain. She was a religious person, and she believed in the church's teaching that every person had special gifts. One of Meryt's gifts was the power to see injury whether it was a broken soul or a broken bone, she could just sense it. One might say that broken hearts were her specialty. There was no better choice for Meryt than medical school and three years of cardiology by way of Uncle Sam.

Meryt was not the typical cardiologist. She was forty-something, wishing she were still thirty-something. Being brown skinned, her nickname in college was *Brown Sugar*. She never liked the nickname, but it had stuck. Meryt had an odd color for an African American. Her skin had the appearance of brown sugar, constantly shifting and reflecting brown, yellow, and red granules. She kept her hair long, mainly because it was easy to keep in a ponytail. A ponytail was Meryt's constant savior for midnight calls to the emergency room. She had run track in high school, in college, and for Uncle Sam's special fitness program, and to this day Meryt maintained her shape by running. After so many years of running, sometimes her knees tried to boycott the program, but they usually got back on board when the scale started to tip too high.

This day, like many others, Meryt had spent too much time gazing out the window during her break. A sound at the door caused her to focus, bringing her out of her daydreams and back to the present where she was sitting in her small, private office space. Meryt had finally earned a corner office with a window inside the main hospital at Saint Catherine's; versus the private office she once had to pay rental fees for located across the street. But who knew the new space would literally be a corner? She had made the tiny space work by adding soft beige colors on the wall, a cherrywood desk, the hospital's standard file cabinets refurbished, and a new computer. The beige office walls were bare other than certificates and degrees. Meryt didn't believe in displaying personal pictures, especially in the workplace. Some things were just plain private.

Dr. Cindy Bloom burst into the office. Her face was a pale chalk white not her normal complexion.

"Meryt, an airplane went down. They are bringing all the survivors into the ER."

Meryt was confused by Cindy's words. They didn't make sense. What could she be talking about? Nothing like that ever happened in upstate

New York. Their town was the inaugural site for Teddy Roosevelt and was once the second-largest city in America; its steel factories and water channels had once allowed the shipping of steel and lumber to Canada, Europe, and the rest of the United States. But those years had since past and had left a ghost town filled with blocks of beautiful, vacant stone buildings and dilapidated wooden homes.

Certain kinds of events happened in upstate New York: snowstorms, yes; ice storms, yes; a few fires, because most of the buildings were vacant and were over a hundred years old, definitely yes. But plane crashes, never.

Meryt had never seen Cindy look so shaken. If there were such a "being" as an angel, it would be her. Cindy always saw the goodness in everything and never had a sour word about others. In addition to being Cindy's friend there were other benefits, her husband was the vice president and chief operations officer of the hospital. Cindy always had the inside scoop and gossip.

At that moment, the "Cindy" who burst into the office was not the Cindy that Meryt knew. She looked off.

Cindy signaled Meryt to follow, and she did. As they got closer to the ER bays, Meryt smelled the injuries before she saw them. It was a smell she was very familiar with. It was the smell of burned human flesh. What followed next were screams of pain from patients and screams from the staff shouting out orders.

Cindy and Meryt walked quickly by each bay to evaluate the total situation. The closest bay had a man with second—and third-degree burns on his left leg. Dr. Dallas Letter and two nurses attended to the man's wounds. Dallas, her red-headed friend, was a pure genius when it came to the opposite sex and medicine. And how he loved them both equally.

Meryt determined the meds were working, because the patient's screams were getting softer with each breath he took through clenched teeth. Dallas had stabilized the patient and attended to his wounds.

The next two rooms had burn injuries as well; they were being stabilized and then moved to the floor. In a few days, they would be transferred to the local burn unit.

The last room had a pregnant woman who was in her sixth month. She had a broken leg and was going into shock and delivery at the same time. Cindy and Meryt stepped into this room to relieve the physician's assistants or PAs as they were called.

They had a huge dilemma. The patient could not fully be medicated due to the pregnancy, yet they had to calm her before shock set in. Immediately, Cindy started removing fragments and damaged tissue from the open leg wound. Meryt reviewed the patient's stats; she noticed they were not adding up properly. Meryt turned to the patient, placed her hand on the patient's cheek, and began asking her simple questions: What is your name? Where are you from? Once Meryt had the patient's attention, she asked her to take slow, deep breaths, no pushing and no screaming, just calm, deep slow breaths. As the patient began to answer through the pain, Meryt saw the fear slowly leaving her face. The patient's name was Melondi Jacobs, and she was a local by way of New York City.

"Why were you traveling today?" and "Were you traveling alone?" were just a few more of the questions that Meryt asked. Finally, Meryt reassured Melondi that the baby was fine.

Meryt had learned the power of touch early in life. She knew that if she could touch a person while redirecting the conversation, she could find the root of the problem. It was a simple mind trick she had acquired while serving her country. Right now, it was working; Melondi's breathing was under control, and the contractions had slowed.

In a blink of an eye, just as Cindy set the leg, the situation changed. Melondi's pressure started to drop. Quickly following, her complexion turned a ghostly white. The anesthesiologist was calling blood pressures aloud as it continued to fall. It was a hunch, but Meryt felt it could be internal bleeding. There were no other wounds, and Melondi's cardiac rhythm remained within normal range. Still, Melondi stopped her breathing exercise and went limp all within three seconds. Her heart rate, which had finally leveled, suddenly slowed down below normal rate. Meryt quickly snatched the hospital sheet off the patient's body. She had to find the new source of Melondi's problem.

There it was. Melondi had another mark on her body. It was low on the left side of her stomach: a small, purple, pen point leading down her leg to a hematoma, a huge deep bruise.

Meryt announced, "She's bleeding internally."

Meryt immediately asked the nurse to prep the area, so she could lance the exact spot. Using her fingers, she opened the wound site and created a pocket by spreading two fingers apart. Blood spilled everywhere. Melondi's femoral vein had a hole in it the size of the top of an ink pen and was gushing out deoxygenated blood with each pump of her heart.

6

Cindy and the nurses immediately opened gauze packages and started counting them off one by one, using some of the gauze to wipe up the blood and stacking the rest around the wound site.

Meryt was able to push her fingers in and grab the vein. She pinched it off and pulled it out.

"Yes, this is our culprit," she said happily. The vessel continued to pour blood onto the floor and all over the front of her clothes. Meryt poured a liquid bandage solution onto the site, which temporarily held while they prepped for surgery. "Get her blood type and have six bags waiting in the OR." Meryt knew they could stabilize her, if time stayed on their side. Melondi should be able to keep the baby until its natural due date.

Tab, the head nurse, called the OR and told them of their new patient. Meryt said she would follow, but first she had to whisk through the ER bays, to ensure the staff had everything under control. As she ran through, Meryt noticed that there weren't a lot of patients, considering a plane had crashed.

Where are all the patients? She wondered. Then she remembered Cindy's statement: it was only the survivors who were brought to the emergency room. That left an even bigger hole in her gut. Meryt yelled at Dallas, "I'm off to OR with a pregnant lady with a bleed. I'm taking Cindy. I'll send her back when the patient is stable." He winked, and Meryt was off to the OR.

Cindy and Meryt worked on Melondi for three hours. Ten bags of O positive, fifty gauzes, and a cast and Melondi was good perhaps, as good as new in a few days if recovery went well.

When Cindy and Meryt walked out of surgery, they quickly remembered the circumstances that had brought Melondi Jacobs to the hospital. She had been in a plane crash. They wondered if Melondi had family on the plane. Melondi never answered all of the questions. So who were Meryt and Cindy expecting to see or going to talk to when they walked out into the waiting room? They looked at each other, knowing at once what the other was thinking. Meryt asked Cindy to check the ER lounge to see if any families were waiting, while Meryt went to check the OR waiting area. As they walked through the double doors, there sat an older couple and a young man about the age of their Melondi. As Meryt walked closer, the family stood up.

They asked with glassy eyes, "Do you know the status of Melondi Jacobs?"

Meryt replied, "Yes, are you family?"

The man stated that he was her husband and that she had been traveling home from visiting her parents in New York City; these were his parents. Meryt explained that Mrs. Jacobs was out of surgery and recovering. Meryt continued, explaining the injuries and the procedure, and saying that Melondi would be available for visitors in thirty minutes. Overall, Melondi and the baby were doing well.

The look on their faces revealed more than a weight being lifted. It was as if they were witnessing the miracle of birth. They had thought the worst for their Melondi, yet here she was with her baby. Meryt had to admit that one of the perks of the job was being able to deliver good news, especially after such a bad circumstance.

The hospital staff eventually discovered that it was a small DC-9 aircraft that went down. It held thirty-two passengers and crewmembers. They thanked God that it was not a full flight. Only seventeen survived the initial crash, and Meryt and Cindy felt confident that in three months the count would go up one more to total eighteen. It was a sad day yet a day of miracles for the survivors. As hard as it was to believe, some people just walked away from the crash without a single scratch.

The story ran repeatedly throughout the day and night, adding a few more pieces to the puzzle every other hour. Attempting to land, the plane had slid off the runway into a ditch. Within a few moments it had burst into flames. Now everyone in town was waiting for the little black box to explain the last few minutes of flight. Meryt knew it was in bad taste, but she was reminded of a comedian who had asked, "How is it that they can create a black box for an aircraft that survives crashes at high and low temperatures, but auto manufacturers can't figure out how to keep a bumper on the car after a little fender bender or a little rust?"

After their shift ended, Dallas, Cindy, and Meryt communed with two PAs at the local drinking hole. It was a jazz bar, a wanna-be club called The Joint. No one really dressed up, yet from time to time the bar had good live performances. Sometimes, if the patrons had too much to drink, they would somehow find their singing voice up on the stage.

On this particular night, none of the staff were up to performing. They just sat, stared, and drank. Cindy was the first to say her time limit was up. She said her husband would be expecting her home soon. She continued, saying she owed him some wifely time.

Meryt sat there thinking, *Wifely time?*

Cindy soon left. Then there were two, Dallas and Meryt. The PAs had moved on, picking up new conversations at the bar. Dallas gave Meryt the once-over stare, the one that sent chills up a girl's spine.

Dallas and Meryt had a little something a while back, but it was over before it truly started. Meryt knew he was not the marrying type. To be honest, she wasn't the marrying type either. Anyway, it was sliced; Meryt was not in love with Dallas. He was not the one for Meryt, but she thought he could be a something, something to do while she waited for the one.

While her little something, something with Dallas was going on, he had some other something, something named Saundra, who began calling Meryt's house nightly. Meryt was mortified. She had never shared a man with another woman. It was a blow to her ego. She was seriously bruised. Plus, to add insult to injury, it was too much drama. Dallas was just a little something, something. It was supposed to be fun! Well, the fun was gone, her feelings were bruised, and Saundra was calling the house at all hours of the night. Meryt had to let this *so-called* relationship go. First, Dallas avoided her, thinking Meryt was a scorned woman, but she wasn't. Truthfully, Meryt was quickly over it because it wasn't a real relationship. If anything, she was a little angry with herself for breaking the golden rule, "Never do a little something, something with a coworker."

Now Dallas was sending her vibes, and chills began to run up and down Meryt's back. He was a hell of a kisser. Meryt could not remember the last time she had hot, tongue-kissing, stripping-your-off-clothes sex. It had been too long, and she started remembering him, his kisses, and his hands. Dallas was a true genius when it came to two things, medicine and women. He knew just how to touch a girl in the right spots.

Dallas smiled, flashing his glassy greenish-blue eyes.

"Meryt, why don't we travel down old roads again and find some new destinations?"

Just hearing his voice with its invitation made Meryt want to say, "Yes, what the hell, it's been awhile and after a day like this a little something, something sounds like a plan."

Then another tiny little voice said, *something, something with Dallas? Remember the social mess!* All Meryt could do was smile. Darn that little voice.

"Dallas, we've been down that road. I don't need to revisit it, but I do need a refill on my Jack and ginger. Thank you for the offer, but I'd rather tease you with a 'What if,'" Meryt said as she pulled his fingers that were rubbing her arm gently and kissed each one, returning the tingling favor. "Now go, get me another drink and call another friend if you want to drive down roads tonight."

He smiled as he switched position in his chair. "You know me too well. Why won't you marry me?"

Meryt shot back with a smile, "First, you never asked me; and secondly, because I know you too well."

Chapter 3

It was a new day, draped in heavy fog. The fog blinded the morning's sunrays. It looked like dusk when it was already 8:30 in the morning. The fog made it feel like an extension from the previous day. Meryt couldn't tell if it was the fog or her headache from too many Jack and gingers from the night before, but she felt like she lost track of time. Meryt felt as if she had never left the hospital.

As she conducted rounds, Meryt thought, *Maybe I'll check on Melondi. I know she'll give me the power to smile today.*

Needless to say, the crash had left a black cloud on Niagara. Time has a way of changing things. Niagara used to be a huge honeymoon destination; to see one of The Seven Forgotten Natural Wonders of the World, Niagara Falls better known as The Falls. People had traveled there from all over the world. Some tested their survival chances and went over The Falls in a barrel. For the most part, other than an occasional suicide attempt, things were calm. Nothing like the plane crash had ever happened there before. Meryt often wondered why, because The Falls are the main source of electricity for five states and the second-largest fresh-water supply in the United States. Back in her army days, they would have called The Falls a high-payoff target.

It was a nice tight community with a little more than fifty thousand residents. It seemed that everyone had known someone on that disastrous flight. It was either a miracle or a sad incident, based on who you spoke to. The horror of the crash lingered in the air, and the air became stagnant. The plane crash added a new level of bleakness to the winter months that were rapidly approaching in the hearts of the locals. It made for a long October and not a good start to the holidays.

The days continued to roll on; everyone whispered about it, yet no one talked aloud at least not openly. The morning had been quiet and so far eventless. Meryt sat at her desk, not looking out the window but at her calendar. A friend in Virginia had requested a meeting. She needed to take a few days off again, but this wasn't the right time to leave. Her staff had not gotten their wind back since the plane crash.

"First or second through the tenth of December, hmmm," Meryt pondered, when a knock at the door broke her train of thought. But before she could look up, Karl Bloom, Cindy's husband, came in with two new doctors.

"Dr. Meryt Brownstone, I would like you to meet Dr. Fritz Daniels and Dr. Rene Daniels. They are brothers who have just transferred in from the West Coast. If you recall, I told you they would be coming soon to help out the team." Karl looked back and forth during the introductions. "I need you to be a team player and show them the ropes and get them quickly up to speed."

Meryt's single thought during the entire introduction was what happened to asking before entering a room? That would be the purpose of a closed door. What happened to common respect? Their unannounced interuption immediately left a bad taste in her mouth. She took a deep breath, thinking, *Let me fix my face; this has nothing to do with the new guys, it's just Karl needing to learn respect.*

As she looked up, Dr. Daniels said, "Just call me Fritz. I read your research paper. I would to love see more of your research materials. Karl said that you specialize in patients with heart failure. He said you've had some success with remodeling both ventricle chambers?"

Meryt was taken aback and a little impressed. Someone had actually read her research paper other than her mother. "Well that's not exactly true. I've been working on creating healthier hemoglobin that has the correct balance of electrolytes before they start converting bad enzyme inhibitors—therefore stopping the deadly roller-coaster ride for the heart failure patient. This synthetic hemoglobin is similar to the patient's healthy blood; it literally tricks the heart into behaving like it's healthy, preventing any remodeling. My synthetic hemoglobin is similar to a patient's blood with the mixed-cocktail drugs they are forced to take, but without the orginal side effects of drugs because it behaves like normal blood." She said all of this in two breaths while creating an imaginary pumping heart in the air with her hands.

Fritz watched in amazement, "Very interesting I have been playing with modular structure of blood. Perhaps I could help out? I would be honored to continue my trial with yours. Can I see your lab?"

Meryt closed the calendar, not sure if she were being made fun of or if she had received a compliment. "Sure."

Karl chimed in, "Great. Meryt, take over the tour, and bring them back to the administrative office to complete their paperwork so they can get their badges." Karl was gone before Meryt could agree. She wasn't certain where to begin the tour. Meryt had to take a few moments to gather her thoughts and finally looked at the two men before her. They definitely did not look like any men she had ever seen, other than on touched-up magazine covers. To say they looked gorgeous would be an understatement. Their clothes weren't anything special, but the clothes became special on them. Local stores in the Falls just didn't carry that quality of clothing. Fritz had on dark brown, almost black, dress slacks with a custom-fitted, button-down, pale eggshell shirt. His hair was salt and pepper, but mostly pepper, a little longer along his neckline, but nicely manicured. Fritz's smile was so inviting that no woman could deny him any favor. Meryt began to feel inadequately dressed as she looked down at her gray slacks and white cotton V-neck T-shirt. *Who knew?* She should have worn a silk blouse and taken down "Old Faithful" the ponytail.

Next she looked at Rene. Her heart stopped. There was no more time. There was no more air. Meryt was standing four feet away, behind her desk, but in that instant when their eyes met, she was inches away from his face. He had the most incredible face. It was masculine, yet soft. He had a strong chin line, and his hair was perfectly parted to the side as if he had just walked out of a high-end spa. He had deep piercing blue eyes, and she could see nothing but endless skies and rolling waves coming from him, inviting her into his arms. His beauty spellbound Meryt. She was no longer in the office but with him someplace else. It did not matter where, it only mattered that they were together. Her heart, which had stopped beating on its own, was now beating on his command. Her breathing was not her own, but his. Meryt had never believed in love at first sight until today. She never understood how young girls could stop in mid-action when their secret crush walked by. Yet here she was, not knowing anything about the man who stood before her, yet this heightened her desire even more to be held in his gaze and longing for his touch. Meryt had no idea how much time had passed or who was watching.

Chapter 4

"I hate ceremonies. If I'm here to protect the pharaoh and his queen, my sister Nefertiti, why do we need to put on a show? My people are well-known warriors. We do not partake in this pomp and circumstance for the Egyptians. This is a complete waste of time." Queen Nitocris shifted the sheer drape from the carrying chair while talking to her second in command, Pliny. He had always been by her side during training, and after her father died his relationship had grown into something more of a father figure.

"Behave. Your father taught you better. It is important to honor their culture." He propped up closer leaning on one arm, trying to get comfortable in the tight quarters, and said with a naughty smile, "If you think this is too much, wait until nightfall, when the true ceremony takes place. Then you will know the true definition of decadence."

Queen Nitocris returned the smile, "I sense evil in your heart. Be careful." She returned her gaze to the masses filling the streets. It was a bright, sunny day. Giza, the city of pure gold, looked beautiful. The Egyptians could build like no others.

The parade finally came to halt in front of the queen's main home. A Nubian soldier came forward and queried, "My Queen, should we carry you to the main chamber?"

"No, I can walk." Nitocris's back ached from the two-week march to Giza. She had ridden most of the way on horseback, but Pliny insisted that she use the official carrying chair once they entered the city's main gates. Nitocris insisted that if she had to ride in the carrier, he would ride with her to ensure she stayed. The servants lowered the carrier to the ground. The Nubian soldiers positioned themselves to the left and right as she and Pliny exited from the shade and coolness of carrier to the sun's powerful blaze. She blinked a few times, temporarily blinded from the sun's direct rays. Perhaps Pliny was correct in having her carried. On horseback in this sun, she would have smelled and looked like that putrid beast the camel.

Pliny was there to guide her hand to help maintain her balance. Queen Nitocris viewed the area, her eyes now fully adjusted to the sun's light and now she considered what lay before them: a series of stairs leading up to the main house. She regarded the stairs as good fortune, in hope of stretching out her back muscles, but more than that, she knew the stairs were the final obstacle she must negotiate before she saw her beautiful sister, Nefertiti. Nitocris had not seen Nefertiti since her arranged marriage to the Pharaoh of Egypt, Akhenaten. Nefertiti had left home over a year ago for the wedding that had been arranged since her birth to unite the expanding Egyptian empire to the firece Nubian Warrior Empire. Nitocris wanted to be her best not only for her sister, whom she missed dearly, but also for her father, who had passed shortly after Nefertiti left to marry. It had been her father's goal to see both kingdoms as one without war.

Nitocris wore a dress made of white fine linen with gold-threaded details along the hemline. She had on her best gold-jeweled necklace with matching cuffs. She would not be completely dressed without her matching khophesh swords. Her father had had them made especially for her several years ago. They were matching fighting swords, made of a special metal, and each had a secret second blade on the back end of each handle. With a push from her fourth finger, a six-inch blade extended or retracted. The weight of swords was light enough that a woman could swing them both simultaneously with ease, yet they were strong enough to cut through any man. The handles were perfectly fitted to each hand. By far, they were her favorites of all the swords in her collection. The swords themselves shined like gold and the handles had three small diamonds embedded on the outside, similar to the three main stars in the Orion Belt seen in the night sky above Egypt's great desert. The twin twenty-two-inch swords hung from her hips, midway down her leg, and were tied together by a golden belt.

As Pliny and Queen Nitocris approached the top step, the pharaoh's elite guard awaited. One guard stepped forward and said, "Good afternoon, Queen Nitocris, my name is Atem, and this is my brother Atum. We are to escort you and your party to the pharaoh and the queen."

Pliny released her hand so Nitocris could properly address the two brothers. Queen Nitocris bowed her head as Atem kissed her hand, and his brother, Atum, stepped forward to follow. Nitocris watched as Atum lowered his head to the back of her hand, while continuing his gaze. His piercing blue eyes never looked away from hers. His hand was cool to the touch, but what nearly dropped her to her knees were his cool lips touching her bare skin. Nitocris felt an electrical charge shoot through her body. If it were not for Atum holding her hand, Nitocris might have lost her balance. She stared for a moment, wondering, *who is this beautiful man still holding my hand with his lips still pressed against my skin?*

Chapter 5

Meryt closed her eyes to regain control of her senses. Rene was gone. "What? Oh . . . I'm sorry, Fritz. I've never been so rude . . ."

Before Meryt could finish her apology, Fritz completed her sentence. "Sorry that my brother had to leave so abruptly. I believe he had to take a call."

Meryt whispered, trying to find her voice, "How long was I staring?"

"Staring? You were not staring. You were telling us about your staff and explaining where our tour starts. Can you take me around? And afterward, can we stop by your lab?" Fritz questioned.

Meryt rubbed her hands through her hair to buy time as she continued to regain her composure. "Sure, just give me a few moments to collect myself and alert the ER staff that I'm leaving the area."

That was day one of meeting the brothers, Fritz and Rene. Fritz and Meryt hit it off well. They were a good working pair. After a few awkward moments, the rest of the day flew by. Meryt had to admit that Fritz was a nice addition to the staff. By noon, she'd noticed that Fritz had a slight English accent that intermittently morphed into something *older* or *more proper,* perhaps a different dialect. It was odd, but it was still cute. She had always enjoyed an English accent. She found it to be sexy. Meryt thought to herself, *Job well done, Karl. I forgive your rude behavior.*

Rene did not return that day. Fritz said there was a family emergency. She had been about to inquire about the type of emergency, and Rene's marital status, but then thought better of it. She figured she would probably have sounded like a giggling teenager, and Meryt had already had her teenage moment earlier. She did not desire to revisit that moment again.

The following weeks went extremely well. Fritz and Meryt worked the same shift: ten in the morning until ten at night. His specialty was hematology, the study of blood and blood diseases. He did his normal rounds but he spent most of his time in the lab. He also liked manning the emergency room. Fritz never grumbled about the long hours. He fit right into the flow of things, as if he were always a part of the staff.

Apparently, Rene had had a rather large family emergency as he had to take off the rest of the week. Fritz never really commented on it, so Meryt never pushed the subject. She only hoped and prayed that Rene's absence was not her fault. She would be embarrassed if he was married when she had all but given herself to him upon first sight. *If I were his wife, I would not approve of my behavior*, she thought. She reminded herself, *I hate drama.*

When Rene finally returned to work he was assigned to the pediatric floor. He did come down to the ER from time to time. He and Fritz lunched together when Meryt had conflicting plans. She found it odd. It only confirmed her belief that she had embarrassed him and herself at that first meeting. All she needed was a sexual harassment complaint!

The nurses were in heaven as the news of two handsome doctors spread like wild fire all over the hospital. Doctors Daniels and Daniels were the subjects of conversations in every breakroom. Perhaps, Karl insisting a picture be hung in all staff break areas to introduce the new doctors encouraged such conduct?

Meryt did ultimately get the scoop. Fritz was forty-seven years old and married with no children. He was taking care of his niece and her two children, a boy, seventeen, and a girl, sixteen. The children were homeschooled. They were planning to put the children in private school in January. Rene was forty-four years old, single, and had no children. Currently, they were all living together in one large house. Because they were new in town, they were trying to get a feel for Niagara Falls, a small town in upstate New York, before they purchased any more homes. They were from England, by way of California. Cindy continued, saying that they had asked to work at Saint Catherine's. The brothers had responded to Karl's postings for help, and they had been willing to take a significant pay cut to move from San Diego to Niagara Falls.

Fritz and Meryt continued to work together, and they worked together constantly. They were almost on the same wavelength, with the exception of urgency. Meryt always thought of her studies on synthetic hemoglobin (SYN) for heart failure patients as a hobby. She had had a few heart failure (HF) patients that she could not save, and it was a long, painful ride to the end. So she started this research because she felt there had to be more. There must be a cure or at least a way to slow this disease down rather than take its ugly roller-coaster ride of ups, downs, and turns that ended in pump failure or sudden cardiac death. At best, Meryt figured she could come up with the foundation for a trial. Then she would turn her research over to a true teaching institution like the Cleveland Clinic or Harvard. Meryt wasn't looking for fame. She just wanted a better life for HF patients.

Fritz, on the other hand, had a true passion. He believed and worked feverishly as if they were going to cure HF disease. She couldn't imagine how they could accomplish such a feat. They didn't have the money or the equipment it would require for such a huge trial. When did small hospitals without endowments or pharmaceutical company backings have groundbreaking cures? Never.

Fritz started bringing in samples from his home into the lab, which meant he was working at home with this same intensity. Meryt knew it had to be personal. He had someone he wanted to help, but who? He never talked about anybody other than his family. From time to time, they had all come by, and each had seemed as beautiful as the next, but more importantly, all were healthy.

Three weeks before Christmas Eve, Rene started coming around. Not around Meryt, but around the lab. She assumed Fritz had pulled him into the study. Meryt calculated that the more bodies they had to work the trial, the better. Fritz was all about analyzing the data from the trial, and nothing distracted him from his research. In fact, Meryt was starting to get the impression that it was his sole purpose for coming to the Falls.

Chapter 6

Meryt loved the holidays. The season seemed to always bring out the best in people. Holiday decorations were being hung throught the hospital. The hospital staff started to thin out as the holiday vacations began. But the best part, finally the dark cloud from the crash was replaced with a bantam of holiday cheer.

Meryt was in the lab, which had become her second home since the Daniels moved to town. After two years of begging for a lab, Karl had finally agreed to give Meryt space in the basement. The reasonably sized room was the old morgue, so there was plenty of countertop space for petri dishes, computers, mini refrigerators, and notepads. It also had a full-size, walk-in refrigerator great for storing tissue and blood samples.

Meryt was completing data input into the mainframe from the last test results when Cindy dropped in to visit. Cindy was clearly in a good mood and in need of a little girlie conversation. "Do you have any special plans for the holidays? Is there any *special* man in your life? You know I live vicariously through you," she said with a devilish smile.

"None," Meryt replied, not looking away from the computer. She was trying to focus. She had a tendency to flip the numbers around when typing, so she spoke slowly trying not to mistype, "I'm planning a trip in the new year. I have no crazy love affair, not even a something, something." Meryt never missed a keystroke, still making the clicking sound on the computer keypad.

Cindy shot back, "Why not? Dallas has been sniffing around since last October."

"And why has he? Because he knows I'm safe." Meryt continued typing, "He knows I do not wish to travel down old roads again. What's the old saying? 'Fool me once, shame on you; fool me twice, shame on me.' Do you have any idea how foolish I felt about that girl calling my house?

Telling me how in love she was with Dallas and that I should leave her man alone. *Her* man?" Meryt finished the last set of numbers, saved the new data, threw her pen down, and stretched back in the chair, taking her ponytail out to let her hair hang freely. "When has Dallas ever committed to any one woman? But what if she was his love? I would be considered a blocker." Meryt knew she didn't love Dallas, nor would she ever fall in love with him. They were just good friends passing time. But what if she was blocking his one true love?

The real killer in the back of her mind was who else had that silly girl told her scandalous story to? Meryt hated to be a part of hospital gossip.

Meryt continued, "Would I have to go to work hearing whispers of a twisted love affair? 'Dr. Brownstone is sleeping around'?"

Cindy started singing, "Downtown Brownstone sleeping around, Doo-wop, Doo-wop."

"Like I said, I can't go down that road again. It's fine just the way it is: a little flirting here, a smile there, and a great friendship."

"What about Darren?" Cindy continued. Darren was a vascular surgeon who had been tracking Meryt since she joined the staff. When she first came to the hospital four years ago, he had been the one to show her around. He showed her the local spots to hang out. They even went to the movies a few times, but Meryt sensed that he was taking their friendship all too seriously. She knew right away that he was not a one-night-stand guy and definitely not a something, something guy either. A *something, something* was a boyfriend or girlfriend with no intention of being anything more. Both partners agreed they were not "the one," but who wanted to wait alone in the house for true love? That's what a something, something relationship was, something to do while a person waited for true love.

Meryt had to slowly backtrack, because she did not want him to get the wrong impression. He was handsome: he had a light-brown complexion, was about six feet tall, and had a nice physique and a great heart. And on top of it all, he had the most irresistible smile; it was impossible not to smile while in his presence when he smiled. Even with all of these outstanding qualities, sadly, he was not the one for Meryt. He was definitely the kind of guy who dated with the intention to marry. She doubted if he had ever participated in a one-night stand. In fact, he had told her the next relationship he entered would be with someone that he planned on marrying. That was Meryt's signal for "Let's be friends and only friends."

This did not stop Dr. Darren Tidwell. At every opportunity, he was quick to show her the error of her ways.

"You must be kidding!" she told Cindy. "He was the whole aftermath of Dallas. Do you know that that fool had the nerve to come up to me after the Dallas thing blew up and say that if I had stayed with my own race, meaning if I were with him, this mess would have never happened? Darren made it clear that if we were a couple there would be no other women. He wanted to make me an 'honest woman.' I thought I was an honest woman! That man followed me around this hospital for a month." Meryt shook her head in disgust. "I don't need that kind of drama in my life. I hate drama. I like it clean and simple. Let's stick to the facts."

At that moment, she heard a laugh directly behind her. She turned around, thinking it was Darren, because she had this uncanny habit of talking about people while they were standing right behind her. To her surprise, it was Rene in the flesh.

Crap! It literally took her breath away. This was the first time they had been this close since the day they had met. She remembered all too well how that went down. She had made a fool of herself.

"Oh, Rene, what a surprise! Your brother is gone for the day, and I'm just finishing things up and gossiping with Cindy." Meryt said it rather slowly to ensure her confidence and professionalism.

Rene quickly said, "I know; my brother asked me to pick up a few things to take home." While Rene was speaking, he continued walking closer and closer into her personal space. Meryt's sole thought was Rene; *He is too handsome for my own good.* He had the body of a Greek warrior. But what took her breath away was his powerful, piercing blue eyes that sat deep beneath his brow. She felt them studying her every movement. He had thin, yet confident lips with just a hint of pink; his skin was pale, but firm. He had no body fat from eating too many late-night dinners or unhealthy snacks between cases. Altogether, it was unbearable for Meryt and it only spelled trouble. She could feel his piercing blue eyes probing her mind. His chin line was cut perfectly; his nose was a little short, but it added to his look of being wise and mature beyond his age. He had the manners of a knight on a mission to save his queen and a presence as if he just knew everything and had authority over everyone.

His cologne smelled of leather and jasmine. If love had a smell, he smelled of it. Ralph Lauren needed to bottle his scent and sell it. They would make millions. No woman could resist; she would simply surrender once she smelled the enchanting fragrance.

Crap, Meryt thought, *I would be first in line to buy a bottle to take home to sniff at will.* She needed to get a hold of herself. Her heart was off to the races, and her mind was spinning with thoughts of making love. She said to herself, *One . . . two . . . three. Breathe. Speak slowly.*

"How much of our conversation did you hear?" she asked.

Rene smiled. "Enough to know that you and Darren would make a fine couple." Cindy chuckled at this little smooth joke made at Meryt's expense. It wouldn't be funny if it were her personal life laid out on Front Street.

"Oh, you've got jokes?" Meryt continued. "Well, if I make a fine mate for Darren, you must make a fine mate for half of the nurses on staff, not to mention about seven physician's assistants."

Rene said with a grin, "Since you are counting, make it seventy-two nurses and ten PAs. I believe in spreading my love around. Wasn't it John Lennon who believed in peace, love, and happiness? Don't you believe in sharing love? Or do you believe in one true love?" His accent wasn't quite English, but he sounded so cute when he shortened the pronunciation of *don't.*"

"Yes, I do. I believe in sharing a certain level of love, peace, and happiness. If I didn't, I could not have taken the oath as a physician. But giving my full heart to another that's a matter of a different nature. It has to be true love."

Rene raised one eye. "How will you know this true love?" He leaned over the counter, staring directly into Meryt's eyes as if he thought of her as a fool to believe in true love. Something in Meryt was no longer afraid; rather, she was infuriated that a man who barely knew her was questioning her judgment.

Meryt leaned across the counter to get closer and prove that neither he nor his comments intimidated her any longer; Meryt spoke in her smarty-pants voice. "Well, Mr. Lyrics, I remember a verse or two from a song that sums it all up perfectly: 'It doesn't take all day to recognize sunshine.' When true love comes, you will know it; the rest is just spreading yourself around."

Rene pulled back on his heels, backed away from the counter, and picked up his brother's notepad and said, "What if this sunshine is only the eye of the storm, a peaceful place filled with sunlight, no rains, and no blowing winds, which will only last a short time before the storm hits again?"

Meryt replied, "'Again' is the key word. Apparently, this person has already weathered a storm and now is being rewarded with sunshine, and maybe that little bit of sunshine is enough to weather the second half of the storm."

Rene looked as if he was in deep thought. As he turned to walk away, he said, "Maybe."

Then he was gone.

"What on earth was that all about?" Cindy blurted out.

"I have no idea. That was the first conversation we've had since he joined the hospital back in October, and now it's December. How dare he eavesdrop on our conversation and then begin to question my ability to love or spread love around. Please! If you spread too much love, you might spread a little STD. I like to call it 'something you catch but you can't throw back'."

"As I said before, what on earth was that all about? I have never seen him openly talk to anyone. And you? I have never seen you look at a man the way you drooled over him. He's 'the one'! I know it. He is the one. I know you and I know that look, and you cannot say anything to make me change my mind." Cindy held up her hand in defiance.

"Cindy, Cindy," Meryt said as she shut off the computers in the lab, "don't you think you are getting a little carried away with all of this? Plus, lower your voice before someone overhears you talking all of this nonsense. The last thing I need is another rumor about my nonexistent love life. Rene is not the one. He is interesting and extremely pleasing to the eyes, but being the one? He is being 'the one' who is starting to work my nerves. Speaking of the one, don't you have to be somewhere? Like at home with your 'the one,' Karl? It's Friday night, you don't have call, and you are still at the hospital. What's up with that picture?"

"Meryt, you cannot throw me off the scent that easily. But you are right. I need to head home. Karl will be home soon and expecting dinner. Your secret is safe with me. I won't tell a soul."

"Cindy, there is no secret; just go home and fix dinner for your man."

With that, Meryt walked Cindy to the door, shut off the lights, locked the lab's door, and they started heading towards the parking lot. By the time they got to the lot, Meryt had her talking about shoes. It was their shared passion. Gucci had already started showing its spring collection before Christmas. Cindy was wondering how she could get a pair without Karl knowing, but what she really wanted was a new car. She had her eye on the new Mercedes C-class, but she would settle for a new pair of designer shoes. Well, maybe a few pairs of new designer shoes. She didn't think Karl would go for the Mercedes. If only she knew how much Karl loved her. He would let her buy and do anything her heart desired as long as she remained his wife. She was his life. Meryt never knew him before they married, but she had spent enough time with the couple to know, that Cindy was his life. Cindy was a good woman, great friend, and even better wife. She would never do anything to hurt Karl. Her only goal was to show him how much life and love there was in the world. She was his ambassador to love.

Meryt watched Cindy get into her car, and then she headed to her BMW 750. She always liked a full-size luxury car. She used to drive a little Honda DelSol back when she served in the army. She had loved that little car. It was fast, cute, and small enough that she didn't need to share because it was a two seater. During the three years she had owned it, it had stayed in the bodyshop. At some point, every exterior piece was replaced. Meryt was done with small, fast cars. She never looked back. Meryt also owned an older truck for snowy days. She should have had it out now, since it was December, but there was no snow on the ground and nothing compared to a BMW seven's ride, except for a newer seven series.

She turned on the car and sat for a few seconds to unwind before putting the car in gear. Meryt was thinking about "Maybe." Rene had not spoken to her in months, and he ended their conversation with a maybe. Maybe what?

A knocking at the driver's side window startled Meryt, which caused her to focus on the current moment. It was Mr. Maybe. What could Rene possibly want tonight?

Meryt let the window down, "Can I help you? Did you forget something?"

"No, I was wondering if you were free. Well, not free, but available. I would like to discuss my brother's work," Rene said with a concerned voice.

"Sure, I have time. Do you want to talk in the hospital?"

Rene recommended they meet at the local spot, The Joint.

Before he could say anything else, like "let's ride together," Meryt abruptly ended the conversation with "I'll meet you there." She needed her alone time before she engaged in any more conversation with Rene. The idea of being alone in his car or hers was beyond anything she was prepared to handle. It took her fifteen minutes to drive to The Joint, which equaled half of the *Who Is Jill Scott* CD. The second song, *Do You Remember*, resonated with Meryt. When Jill sang her beautiful, soulful music each note massaged the stress away and restored her strength and courage. In Meryt's favorite song, Jill sang about remembering an old fling from back in the day and how it made her feel, Meryt could not resist humming along with a delicious smile. Meryt arrived at The Joint still humming the song, "Do you remember, you and me and what we did?"

If Meryt had been to this bar once, she'd been there a million times. The bar had an odd shape, narrow and long. Right at the entrance was the dance floor, followed by the bar, which was done in neon baby-blue lights with a glass countertop. The blue lit bar immediately placed the patron in the mood for a sexy martini. The bar had a "Miami" feel. Once the patron walked past the bar, there was a choke point, a narrowing to three steps down into the cozy section. The rear of the bar was decorated totally different from the entrance. The front was well lit, done in neon lights, and loud dance music; in contrast, the rear of the bar was decorated in dark brown and black velvet, and featured a jazzy-blues flavor of songs and dim lighting. Velvet curtains hung from the ceiling to the floor creating a soft atmosphere. Copper 3-D starlights hung down from the ceiling, delicately illuminating this area. The lights weren't as bright or as shiny as Christmas lights, yet they were perfect for the room and gave it a special intimacy. At the farthest end of the room was a small stage for the entertainers or for patrons who had had too much to drink. This room always smelled of incense, which burned constantly.

As her eyes roamed this familiar place, which was a little on the empty side tonight, she spotted Rene in the corner. He'd beaten her there and already had a little table in the back.

Meryt sat down and greeted him. "Hello, Mr. Maybe."

He looked confused; he repeated her words with hesitation. "Mr. Maybe?"

She said, "Yes, when we last spoke at the lab, you walked away and said 'maybe.' Maybe what? I don't know. Maybe world peace or maybe true love or maybe the end of world famine?"

Meryt knew she sounded young and overanalyzing. It was a dirty rumor that she, at times, over analyzed things. Meryt abruptly stopped talking for a moment. She required silence as she regrouped her thoughts.

"Let's talk about your brother. You sounded concerned about Fritz."

Before Rene could answer Meryt's question, the waitress walked over and asked them for their drink order; but instead of greeting both of them, she focused only on Rene.

Meryt thought, *Well, that makes seventy-two nurses, ten PAs, and one waitress.* Rene glanced over at Meryt with a grin. She returned the grin and said, "I'll take a Jack and ginger."

He politely gave the waitress their order; "I will have the house red wine and one Jack Daniels and ginger ale for the lady." The waitress never acknowledged Meryt; it was as if she was not present. Rene ignored the whole ordeal and returned to their conversation. "What are you thinking? You look distracted."

"No, I'm just curious. Why are we talking? You have not spoken two words to me since the first day we met, and now we are here because you want to talk about your brother, Fritz. The very brother who you see every day and I know is not secretive about his trial work. Well, at least not with you."

Rene smiled warmly. "My brother said you were direct and like to get to the bottom line quickly." He leaned over closer to Meryt while sitting in his chair. "I want to assist with your research. I feel as if Fritz is getting close, and I figure three working must be better than two."

Meryt was still a little confused and nervous. "So, you needed to tell me this on a Friday night in a bar?"

"No, I guess not. I wasn't ready to go home, and I really enjoyed our conversation in the lab. I was hoping to continue it," Rene said in an intoxicating voice.

At that moment, the rude waitress returned with their drinks and her top button undone and her hair down. Meryt giggled and said softly to Rene, "I guess that makes three of us being direct tonight."

Rene grinned and gave the young lady a credit card and told her to start a tab. The waitress placed her hand on his and slowly pulled the credit card from his hand. He never looked back at her, as if this was normal behavior. Meryt supposed it took all kinds to make the world go round.

Rene raised his glass and said, "Cheers. How is your drink?"

"What can I say? It's a Jack and ginger. I can tell it wasn't made with tender, loving care."

Rene responded, "You say the oddest things. I can see why my brother enjoys you. At home, you are all he talks about. If I did not know how much he adores his wife, I would be worried."

Rene closed his eyes to enjoy her scent mixing with the alcohol and the incense in the room. He was thinking the better word choice would be jealous. If Fritz were not so in love with Lolita, his wife, he would be jealous of Fritz's stories of Meryt and their trial work. Rene had been dying to spend time alone with Meryt. He had fantasized about his own private conversations with Meryt, and none of it had to do with the trial. But Rene knew the trial work was important. He did not want to jeopardize the progress, since time was of the essence.

Fritz did not help matters by continuously talking about Meryt. It only heightened Rene's curiosity and lust. Upon their first meeting, Rene had lost control. He had mentally pulled her across the room and was a millisecond from kissing her and relieveing her of a few ounces of blood at first sight. He was behaving like a newly made dark angel and not the 625-year-old dark angel that he had become.

Tonight would be different. He had gone home earlier and fed, only to return to the hospital to invite Meryt on a date. This time, he would be prepared. He hoped to discover more about this mystery woman who continuously amused his brother, Fritz, who was never fazed by humans. Rene wanted to know more about this woman who had almost made him lose control at first sight.

Meryt had continued talking unaware of Rene's yearnings, "Believe me, you do not have to worry about a thing. Fritz is not my flavor."

Rene wrinkled his nose and opened his eyes, coming back to the conversation, repeating Meryt's words. "Not your flavor? What flavor is Fritz?"

Meryt took another sip. "Taken. I don't do 'taken.' It brings too many problems. Problems I don't need. Plus, your brother is not into me as much as he is into my work. I would be surprised if he noticed I had on clothes. You can tell his wife that he is solely into my mind. He does not know there is a female body connected to it."

Rene laughed because he knew it was true. Nothing separated Fritz from his work.

Meryt started to work on her drink and it started to work on her. She could smell Rene's scent mixing with the incense in the room drifting across their tiny table. She knew this meant it was a one-drink night. She had to stay focused.

Rene broke the moment of silence by asking, "What do you know about true love?"

"What?" Meryt nearly choked on her ice. She felt the liquor burn as it slide down her windpipe. "What do you mean? I do not know true love." She said in a sharper voice, "true love and I have no history, but I've seen it and I know I want it. Now, when will it come? That's the million-dollar question."

Like clockwork, her phone rang. She looked down at the caller ID. It was the call she had been waiting for.

She quickly answered it. "Okay, I need to call you back in a few minutes. I'll be there." She hung up the phone.

"Well, Mr. Maybe, I gotta go. I need to take this call. It was nice to finally have a moment with you. I'm sorry I can't stay. *Maybe* another time?"

Rene, being a gentleman, walked her to her car, wondering what had just happened. He had wanted the conversation to go on a little longer. He wanted to know more about this brown beauty that smelled as sweet as she looked. Rene was similar to his brother in that it was rare when things threw him for an unexpected loop. He normally remained calm and stayed on track. But Rene was not expecting a phone call to end his planned date. He was prepared to handle any situation, but a cell phone call from a friend? What friend? He had been watching her for months. She had no friends outside of the hospital. Could she have a male suitor? Rene thought to himself patient. That was one thing he had learned during his six-hundred-plus years of life: "Patience, and in time everything comes to light."

Rene leaned over the driver's-side window, smiling, and said, "Maybe another time."

At that moment, Meryt's entire body wanted nothing less than a kiss from Rene. Her mouth began to water; her body temperature jumped ten degrees. In a faraway place, next to common sense, a little voice was screaming *No!* But everything else in her body was saying *Yes!* And drowning out that little voice. Meryt looked into his eyes; in the night air, his eyes flashed from jet black to a deep rich red back to blue. She wondered if this was what being delusional felt like.

She leaned forward, waiting for her kiss, when the waitress who serviced them called Rene's name. "Mr. Rene Daniels, you left your credit card!"

As quickly as the moment came, it was gone. Meryt was no longer hypnotized by his presence. "Handle your fan club, I gotta go."

Meryt put the car in to drive. They were both in her rearview mirror within seconds.

Chapter 7

Meryt kept thinking to herself, *What's up with Rene? Am I attracted, or am I not? This is crazy! I'm a grown woman playing high-school games.* At that moment it made no difference. Her little investigation into her feelings had to continue later. Right then, she needed to get to the airport within fifteen minutes to catch her other baby, a Falcon 2000 private jet. The jet wasn't hers, but it was sent exclusively for her tonight. The jet was a major perk for serving with Uncle Sam and completing unwanted missions. It was a sleek, sexy, white aircraft on the outside and a dream on the inside. It had pale, off-white leather chairs; soft, white carpet; and cherrywood doors and trim. The cockpit contained two leather seats and a dashboard that looked as if it had come from a Star Wars movie. As she pulled into the airport parking lot, she saw the plane. It stood there sexy as ever, looking spotless and shiny in the night's light.

Meryt pulled around to her regular parking spot. She grabbed her purse and ran to the plane. She was ready to leave Niagara, posthaste. Meryt was steaming with emotions over the waitress and the man she had almost kissed and yet barely knew. But now she needed to leave that behind and prepare her mind for Deacon. For Deacon to call late on a Friday night, and needing her in Virginia bad enough to send the Falcon, it had to be serious. All her hormones had to be put on hold. She required a clear mind for Jed Deacon.

Once on the plane, she took her seat. She always sat in the first seat to the right, so she could see the door of the plane. The flight attendant asked if she wanted a drink, Meryt replied no but asked for a blanket instead. She was soon off to sleep. It was 9:30 p.m. The flight would land in Virginia by 10:45 p.m., which meant the meeting would take all night.

Chapter 8

Jed Deacon was an old friend. He and Meryt had crossed paths while she was serving payback time to the army for footing the bill for medical school. They created a camaraderie that no man could break. He had taught her the importance of knowing who she was, what she stood for, what she was willing to die for, and most importantly, what she was prepared to sacrifice to save her own life. It may have sounded silly, perhaps even juvenile, but those were intellectual questions, which had to be answered when it came to leadership, and when it came to hand-to-hand combat. The answers made the simple difference between life and death. They were the fundamentals of being aware of your commitment. One of man's biggest challenges in life was to know himself. Shakespeare wrote, "This above all: to thine own self be true, And it must follow, as the night the day, Thou canst not then be false to any man." Meryt once heard an old saying, that it took more courage to stand and face one's true self, than it took to stand and fight on any battlefield.

The bottom line remained constant: once people were assured of themselves, the world was open. If you loved yourself, you could love others. If you were strong for yourself, then you could be strong for others. If you were honest with yourself, then you could be honest with others—or you could manipulate others because they refused honesty and truth.

Deacon and Meryt had met at Survival Evasion Resistance Escape School known commonly as SERE. SERE school was special operational training that taught soldiers how to cope with the stress of being a prisoner of war (POW). Meryt was one of two women in that particular cycle. Deacon was amazed at their endurance. The women had lasted longer than expected. Female soldiers were recently allowed to participate in this type of training, and the few that did never lasted longer than twenty-four hours. Meryt's class started with twenty-one soldiers, nineteen males and two females. Two weeks later, on graduation day, five soldiers received certificates and Meryt was only the female.

The training started when soldiers were dropped off two miles from the camp with no food, no equipment, and no weapons. They were given the mission to return to the base camp without being captured in enemy territory. Within a few hours, enemy personnel had captured all twenty-one soldiers. They were shackled at their hands and feet forced into a double-barbed-wire encampment. It was a simulated POW camp. As soldiers entered the camp, unmarked graves were stationed along both sides of the walkway. It was November on the east coast, so there was a fine gloom that sat over the compound at dusk. There was no vegetation, no small lively, furry creatures running about within the compound, only dead leaves lingering in the wind. Nothing lived there but soldiers preparing to inflict pain and soldiers entering the compound hoping to survive the pain. A large sign should have been posted above the barracks, barely hanging on by one rusted nail, that said, Welcome to Hell. That was how Meryt felt as she entered the camp. Gunmen were posted along the camp boundary. The prisoners were held captive for two weeks for hourly interrogation and torture.

If anyone was looking to lose weight, it was an excellent method. Meryt dropped twenty pounds during the program. At first, she didn't remember why she had ever signed up for SERE School. She had nothing to prove, but then she remembered. She had been assigned as a medical officer to a small tactic human intel cell. On their last mission the entire cell was destroyed. Meryt was the only survivor. She figured a little POW training could keep her mind off of her current heartache.

SERE school was hell on earth wrapped in lies. The prisoners were told that if they escaped it would be considered an automatic graduation from the program, similar to real life: if a soldier escaped his captors, the soldier was no longer a POW. It was simple game over, the soldier won. But most important, once the soldier escaped, he got a meal. Immediately, the soldier would receive a peanut butter and jelly sandwich. A peanut butter and jelly sandwich was the gold-standard meal for the Army. It contained high levels of protein and sugar. Plus it could be stored in supply cabinets or sealed in a plastic brown bag in a foxhole for years.

Meryt couldn't tell days from nights most times because they were inside. She rarely saw the sun. The only way she could keep up with time was by counting seconds. There were 86,400 seconds in a day. Meryt knew this because, as a cardiologist, she was constantly calculating heart rates and cardiac output. The number broke down to 3,600 seconds an hour and so on. She found it better to count. It distracted her mind from the hourly interrogation and torture.

The culminating point happened on the tenth night. That's when the program became hell wrapped in lies. It happened during one of her interrogation and torture session. She had been in the same room for roughly six hours. Meryt lost count a few times while choking on water, a gift from the Asian culture on how to torture. There were two officers taking turns dunking her head in a bucket of water. Meryt had no idea why people were afraid of pools or any large body of water, when the plain truth of the matter was that a person could drown in less than ten ounces of water.

By the tenth day, Meryt had no more clothes. It was all part of the psychological breakdown to take away basic privileges, ration food and water, and remove all personal possessions, thereby leaving a soldier holding onto name, rank, and serial number. Meryt was naked, with her hands bound behind her back by a leather strap. The two guards were taking turns throwing her around the room and dunking her head either face forward or backwards into a wooden bucket of water. When she wasn't counting, she was trying to figure out how to break the stinking bucket. They were in a small, nine-by-ten cell containing a wooden table, two chairs, and one wooden picnic bench. Meryt knew its exact size because they had thrown, pushed, and beaten her against every square inch of it. And each time, she tried like crazy to fall on the bucket to break it.

When she chose to focus on the routine, it was always the same questions and the same cursing. Occasionally, she heard screams from the other POWs located somewhere in the barracks. She often wondered how many soldiers remaind in her class. After a few rounds of being attentive during the interrogation and torture, Meryt would focus either on counting again or on how to break the bucket.

At some point during the interrogation, one of guards walked out of the cell leaving Meryt alone with the other guard. She was naked, bent over the bucket, being held by her hair with her face literally inches from the water waiting to be submerged again into the bucket. The remaining guard was holding her weight by her hair. He leaned in close and whispered a new threat in her ear. The gurad was threatening to put his fingers between her legs to invade her private area if she did not answer his next question. At first, Meryt thought it was just another threat, but when he followed through, Meryt was in shock. She couldn't believe this was happening. It was one thing to be threatened and another to follow through. Meryt expected to be physically beaten, that was part of being a POW, but she was not counting on sexual assault from a fellow soldier who wore the same uniform. This was not a part of regulation training. He was clearly breaking the rules. Which meant she was going to clearly break his hand. This was no longer a game of endurance; it was now a test of willpower. No man had ever disrespected her body and not experienced her revenge.

Meryt allowed the revenge to grow and encompass her whole spirit. Her body temperature dropped. Her fingers began to get cold. She was waiting for the right moment; just a split second was all she required. The guard would soon discover her second special gift was killing. It was second nature, just like breathing.

Still bent over the bucket, the guard continued to dunk her head into the water for another ninety seconds. While she was bent over underwater, he slide three fingers into her again and whispered in her ear, "Tell me you like it. Tell me you want more, you dirty bitch." He kept pushing his fingers harder and deeper. With her remaining strength, Meryt kicked him off. He fell back against the wall, and she fell to the floor, out of breath and outraged. Her breathing was out of control. Her chest was heaving in and out as she tried to cough water out of her lungs. She desperately wanted to wipe her face and regain some form of dignity as more water ran forward down chin from her soaked hair.

The first guard returned to the room. Meryt assumed he would want to know what happened, so she tried to explain while still taking in deep breaths. He just laughed and walked out, as if this was common behavior. Meryt now knew why women have never completed SERE school.

She was done. It was final. The guard's fate was sealed. Meryt could think of nothing else but revenge. The guard and Meryt were alone again. He became her whole world. He held her total attention. Counting seconds or trying to remember the basics of name, rank, and serial number was a waste of her concentration. Every brain cell was dedicated to planning the attack.

The guard picked her up from the floor and slammed her into a chair next to the table. He told Meryt he would kill her if she repeated a word of what happened. Her head was lying on the table and her hands were still tied behind by her back. She was still gasping for air, trying to control her breathing and focus her vision. *Just think.*

The guard leaned in close to speak. Meryt could smell the tobacco on his breath. The guard mistook her breathing out of control as fear versus anger. He gave her the moment she needed. Before he could inhale his next breath, Meryt swung her arms from around her back and over her head and slammed the guard's face down onto the table. The wooden table broke from the force of the blow. Meryt quickly grabbed the broken leg from the table and cracked it over his head as he tried to stand up. The guard stumbled back a few steps and fell down to the floor on his knees, using his hands to balance his weight.

While he was down on the ground, Meryt took the wide end of the broken table leg and targeted his left hand, the very hand that possessed the three fingers he had forced inside her. With both hands tightly holding the wooden leg, Meryt raised it above her head. Like a martial artist, she visualized the energy from her core traveling from her center down her arms, into her hands, and through the broken wooden table leg to his left hand. The power from the blow literally left his hand unrecognizable. The soldier pulled what was left of his hand close to his chest and screamed, "You bitch!" His pain was a burst of energy to her soul. She felt a little sad he forgot the word *dirty.* She understood that pain did that to soldiers, it shortened their memory.

The guard huddled next to the turned-over, broken table trying to apply a pressure wrap to his hand in hopes of control the bleeding. The wooden leg that Meryt held had split into three pieces from the impact. She used one of the sharp pieces as a shank to cut through the leather ties around her hands. Once her hands were free, she wrapped the leather around the opposite end of the shank to create a handheld knife. Meryt pulled her new friend to his feet and told him that they were going to walk out of that hellhole together. If he chose not to, she would kill him as easily as she spoke her own name.

Meryt couldn't believe what happened next. The guard started crying. She asked him, "Who's the bitch now?"

Two more guards ran into the interrogation room with guns drawn. She used the soldier, her new friend with the broken hand, as a human shield. With the homemade knife to his neck, she told the two soldiers to drop their weapons or she would kill the guard. They dropped their weapons like obedient soldiers. As she walked past, Meryt recognized one of the guards. Meryt kicked him in the family jewels because he thought her assault was not newsworthy.

They snaked their way through the camp to the front gate. By this time, twenty soldiers were lined up with M16s locked and loaded. They ordered her to drop the weapon and release her prisoner. She dropped the knife and released the prisoner, but not before she side-kicked him in the knee. She heard it snap in two. He fell to the ground with his shoulder breaking the fall, the same way he threw her to the floor less than twenty minutes earlier.

Within seconds, she was pinned to the ground and thrown in "the hole." No food, no water, definitely no automatic graduation, and no peanut butter and jelly sandwich. The hole was actually as it sounded. It was a tiny space. There wasn't enough room to stand. There wasn't enough room to lie down. Even while sitting, there wasn't enough room for a soldier's head to rise up to a natural level. The soldier had to bend his or her head forward because there wasn't enough height. There was no light, just darkness. No one came to take a statement, and there was no military police investigation, only darkness and silence. Meryt stayed in the hole for two days. She returned to counting. One . . . two . . . three.

Meryt remember meeting Deacon for the first time on graduation day from the program. She was severely dehydrated, malnourished, and mentally beaten. He came over to her, wanting to shake her hand. As he reached for her hand she remembered that she had seen him briefly on the night of her assault and escape. He was the highest-ranking officer present, and most likely the one who had ordered the cover up. As he moved to touch her hand, instinct took over. Meryt twisted his hand, turned it around his back, and used his arm as a choke collar. The action was so quick that everyone stopped and stared. Meryt whispered in his ear, "What would you want to say to a sexually assaulted victim on such a fine afternoon?"

He had calmly replied that he did not condone the guard's behavior, and that the guard was being detained in a military prison, awaiting trial. Deacon further explained that the trial most likely would not take place considering the guard's left hand had been amputated and his left knee was completely shattered. The guard was headed for a dishonorable discharge. Deacon went on to say that he wanted to recruit her for the program to train the trainers and candidates. Meryt slowly released her grip. Deacon could now breathe freely. He said, while rubbing his neck, "You still have the strength to choke a man twice your weight."

Meryt replied, "The human will is a powerful tool."

He finished her statement. "Exactly! That's why you should join me. Go home, rebuild yourself, and then call me."

That was the beginning of a great relationship. He was her trainer, her father, her mentor, and her friend all rolled into one. She became his trainee, a daughter, and a friend. There was nothing she couldn't trust him with. He was the one who showed her true love as a friend. When Meryt met his wife, there was no doubt that his spouse was his true love for life.

Deacon and Meryt worked together on a variety of classified missions. Some were based in human intel and others on small unit warfare tactics. They served four years with the Army before the Clinton administration suspended all funds. Deacon took his brand of small-unit large-return offense/defense teams and became a government contractor. Meryt left active duty after ten years of service and started working for Deacon in his private group. Deacon's organization was employed when the US government could not afford to have its name tied to an incident but required action to be taken. Over the years, Deacon had called Meryt in on different missions, ranging from small-arms warfare to simply having a second pair of eyes reviewing classified documents.

She wasn't sure what to expect on this night. He did say she could return home by morning, but his voice had contained a touch of concern. Meryt tried not to worry about the future because the only guarantee the future held was it would one day become the past. She closed her eyes and pulled the blanket up over her arms. She shut off her brain to get needed rest before the flight ended.

Once the plane was on the ground, Meryt disembarked. A black sedan was waiting. Meryt got into the backseat of the car with no questions asked. She was on her way to Deacon's office.

Meryt walked into Deacon's office, which was a battle zone torn among traditional, historical, and new-age warfare. He had a large, old, cherrywood desk that sat slightly off-center in the rear of the room facing two oversized, deep-cushioned, highback brown chairs. The desk sat off-center because there was a second entrance in the rear of his office. The doors were on opposite walls. The space perpendicular to his desk had a wall-to-wall computer screen with motion sensors. A person could touch and drag images all along the wall. Meryt had only seen a screen like this in movies. The one remaining wall was a bookshelf. Deacon was a devoted reader. Between the books he purchased and the books he received as gifts, the shelves were never empty. The collection was priceless. Whatever space remained on the walls was covered in plaques and pictures taken from the span of his military career.

Deacon was sitting behind his desk drinking his favorite cocktail, a white Russian.

"Hey, how was your trip?" Deacon inquired as he stood up with a warm hardy smile and arms wide open for a hug. "I hope very accommodating."

"Sure, nothing less than the best." Meryt beamed with pleasure, and she happily fell into his hug.

"So who were you with? I know it had to be a man by your hurried tone."

"If I told you, I might have to kill you. It's top secret." Meryt jabbed Deacon in the stomach. "He's a new doctor at the hospital. Can you believe he hasn't spoken to me since the day he arrived, and today of all days, he asked me out for a drink under the disguise of helping his brother? And when he started asking me about love, like clockwork, you called. It must be a sign from God," Meryt added as she laughed. "It's official. You are a blocker. So why are you calling me away from a potentially interesting evening with a single man?"

"Meryt, we've been collecting some interesting intel hits." Deacon walked over to the wall-to-wall screen and opened a file, which started downloading images. "I can't call it, but I think we may have a hit on Eagle One."

"You called me in for the president? There are always plots on Eagle One. That's part of being the leader of the free world. There must be more."

"I know. I can't put my finger on it. That's why I called you to Virginia. I want another pair of eyes to look at it. It's too loose, too unrelated, and yet related at the same time. We picked up a rookie down in South America. We were tracking him from the Middle East and Africa. He had these pictures on disks." He pressed the *OK* command on the screen, and pictures appeared one by one on a glass before them. He had about fifty.

"Are they real?"

Deacon answered, "Yes" as he sipped his white Russian. Meryt began to study the pictures one by one. She recognized they were of the president and his family at close range. She could tell by the quality that they were not from a long-range lens. Some were of the president alone, but most of them were with his family. Yet, all were shot within a close range. It was as if the person taking them always maintained a distance of ten feet or less. The person must have had VIP privileges to be in close range at so many different venues.

Meryt immediately followed up, "Were all these trips announced ahead of time? Did you check to ensure the pictures were not public pictures? The rookie could have collected all the pictures from the media."

Deacon reassured her they were not publicly held prints.

She continued firing questions, "How does this person get so close in every shot? You must have a record if he or she has a VIP pass."

"Nope, that's not it. For some of these events, the president decided to attend at the last minute. The pictures taken are a combination of preannounced visits and unannounced visits," Deacon replied.

Meryt asked, "How does someone always know where the president will be? They must have unlimited resources to spend to have assets onsite, or—"

Meryt stopped and looked back at the pictures. "You have a leak. And if you have a leak, the next question is who?"

"Hence your presence. I believe we do have a leak, and that's what makes this hit believable. I don't know where the leak is, but I'm sure it's inside the White House. Some of these events Eagle One did not decide to attend until two hours before arriving. Not even his wife knew until she saw it on the news."

"Deacon, it can't be this obvious. There is more to this story; let me look at the pictures again." Meryt spent the next two hours reviewing the pictures against the itineraries for each. She reviewed who was assigned to Eagle One's protection detail on each day. It all added up, yet it did not explain a thing.

"What did the kid say when you picked him up?" Meryt asked.

"He knew very little. I think he was a mule. He was hired to carry packages. We caught him with pictures and routes. He was new in the game. We tagged and released him back into the wild. I put two surveillance agents on him and within three days they all were dead, the two agents and the kid."

"You're kidding me? You've got a problem," Meryt whispered.

"Meryt, that's what I needed you to say. I'm in the process of reinvestigating all top-secret clearances on Eagle One's detail. I need you to start preparing for a mission."

"You know all you have to do is call. But, when you call, it better be from your mama's or sister's phones until you find the leak." Meryt gave him another hug and headed back to the airport.

The whole time on the jet, Meryt kept thinking about the pictures. A hit couldn't be this obvious. They must have overlooked something. The person who ordered the pictures would know that someone had them, so why continue with the plan if he knew that someone else knew? But more importantly, who was the leak? It could be anyone. The bottom line remained the same, the leak still existed, so the plan must still exist."

Thoughts kept rolling around in her head, *What's more important, the leak or the plan?* She did not sleep on the way home. Flashes of the pictures appeared in her head. In each one, the person taking the pictures was within ten feet of the president and his family. Someone in the president's escort had to recognize the same person in the crowd unless it was a different person at each event. But who told the person or persons to be there and take pictures? And why now? Nothing in the news stood out. What was coming up or what actions had the president taken that didn't appear in the national news? Deacon had homework to complete. There were dozens of angles to comprehend before solving this riddle.

Chapter 9

Why now? Meryt was thinking as she got into her car and drove home. It was Saturday afternoon. She was glad it wasn't Sunday. She still had a whole day to rest, prepare for the workweek, and start planning her conditioning. Conditioning for what? *What* she didn't know, but deep inside her gut, she knew the *where*, and she knew the *where* would be hot. Meryt added hot, dry, and sandy weather training to her To Do list.

Sunday came and went fast, and the next thing Meryt knew, she walking towards the lab at the hospital shaking her breakfast in a can, preparing to pop the can open. When she walked in, Fritz and Rene were bent over a laptop at the main counter in the center of the room. This was a far cry from the computers she had seen at Deacon's office. No wall-to-wall glass screen with lights and sensors, and no expensive book collections or deep-cushioned chairs. There was just a plain laptop computer on a high countertop and two black stools. The brothers looked up together like perfect models. It had been awhile since she had seen them together. Meryt had gotten use to Fritz's perfect posture, but now two?

"Good morning gentlemen. How was your weekend?" she asked.

Rene answered, "It was nice. I had a few drinks at the Joint, hung around the house, and worked with Fritz on the numbers. And yours? When I last saw you there was an urgent matter you had to attend to. Did it go well?"

"Yes, it was an old friend who needed help. You know me. If you need help, just give me a call," Meryt said as she shook her breakfast in a can. "How are the tests results on Fritz's new formula?"

Fritz replied, "Not good. They're reacting too slow."

Rene had not taken his attention away from Meryt. She thought about looking away, but why should she? He had started the staring game.

Meryt finally spoke. "What? Is there something I can help you with?"

Rene answered without changing his glare. "I've never seen you drink that before, and you look stressed. Did something happen during your visit?" It bothered Rene that another man he had never met could call Meryt away at a moment's notice without an explanation.

"No, no nothing out of the ordinary, I'm just starting a new health diet. I started conditioning again. Maybe that's why I'm looking a little bushed. I'm getting old and out of shape. I have to be able to keep up with the young busty waitresses of the world."

Rene fired right back, "Did your friend make you feel that you need to condition?"

"No, Rene, it's not like that. It's two separate events: I visited a friend over the weekend, and I want to start conditioning for myself. What's going on with you? I was just playing with you. Why all the questions?"

Before Rene could answer or take another step forward, Darren came into the lab. The tone in the lab immediately changed. Darren pulled Meryt aside, asking if they could speak privately. Meryt told Fritz and Rene she would return later.

Darren and Meryt walked to the courtyard. It was a nice, quiet area that had been dedicated to the hospital a few years back. It was for the staff and patients to sit and relax while enjoying the outside from inside. The whole room was paneled in heated glass. The room sat in the middle of a small outdoor courtyard. During the warmer days, patients and their guests could go outside and when it was cooler, they could just stay inside and enjoy the view. It was one of Meryt's favorite places in the hospital. The acoustics were amazing. No matter how full the room was, the noise level never matched the crowd. In addition, there was a beautiful koi pond with a small waterfall. If peace was not found here, then peace was not meant to be found.

Darren and Meryt sat in a corner next to the window, looking out onto melting snow and overcast skies. It was a rainy, sluggish, cold day, like most other days in the winter. "What's up Darren? Is everything okay with your family?"

Darren answered, "Yeah, everything is cool at home. You are 'what's up.' What were you doing hanging out with Rene?"

Meryt was a little taken back, amazed at how fast gossip had traveled. She was not hanging out with Rene. They had met for one drink, and she didn't even finish it. This was ridiculous. It reminded her of the army days when everybody's business was fair game. It was a daily soap opera:

As the Armed Forces Turned. Meryt thought it only happened in the army because they worked such long hours together, the soldiers couldn't help but be nosy. They all were so close in the army, sometimes closer than blood family. This is not the case in the hospital. Then again, they did work long hours.

"Darren, are you kidding? You are asking me about Rene? We met for a drink that ended with me leaving early because I got a call. Why does this concern you?"

Darren started with his soapbox speech: "Meryt, I thought if you were going to start dating again it would be me. We get along so well. We come from the same background, the same gene pool. We can use the same comb and brush. Why can't we try dating? Why are you always with these white guys? It never ends well for you." He looked as if he believed the nonsense he was spewing. "I'm a doctor. We have things in common. Meryt, you know I make good money." He started laughing. "You know I've got benefits, and a brotha ain't bad on the eyes."

Everything he said was true minus them dating. He was a cutie pie. Any woman black, white, brown, or yellow would be honored to be involved with him. He loved to play basketball, and before or after games he hit the weights. He had light brown skin with hazel eyes. His eyes always changed colors based on his mood. And yes, Lord, he had them, meaning the mood swings. He was worse than any woman Meryt knew. Darren was fun to be with, and her mother would be all too happy for her to bring him home, but he was not for Meryt. On a scale of one to one hundred, he was an eighty-nine. Eighty-nine was not his looks or the total package, but a number her heart assigned to a mate. Meryt knew it sounded crazy. Maybe she was crazy. Her heart was looking for a ninety-five or better. She figured a ninety-five or better would have greater chance of making a happy, long marriage.

She'd been around too many unhappy marriages. In some cases, they wouldn't even divorce. They just cheated and lied to themselves and to their spouses. They thought they were doing the right thing by not divorcing, but they were simply wrong. They ended up hurting themselves and everyone else. Sometimes the very person or persons they tried not to hurt, they ended up hurting the most. But at least they tried to make it work. She least admired the ones that married, and before wedding gifts were unwrapped and thank-you cards were sent, they got divorced. Meryt wondered, *How do you divorce that quickly? So that means, five minutes after being married, the person realized a mistake was made.* Meryt figured those were her demons, and she probably was overanalyzing.

But, back to Darren; he was a hottie, but not her hottie. Meryt loved him like a brother. But to pursue this relationship when she knew he didn't make her heart beat fast was not fair to him or to herself. And Darren was not a something, something guy. Either a person was in it for a lifetime commitment or a friend on the sidelines. There was no middle ground.

"Darren, we are friends. You know I'm your girl, but I can't be your woman. There is a young lady or maybe a young man for you, but it's not me," Meryt starting chuckling. "Furthermore, who I chose to have a drink with should not be your concern. Now, are we done with this conversation? Or am I going to have to start charging you therapist fees?"

Darren started laughing with Meryt saying, "Please!"

She continued, "Are we good? Can I get back to my paying job?"

They hugged and went in two different directions. Meryt walked toward the elevator; looking down at her cell phone she saw she had received two messages during her free consulting session. None were from Deacon.

Chapter 10

After a long day at the hospital, Meryt knew there was nothing better than pulling up into her own driveway. She came home to no pages, no intercom messages, no this, no that just peace and quiet. Meryt needed to start twice-a-day workouts. Endurance always beat strength. That morning, she swam for forty minutes. After work, she promised herself a rucksack run. She got out of the car and strolled over to the garage cabinets looking for her old running partner, the rucksack. She found it folded up under a dirty bucket. Meryt kicked the bucket across the garage into a corner. She hated buckets. She pulled the ruck out, shaking the dust off, while looking around the garage to see what she could pack in it. Meryt figured she'd start off with a fifteen-pound ruck. *It's funny,* she thought. She watched people running in the parks with latest in lightweight running gear. She was fascinated by people running without any additional weight. What was the purpose of running with nothing but bare skin? When she ran, she always carried a few days of supplies, such as food, water, and ammunition. Weight meant everything to Meryt. There she went again, putting military standards on civilians. The people Meryt saw running in parks were running for fun, trying to stay healthy; when she ran, it was to save her own life. Every three pounds of weight was a day's rations or ammunitions. Deciding to drop the weight to gain speed meant the situation was dire.

Meryt entered the house and quickly changed into her running gear before she changed her mind about the run. Actually, she loved running. She loved hearing her heartbeat. Meryt loved pushing herself further than she had the day before. In the garage, she had found some old sneakers, a few paperbacks, a few bricks, and black trash bags to shove into the ruck. She threw the ruck over her shoulder and pulled her arms through the straps and then tightened them down. Meryt reached for her earplugs and put the mini MP3 player in her pocket. She positioned the earplugs in her ears and pulled her black knit cap down over them. After a little stretching, Meryt was all set for a ten-mile run.

She had a preplanned route. Meryt changed them every few weeks. She dreaded running the same routes, because she got bored. Her body started to anticipate the turn-around points. No matter the time, it was always the last two miles that hurt the most, regardless of the distance. In this case, it held true. Meryt was two miles from the house, averaging a six-minute mile, when her knees started complaining. Every time her foot hit the ground, her knees sent shooting pain messages up her legs saying, *You're getting too old for this. We did not agree to this program.* Meryt ignored them. She was accustomed to their complaints during the workout sessions.

She completely stopped annotating body-part complaints and started to pick up the speed for the last two miles. As she crossed the parking lot that led to her street, she noticed a car pulling alongside her. Meryt slowed down to see if she recognized the car. It was Rene and Fritz. Fritz was driving, and Rene was on the passenger side. Fritz stopped and Rene put his window down.

Meryt squatted over, resting on her knees while gasping for air. "What's up guys? Are you trying to race me across the parking lot?"

Rene smiled. "What are you doing out here at eleven thirty at night? It's not safe."

"What is this? You are starting to sound like Darren. Did it ever occur to you that I might like a little trouble in my life?" Meryt said, stretching her legs. It was thirty degrees outside, and she didn't want her legs to stiffen-up.

"Trouble is exactly what you'll find out here so late at night," Rene said. He was wondering, *Why can't she do normal things? What woman runs around in the middle of the night with a backpack?* The only thing that gave him relief was the fact that at least she was heading home. He knew her house was just around the block. As relief started to settle in, he saw the top of a sneaker peeking out of her backpack. Rene immediately assumed the worst; *Did her friend kick her out in the middle of night and forced her to run home?* Rene's temper started to flare. He felt his vision changing and quickly looked away before Meryt noticed.

"Rene, what's up? What are you guys doing out so late?" Meryt started to worry. Rene didn't look well. Instinct took over. She reached into the car and touched Rene's face as he was turning away to check if he had a fever. Rene pulled away. He grabbed his eyes as if something irritated them.

Fritz spoke-up, "Oh, I needed to pick up a prescription. This is the only twenty-four-hour pharmacy in town." He pointed to the drug store sign behind them flashing its neon lights.

"All right, I need to finish this run before I find any more trouble, like these old legs giving out. Good night. See ya tomorrow at work." Meryt took off running, trying to regain her six-minute-mile pace.

All the way home, she thought about Rene. What was his problem? One minute he wanted to talk, have drinks, have conversations, and then nothing. Odd. She made it home with no further complaints from her legs. She dropped the ruck on the garage floor and took off her running shoes. They were soaked, and she didn't want to leave dirty tracks on the house floors. Once inside, she armed the house security. She took out her cell phone and checked for missed calls from the hospital or Deacon as she walked upstairs to the master suite. The only things that occupied her mind were a hot shower and Rene's strange behavior.

Chapter 11

Pliny was correct. Indulgence was an understatement. The ceremony to unite the two kingdoms, Egyptians and the Nubians, had commenced one year ago with the marriage of Akhenaten and Nefertiti. Today's ceremony was dedicated to uniting the armies. The pharaoh had requested additional security following the birth of his new daughter.

Smenkhkara, the pharaoh's best advisor, insisted that the armies be united quicky. Smenkhkara was very pleased to see the union finally materialize. As the senior advisor, he knew the importance of having the military strength from the Nubians to help protect Egyptain's growing empire.

The ceremony started officially, exchanging vows and reciting rituals asking for blessing from the Creator. Nitocris thought her father would have been proud. He had orchestrated this union soon after her sister's birth. He noticed the multitude of people growing every day, not only among his people, but also in the population along the trade routes. Her father wanted neighbors as allies. This allowed for a better defense against foreigners.

The official ceremony ended, allowing time to change for the unofficial celebration, which started at dusk. Queen Nitocris was most grateful. After riding all day, and going directly into the formal ceremony, she needed a bath. She 'Thank the Creator', Pliny had convinced her not to ride in on horseback in the sun. She would have been a mess. Back in her quarters, the servants prepared her for evening festivities.

Refreshed and dressed, Queen Nitocris arrived at dusk with Pliny on her right. The temple was alive with colors, movement, and laughter. There were pillows of different shapes, colors, and sizes along every wall and surrounding every fountain. Entertainers were everywhere, painted from head to toe in shimmering gold. They appeared to be almost magical as the circled the room dancing and singing. Nitocris wondered how they were going to come clean from that much gold paint. There were magic acts and jesters doing flips and spins. The ambiance of the room was only surpassed by the abundance of food presented. Nitocris had never seen so much food laid out; large copper plates were spread throughout the room. Servers maneuvered in and out of the crowds, offering more food and more beer.

The Egyptians loved their beer and lived by their legends. It was only natural that beer's recipe was born from such a tale. It was believed that the Creator became disenchanted with his people because they began to question if he was truly the Creator. In his anger, he sent forth his favorite goddess, Hathor, to kill the rebels, the nonbelievers. When the Creator witnessed Hathor killing his people and rejoicing in their blood, his heart grew soft and mourned for the mortals' deaths. No one loved man more than the Creator, but he also loved Hathor. So he gave mandrakes, the love apples, to Sekit, goddess of love, and commanded her to crush and grind up the fruit and mix it with human blood and wheat to form beer. Once the beer was complete, the Creator brought forth the offering to Hathor with its hidden intent to lessen her desire to kill man and instead make merry. The offer was successful. Over the generations, as the story had been passed along, holy men had used beer for many things, from treaty negotiations to drugs for fertility. Nitocris's teachers would remind her daily of the multiple purposes of beer. She always laughed; who would not want to make merry after beer? Wasn't that the hidden intention?

Pliny escorted Nitocris to her sister, Nefertiti, who was sitting by the water fountain made of rubies. Afterwards Pliny bowed and stood off to the side allowing the sisters their privacy. The two women embraced for a long moment to commemorate their love, it had been a year full of change and growth for both women. Nefertiti had gotten married and became a queen in a new land. She had given birth to her first child. Nitocris buried their father; she had become the queen of Nubia, and assumed the reign of her kingdom. Once the family moment passed, the queens did what they loved to do together gossip and giggle at the room's entertainment and guests.

Nitocris scooted close and asked, "Are you sure, you want to remain here in Giza? You should bring your baby to her homeland. Do you really trust these people?"

"Oh, you worry too much. Egyptians love to celebrate, but they are good, hardworking people," Nefertiti replied as a man danced in front of them, dressed as both a woman and a man, changing directions pretending to dance with himself.

Nefertiti continued, holding back her smile, "They are different." Both ladies laughed.

"Can you tell me about the brothers, Atem and Atum?" Queen Nitocris asked.

"They are definitely different. They are not originally from Egypt, but they have lived here longer than most. The concubines often joke about their ages. It is believed that they have the gift of life," Nefertiti said as she looked around the room, locating her husband and Smenkhkara together talking. "Atem and Atum are handsome. If I were not promised to the pharaoh, I would allow courtship with Atem," she added, scanning the room for the brothers' location.

"You talk blasphemy! Can you compare the pharaoh's love to a mere immortal?"

"I know duty and honor, but you are my sister. If I cannot speak truth with you, whom can I speak it to? I have every intention to remain a faithful wife to the pharaoh." Nefertiti gave her a smirk. "I can tell you this: study your words carefully when you speak to the brothers. They are always plotting and planning. And they are almost always together. The brothers are part of an elite guard from the pharaoh's father. They started providing protection for Akhenaten since the death of his brother, Thutmos. I rarely see them during the day. They are mostly out at dusk. Once I saw them during high sun, and" Nefertiti moved in closer, "they wore the oddest things. They were covered from head to toe in cloths. It is rumored they have a skin disease. I've never seen any markings or bruises, but I have seen them practice swords." Nefertiti smiled, remembering home. "They remind me of you and our father practicing back home. Normally, they stand off in the shadows, like right now, just watching." Nefertiti had finally found them, standing together in the shadows of the drapes.

Queen Nitocris looked over in their direction. They were surveying the crowd. No, they were both watching the queens in their conversation. She thought Atum nodded his head with a grin. "They are staring at us," she said softly. Nitocris's heart began to rush at the thought of his grin.

"Don't worry. He's been watching ever since you entered the room," Nefertiti said and looked back in Atum's direction. "Well, if you are going to worry, worry now because it looks as if he's coming over."

Nitocris looked up. "What! What do I do? How do I look?" She tried to adjust her seated position to appear regal.

"How do you look? What do you say? When did you start to notice men? I must have been gone too long." Nefertiti laughed.

"Stop laughing. Look official. He'll think we were talking about him."

"We *were* talking about him. Now I know why you asked me questions about the brothers! At first, I thought you were concerned for my safety, but you are interested in Atum."

"Stop. He's close now," Nitocris whispered.

"Queen Nefertiti and Queen Nitocris," Atum stated as he bowed his head. "Are you enjoying the festivities?"

Nefertiti spoke first. "Yes, we are enjoying the night's festivities. My sister was just commenting that she would love to dance, but unfortunately she knows no one. Would you offer your service?"

Nitocris couldn't believe the words that were coming from Nefertiti's mouth. If they were home, Nitocris would have pushed her sister back into the pillows and tried to smother her with another. Truly the heat had taken hold of Nefertiti's mind.

"Yes, my Queen, as you request."

Atum held his hand out for Nitocris to touch. *One . . . two . . . three . . . breathe. That settles it. When I return from this dance, I will kill my sister.* Nitocris thought to herself.

As Queen Nitocris reached up for Atum's hand their eyes met again for the second time that day and Nitocris refused to look away.

Chapter 12

Time marched forward; even the Mayan's knew time continued to move, repeating the cycle over and over with minuscule differences. Meryt blinked and December was gone and new year was here. She was working another night shift in the ER. The only thing making it bearable was Fritz and his demanding trial. Fritz was still pushing the limits of her mind on the new equations. Still, the time allotted for the reaction to break down and rebuild was the major obstacle they could not pass. They hadn't developed a compound that would break down, attach to human modular cell, and rebuild before the host's white cells would destroy it. Fritz and Meryt were in the lab when a stat call came over the intercom. They both made their way to the emergency room. When they arrived, a woman and her daughter were being prepped in two separate bays. Fritz went to the mother, and Meryt went to the little girl.

As Meryt walked into the room, Tab, the head nurse who always shared the same shift as Meryt started rattling off the child's condition: ten-year-old female, barely conscious, broken left hand, concussion, and possible spinal injuries. The child was lying on a board in a blood-soaked t-shirt and shorts, looking up at the ceiling light, calling softly for her mother. Meryt ordered X-rays stat.

"What's her name?" she asked.

Someone replied, "Rochelle."

"Listen, Rochelle, you're in the emergency room it's going to be fine. Are you in pain? Can you tell me where it hurts?"

Tab screamed, "She coding!"

"Get me the paddles and injections of nitrates and epinephrine," Meryt ordered as she scanned over Rochelle's body. "Hold on, Honey, don't do this! Stay with me!"

Tab passed the injection, and Meryt jabbed the needle directly into Rochelle's heart as another nurse placed grounding pads on Rochelle's sides. Tab gave Meryt the paddles from the defibrillator.

"Stand clear!" Meryt called as she delivered 360 biphasic joules to Rochelle's chest. The little girl's body jumped off the table from the energy delivered.

Meryt rapidly assessed Rochelle's condition. She was turning a deadly gray, and the heart monitor was beeping faster as Rochelle's rate climbed to 440 beats per minute; her pressure was nearly nonexistent. She was not out of the forest yet.

"I'm hitting her again. Clear!" Rochelle's petite body jumped off the table, making a thumping sound as it fell back down. The same high-pitched beeping still screamed from the heart monitor.

"Tab, intubate her, and I'll start CPR."

As Meryt gazed into Rochelle's eyes, she felt the little girl say, "It's okay. I'm not afraid. I'm with my mom." And then she closed her eyes forever. At that exact moment, the monitor flat-lined.

"No, it's not your time. Don't die!" Meryt shrieked.

Her words fell on deaf ears. Rochelle was gone. Meryt gave her another shot of nitrate and epinephrine solution and shocked her two more times; still nothing, just a flat line on the monitor.

Tab pulled Meryt back from the bed. "It's been over five minutes. Do you want to call it, Dr. Brownstone?"

"Wait, let me think," she whispered. Meryt needed to stop her own adrenaline. It had been a long time since she lost a patient, especially a child. Rochelle had had her whole life in front of her, and now it was all gone. Meryt had met Rochelle and said good-bye all in fifteen minutes.

"Yes, call it," she finally replied. "It's 12:54 a.m.; Start the paperwork. I'm going to check on the mother. I'll be back."

Meryt sprinted into the other bay. The entire front of Fritz, from his gloves on down was covered in blood. For the first time, Meryt really noticed that Fritz looked as white as a ghost. He turned completely around, away from Meryt, as if he were embarrassed.

He spoke with his back still turned away from Meryt, "She's gone. She had head trauma, and her whole front rib cage was spilt open, as if she had caught a huge medicine ball that tore right through her chest cavity."

Meryt questioned Fritz, "Did she say anything?"

This time Meryt heard the gloves snap as Fritz spoke through clenched teeth, still trying to remove his blood soaked gloves without any more blood spatter. The single snap of the gloves sent a fresh wave of blood aroma into the air, tingling his senses. "She kept calling for her daughter. I told her she was in good hands and everything was going to be fine," Fritz said as he tore off his paper gown, desperately trying not to let any more blood touch his clothes.

"It's not fine, nor is it alright. I lost the daughter. She told me she wanted to be with her mother. Little Ms. Rochelle took her last breath and closed her eyes. What happened? A car accident?"

The medic from the ambulance replied, "Yes, a drunk driver hit them at a red light. They were in a small, two-door '98 Honda Civic. The driver was in an Escalade. It was like a tank driving over a go-kart. We have the driver recovering in our vehicle. All he he had were a few stitches."

Meryt asked the medics as she walked toward the waiting room, "Is there family waiting out front?"

Medic replied, "Only the driver's friends."

She peeked out the window and saw three guys laughing it up. One was under six feet and about 210 pounds, and his two friends over were over six foot two and well over 250 pounds. All three seemed to be thirty-ish with a major case of Peter Pan syndrome. The one under six feet appeared to be the pack leader. Every clique has one. Clearly, he was it.

Meryt heard them laughing again, and the leader started joking. "Did you see that bitch and all that blood? That'll teach her about leaving. How long do you think they'll keep Bobby?"

Her blood ran cold, and her eyes dilated; the killer within was awakened by the killers sitting in the lobby. Only young immature killers find it funny when innocent lives were lost. Meryt blinked her eyes a few times to regain some type of composure, but the rage was too overwhelming. Her cold hands pushed opened the door, and her feet started walking in their direction. As she got closer, she noticed a young lady whose eyes were red. It looked as if she had been crying all night; her mascara had left black circles around her eyes and two long lines down each cheek. She was wearing a gold, shimmery party dress. Meryt could see the stains on the front of her dress where she had wiped all of her makeup off from crying. Meryt must have caught her eye, because she stood up as Meryt got closer and asked her about the woman and her daughter. Meryt asked her to immediately go back and ask for Dr. Daniels.

The whole time Meryt could not take her eyes off her prey. Yes, her prey. They would meet again this evening to further discuss bitches and blood. Meryt was always prepared for a little action as she reached into her pocket ensuring the microchip was there. Thinking about their meeting only excited her more. She felt her body temperature drop another five degrees. As the young lady started to pass Meryt, heading toward the bay area of the ER, Meryt caught the attention of her prey.

She immediately took a posture between the young lady and her prey. Meryt reminded herself, *Control.*

Meryt slowly took her hand from her lab pocket to pat the leader on his shoulder. "Excuse me, Mr. Um?"

He replied with a grin, "Smith."

Meryt continued, "Mr. Smith, we only allow one guest in at a time. She may be awhile."

Meryt had made contact. She touched his shoulder and started sliding her hand quickly down his back, dropping a microchip into his coat pocket.

Mr. Smith responded, "No problem. We won't be staying. I'm sure Bubbles will get a ride home. But you? When do you get off tonight, baby?"

Her temperature dropped another degree. She felt a cool breeze by her ear.

Rene started speaking. "I'm sure we can handle this. Is there a number we can contact you if we have any questions?" At the same time, Rene tried sending mental images for them to leave. Rene knew they were up to no good. He smelled their wickedness from three feet away. He couldn't understand why Meryt was entertained by their company.

The clique spoke as one, "No, we have to leave. We'll be back later."

Meryt thought that the police walking in had changed their minds about hanging around.

"I have to leave, as well," Meryt announced. Rene grabbed her arm, and escorted her back to the ER bay area.

"What were you doing out there?" Rene asked.

"My job. I needed to talk to the family." Meryt made no eye contact and paid no attention to his obvious attitude. The killer in her was awake, and she needed to escape from the hospital and into her car. No one at work had ever seen this side of her, and she didn't want tonight to be the coming-out party.

"Tab, give the paper work to Fritz. He'll finish it. Something came up, and I have to run home quickly." Meryt kept walking to the changing room to get her purse.

Rene caught up. "What is wrong with you? I've never seen you like this? Where are you going?"

"Considering we just started speaking, of course you have never seen me like this. The answer to your second question is 'to my car.'" Elvis had left the building.

Meryt got into her car. She thanked God she had brought her car tonight. Most winter days she took the truck. The truck would have slowed her down tonight. She put her foot on the brake, and pushed the start button to turn on the car. She felt the engine purr in her seat.

Suddenly, a knock came from the passenger-side door. It was Rene. She let the window down. "What?"

Before she knew it, Rene had reached his hand in the car, opened the door, and sat down.

"Rene, get out. I do not have time to play word games with you tonight."

"I'm not getting out, so wherever you are going, we are going."

Meryt didn't have time to argue. She locked the doors and roared out of the parking lot.

"Meryt, where are you going in such a rush? Are you going after those guys alone?" She did not answer any of his questions. She was too busy.

Meryt reached into the armrest to retrieve the tracking device that activated the homing chip she had placed in Mr. Smith's pocket. *Like his name is really Smith,* she thought.

"Meryt, what is this?" Rene asked, pointing at the tracking device.

"A tracking device. Make yourself useful. Turn it on and mount it on the dashboard for me."

Finally a signal came in on the device. They were on the move. It appeared they were heading north toward the highway.

"Listen, you wanted to come. You jumped into my car. Do you honestly think you are the only one with secrets?"

Rene responded, "What does that mean?"

Meryt continued, "You and your family move to Niagara Falls. You all live in one house. You have money. It's clear by your lifestyle. Not to mention, you and your brother are very talented physicians. Any big-name hospital would pay top dollar for either of you, yet both of you are here in Niagara Falls. Your brother is on a quest to create some super synthetic hemoglobin. His first words to me were about the similarities in our trials. The very first time I met your brother, he wanted to start working on a prototype in my lab. If I did not know any better, I would think your brother's research led him to me. But, whatever the reasons, you and your family are here. It is clear to me you want to fly under the radar. You are hiding out."

"My brother was correct about you; he said it would not be long before you caught on."

"Listen, Rene, I don't want to know anything you are not prepared to tell. All I require is a little company. I want to catch up with those thugs, because they look like they need a lesson or two. Now hold on, we've got some miles to make up. Is that Okay with you?"

Rene agreed. Within a few minutes, they were trailing behind their car. Meryt cut her headlights off and turned on her night-vision window shield. The inside of the car glowed green, but the windows were tinted, preventing the light from escaping. With the upstate's normal evening fog, her car became virtually invisible in the night air.

Rene asked, "Where did you get this car?"

"I purchased it through the dealer and added a few extras." Meryt got close enough to read Mr. Smith's license plate. He drove a black 2007 Cadillac. She called Deacon to run the tag.

The car was registered to a Ronald Tuswang. Mr. Tuswang had a nice lengthy rap sheet. assault and battery, trafficking and prostitution. Just her kind of guy. Once she collected the information, she sped pass Mr. Tuswang on the highway.

Meryt drove about a half mile down the road and spun the car around. She switched off the night-vision and switched on her headlights. With full speed, she drove straight for Mr. Smith, aka Mr. Tuswang. They were going to play "chicken."

When the driver saw her lights, he tried to swivel, but Meryt copied his swivel. They repeated mirror maneuvers two more times until he ran his car off the highway. What was wonderful about upstate was there were always plenty of wooded areas that surrounded the highways and never enough cops to cover it all. In addition, the good folks of upstate were normally home asleep after one in the morning.

The Cadillac skidded about fifty feet before it came to a stop. Meryt shut off her lights and stopped her car about forty feet away from them. She reached for her gun under the seat and tucked it into her pants.

Meryt looked over at Rene. "Are you ready to play?"

She was surprised at his response: "I could get used to hanging out with you. Let's go."

Mr. Tuswang and his crew got out of the car slowly, looking over the damage to their car. They had no idea what happened.

Meryt pulled her gun out, pointed it, and shot all three with a tranquilizer. They were out for twenty minutes. During that time, she and Rene strung the men to three separate trees.

The two groupies/bodyguards awakened first to the snug ropes. They tried talking, but it was difficult with duct tape wrapped across their mouths. No one could hear them scream out in pain as Meryt and Rene took turns using them as a punching bag. The more they wiggled, the tighter the ropes became. Before long, Ronald started to come around.

"Mr. Smith, or should I say Mr. Tuswang, I'm so glad you've come back. I was afraid we wouldn't have any fun tonight. I heard a rumor that you were into bitches and blood."

Meryt clapped her hands with excitement, the way a teacher does as she announces day's lessons. "So here I am. I'll play the bitch, and I figure you would supply the blood." Meryt hit him in the mouth. Mr. Tuswang, on queue, supplied a nice small steam of blood from his lower lip.

He screamed, "You bitch, I'll kill you." He began to struggle with the ropes that Rene had tied.

"See, I told you I would supply the bitch," Meryt said, and she hit him again in the mouth and more blood began to flow. "And you'll supply the blood!"

"Who are you?" Tuswang, gasping for air, asked.

"You've got bigger problems; who I am should not concern you." Meryt side-kicked him in the ribs. "Your concerns should be, 'will I be alive in the morning or will I be in jail?' You do realize, you are tied to a tree in the middle of nowhere in the woods with blood running down from your month." Meryt followed the statement with a combination kick to his chest. "Plus, with a few more direct kicks, I'm hoping you'll have some internal bleeding. I've heard rumors of things that put man in their food-chain." She hit him again in the mouth, followed by another sidekick to the chest.

Suddenly, she didn't feel the need to continue the assault. Meryt never intended on killing them. She only wanted to blow some steam off and teach them a lesson. Meryt had every intention on calling the authorities in the morning.

"You and your boys might be something's midnight snack. On that note, I must bid my farewell, I wouldn't want to be confused by the night snake, no, I mean for the night snack. I'm not psychic, but I have a strong feeling your life will be totally different in a few hours. I can smell the demons coming for you." As she wiped the blood from her hands, she noticed Rene standing over in the shadows. She looked over to him and said, "I'm done. This isn't my kill. I want to leave before it's too late."

Mr. Tuswang started screaming at the top of his lungs, "Too late for what?"

Meryt felt her high coming down, her combat exterior collapsing. As they walked away, she felt weak and cold. The adrenaline high left her feeling empty. Rene instinctively reached for her hand. Meryt fell in step, close to his side.

Rene couldn't believe what just happened. What kind of woman was this? She was prepared to confront three men alone? Not only was she beautiful, sexy, smart, and smelled absolutely delicious, but she was also a warrior. He hadn't seen this kind of woman since the 1600s. Watching her cause Tuswang to bleed outside in the night air heightened his senses. He loved the smell of fresh blood outside. It smelled totally different from hospital blood that was mixed with the odors of disinfectants and alcohol. Out here, in the open night air, being this close to Meryt, her scent mingled with the fresh blood, the combination ignited his lust.

They walked a few more feet together as if they were old friends on a late night walk. They hadn't just finished tying three men to trees and torturing them. Nope, they were just friends enjoying an evening walk. By now they were only a few steps away from the car. At the end of the walk, the electricity had built between them. Meryt couldn't help herself. She wanted to touch him. Her hand started wandering along his back, up and down, until it rested around his side. She could smell his sweet, masculine scent jasmine and leather spice. Her mind began to drift and the heat of lust started to replace the coldness in her veins.

Rene could sense the temperament change in Meryt. Without another thought, he picked her up and straddled her around his waist. She was surprised she even noticed he picked her up. Her mind had only one thing on it. Kissing Rene. Meryt need to satisfy her curiosity. She needed to satisfy her lust. She could feel his thin, strong lips against hers. Meryt had fuller lips, but they did not overpower his. He softly sucked each lip, giving each lip it's full due attention, as if either would be jealous. He slowly began to open her mouth, allowing his tongue to explore. He tasted as good as he smelled.

Rene wanted it all. There was no time to explain anything. Hopefully, Meryt felt the same strong pulling sensation he had felt since the first day they met. He couldn't wait for the trial to be complete; he wouldn't wait to manage through a courtship. It had to be now. He felt her pulse quicken as he pushed her up against the tree. He felt her body heat rising. From his lustful vision, she glowed a soft red beneath her brown skin. He had long since missed the true taste of chocolate. Rene imagined that was how she must taste. Rene was losing control of his desires. He wanted all of it: her scent, her heat, her quick wit, and her warrior spirit. But more than that, he wanted her blood. His eyes turned a deep, boiling red. He dug his face into her neck, kissing and licking her carotid artery.

Meryt felt her back against the tree; her legs were still wrapped around his waist. Her fever was rising quickly, even faster as she felt his manhood pressed against her body. It caused her to hold him closer. She felt his cool tongue slide into her hot, wet mouth, followed by kisses around her neck. In that moment, Meryt felt herself slip into another world or maybe she was on the verge of fainting? She couldn't tell the difference nor did she care. Meryt stopped kissing only to feel his breathing against her earlobe as he was slowly moving down her neck. She was holding on to him so tightly, wanting nothing less than to melt in his embrace. Rene was driving her crazy with light kisses along her neck. He started in the front, moving lightly around toward the back arch of her neck. That was her spot! Chills ran down her spine. She could no longer hold on. Wherever they were, it did not matter. All she wanted was him all over her, inside of her, on top of her. Meryt just wanted him.

Meryt heard growls and screams. It felt like some crazy mystical dream, but it did not matter. The noises were not her concern. The only thing that remained important was Rene, the man in her arms. She was holding on to sanity with all of her might, and then she was gone.

Meryt began to dream of first kisses. All of them she knew. She felt them; she felt their love, their lust, and the blood running through their veins. A couple in Egypt was the clearest. Meryt could feel their love, their passion as if it were all her own.

Chapter 13

After the dance, Atum escorted Queen Nitocris out onto the balcony overlooking Giza. The desert breeze lifted her long curly hair off of her shoulders. Atum breathed in her scent deeply. His heart smiled, but his face would not betray his secret. Atum was a protector, a guardian for humans. He was not created to love mankind only to watch and to protect.

He had watched his brother Atem fall in love with Queen Nefertiti, and nothing good had come of it. She was dedicated to the pharaoh and had already given birth to one child. Only a few knew that it almost killed her during the delivery. Between the pharaoh and his brother, Atem, he did not know who was in more pain at the potential loss.

Akhenaten the Pharaoh demanded the high priests give offerings to the Creator. The priests remained in the temple, chanting and praying, for two days nonstop. The pharaoh rarely left her side, pleading with the Queen to remain strong and not cross over to the underworld when she closed her eyes. The pharaoh knew she wanted more children. He promised her as many children as the kingdom allowed. She was Mother to all of Egypt. They would all become her children.

Akhenaten loved her, but more than that, she was the true backbone, the diplomat, to Egypt's new religion. He was never supposed to be the pharaoh. It was his brother who had received the training. Akhenaten was a lover of art, not politics. Nefertiti's strong training in leadership and politics helped him guide Egypt into the new realm of religion and economic monopoly along new trade routes. Her name, Nefertiti, meant *the beautiful one has come*. All would be lost without her guidance.

Atem never left the shadows of Queen Nefertiti's room. He stood watch day and night, never resting, never feeding. His eyes glowed red with the passion and hurt that burned in his blood. Atem felt helpless. Atum knew his brother loved her, but Atem had agreed not to inform the queen of his true feelings. Even if she returned his love, their love had no purpose. Nefertiti was still the Pharaoh's wife. She was human. He knew one day she would die, while he would remain alive to mourn her for all of eternity. It was not common knowledge that she ran the kingdom. But it was her true calling; Nefertiti was meant to rule Egypt. She was not meant to run through the desert sands making love until the sun rose with Atem.

Atum worried, wondering if Atem planned to offer Nefertiti his blood to become a dark angel. One night, Atum caught him praying to the Creator for permission. He asked Atem if that was his master plan. Atem just looked beyond him to Nefertiti, as if he was not present. No words were spoken between the brothers that night. Finally on the third night, the queen appeared to be recovering. Atem finally fed.

Atum made note, falling in love with a human was useless at its best and painful at its worst. But on this night, Atum knew differently for the first time. Falling in love presented faith and hope for goodness. Now he understood how the Creator loved Hathor, his mother, and how Atem loved Nefertiti. Love did not make you weak; it made you strong. Love was the basis of creation. You create for love. You build for love. You live for love. Again, his heart smiled. Love was worth having even if it was not returned.

Queen Nitocris broke his concentration. "Atum, why are you staring off into the night? Do I bore you?"

"Sorry, Queen Nitocris, I had not noticed. My mind drifted to another matter. You are many things, but boring you are not." Atum stood back, leaning over the bannister and watching the stars. "How long will you stay in Egypt?"

"As long as my sister requires. I had hoped to bring her home, but I'm afraid she is as stubborn as I and refuses to leave Egypt. I will stay for few months, but I must return home.

"To your king?"

"I have no king. My father died nine months ago. I am the queen, the ruler of Nubia. I am to rule until my death comes, and then my reign is passed to Nefertiti or her oldest offspring. Plus, there are rumors of a war. The Babylonians are attacking trade routes on the far reaches of our eastern border in the mountains. I must keep a close eye, the reports are starting to be numerous. Now you have uncovered my reason for wanting my niece and my sister to come home. One day, one of them will rule all."

Atum felt a spark of hope. She had no dedication other than her country. She was open to love. He reached over to her and removed a strand of hair that fell in the corner of her mouth. Her hair was as soft as silk. He felt her heart speed up. She began to glow in his vision.

"Why do you insist on taking so many liberties with me? Is your mind on another matter?" Nitocris asked.

"Yes, Queen Nitocris, my mind is on another matter." Atum took another step closer. She glowed even hotter in his vision. Atum knew she was interested. He had seen it in her eyes when they met on the stairs. He had heard it in her voice as he listened to her conversation with Queen Nefertiti earlier this evening.

"Take heed, please don't step so close. You will take no more liberties. Don't tempt me," Queen Nitocris warned as she pulled a knife from under her skirt.

Atum only smiled. This time it showed on his face. "Does your heart beat fast and perspiration build on your forehead when you are tempted to fight or when you are tempted to make love?" Atum took one final step. He now felt her heart beating against his skin. She felt as hot as midday desert heat. There was no denying she cared for him, if only she knew his real intentions.

He leaned forward and lifted her chin for a simple kiss, a kiss that made him a true believer in all things.

Chapter 14

The only thing that changed Fritz's mood from panic to worry was the call he got from Rene saying he was following Meryt to her car. Fritz called home to his family to meet him outside the hospital immediately. He asked his mother, NeiNei to track Rene and Meryt. Fritz felt nothing but disgust. The night had almost compromised all of his work. He was flustered by the amount of blood, which soaked into his clothes. The smell of fresh blood was all over him, it was in his clothes, and it reeked in the air. The blood actually soaked through to his skin. It tested every ounce of his resolve to remain calm. Tonight he demanded restitution. Fritz required more than prepackaged blood to satisfy his thirst.

What was Meryt up to? She didn't even know these people. Humans can be so emotional. When he saw the young lady coming into the restricted area of the ER, with her tear-stained dress, asking for the two victims, he didn't know what to think. Tabatha, everyone else called her Tab, had explained the situation and a collection was taken up. He pitched in $580. That was all he had on him in cash at the time.

Fritz gathered up all the paperwork and went into his office, but first he had to change. Once in clean scrubs, he completed all of the paperwork. Fritz was outside with his family within ten minutes of the initial call from Rene. Someone had to pay, and Fritz was eager to collect. What he found in the woods made up for all the earlier events from tonight. Fritz got his revenge. It had been seven months since he and his family had fed on live human blood.

Chapter 15

"Meryt, wake up." Rene was shaking her face.

"What? What happened? She was still against the tree, barely standing; Rene was still holding most of her weight. "I must have passed out? How long was I out?"

"Just a few seconds," Rene answered. He was concerned. This had been the moment he craved. For a brief second, he thought he squeezed the life out of her as they pressed up against the tree. His own passion had blinded him for a split second. "Are you okay?"

How embarrassing, Meryt thought. The first time they kissed, she fainted! She, of all people, after all the training she had completed and all the things she had seen; she had fainted over a kiss. Thank God that Deacon couldn't see her now. He would definitely have had jokes.

Rene repeatedly asked if Meryt was okay. She assured him she was fine, but he insisted on driving. Meryt didn't argue over the subject. She was in no mood to drive. *Who else would drive? Mr. Tuswang and his crew?* Meryt and Rene barely spoke as they drove back to the hospital. Meryt kept trying to figure out the last time she had fainted. No date came to mind. She had never fainted during any training exercise. She had undergone extensive exercises in how to control her body's natural chemical response to not fainting. Yet this evening she fainted over a kiss. Life.

As they pulled into the parking lot of the hospital, she remembered the true victims, the two lives lost in the ER. Meryt hoped, at least one life was saved tonight. She hoped the lady in the stained gold dress would learn to keep better company. Meryt had also remembered the ton of paperwork that remained. She took a deep breath to steady her nerves and give her strength for the tasks at hand.

As if Rene were reading her mind, he said, "Fritz has finished all the paperwork. Why don't you go home and rest tonight?"

Meryt thought about it for a moment, but she needed to confirm it for herself what remained. Rene reluctantly agreed and left Meryt to her own mission.

Meryt walked into ER. Tab was about to change shifts. She said the paperwork had been completed. Dr. Daniels had finished it hours ago before he quickly ran out. The lady Meryt had sent back had left the hospital with enough bus fare to return home to Canada. Tab must have seen the exhausted look in Meryt's face and asked why was she still at the hospital.

Meryt left the hospital under direct orders from her head nurse. It was true. Meryt needed sleep. She got home and showered the night's events off of her skin. The smell of Rene, his touches on her body, the tree bark in her hair, and the old dried up blood under her nails. *What a night.* Meryt could not have squeezed one more thing into the evening.

She dressed in a silky, soft nightgown. Funny how things changed; there was a time she had hated to have anything on her skin while she slept. Meryt always slept in the buff. It was the opposite now. She couldn't stand the idea of sleeping nude. And her nightwear had to be silky soft and short. Anything other than that she would toss and turn all night long.

But the short gown made no difference that evening; all night Meryt tossed and turned. What did this all mean: the kiss, the fainting, and her feelings for Rene? She had never experience this type of passion before, other than in a dream—it had felt so real.

On the ride back to the hospital they had not spoken a single word. She couldn't blame it solely on him; she had no words to say either. The weirdest feeling had taken over her. Rene had felt strangely familiar. None of her actions made sense, but then again, she had never felt this way before. Not to mention, she had never fainted over a kiss.

Her pride would not allow her mouth to utter such words. The only thing she could do was pray. Meryt did not want rumors flying around the hospital about her and last night's events. She definitely wanted no part of a little girl calling the house about "her Rene." The bottom line was, she did not want to repeat the whole Dallas event. Meryt truly could not stand another, "I told you so" talk from Darren. She would have no choice other than to leave Saint Catherine's Hospital. Meryt might possibly move to another state all together. Yet, she knew in her heart, the way she trembled when she thought of his kiss; Rene was definitely more than a something, something.

Monday came, and amazingly, Meryt was at ease seeing Rene. She was in the lab, working on her original findings in creating a synthetic blood prototype. Rene and his brother both came in, looking rather invigorated.

"You're in early." Rene spoke first.

"Yeah, I couldn't sleep. It was an interesting weekend, especially Saturday night or should I say Sunday morning?" Suddenly the room became quiet; Rene and Fritz froze in their steps. "Did I say something wrong? I was the one who dragged you out in the middle of nowhere to play Rambo. When the evening started to show some promise, I passed out."

Rene smiled. "That's how you remember the evening?" He came over and put his arm around Meryt and said, "Well, let's just leave it at that; what happens in the woods, stays in the woods."

"Agreed," they both said with a smile.

No rumors for Meryt meant that she didn't have to think about relocation.

Cindy came in the lab spreading morning cheer. "Meryt, it's a week before the ball. Do you have a date yet?" She said it loud enough for everyone in the room to hear.

Rene and Meryt were still embraced.

"Oh, well maybe you have?" she added. "Am I disturbing something, something?" Rene and Meryt looked at each other and quickly released.

"Cindy, you always know how to make an entrance. No, you are not disturbing anything. We were just playing around. There's nothing but work going on. And you know, I go stag every year," Meryt said with a giggle. "So should I be expecting you there with no one other than our fearless leader, Karl?"

Cindy said jokingly, "I don't know. I've had my eye on this cute little number." She winked at Rene.

Meryt said, "Really?" with one eye up. "Anybody I know?"

"You may; it's silver from the CLK550 family!" she said, holding out her brand new key chain and key.

"No way! Karl finally got it for you!"

"Yes! I got it last night during dinner. The Mercedes dealership drove it over to our house. Let's take it out for a coffee run." Cindy changed the mood in the room. Cindy asked Rene and Fritz if they wanted a cup. They both were laughing and declined her offer. Meryt told the guys she would see them later.

The car was beautiful. Karl definitely had taste. CLK 550 Mercedes-Benz, metallic silver, all-ash leather seats, door and matching carpets all the same color as the leather. It had just a touch of wood grain on the door and around the driver's command seat. Cindy glowed with so much happiness. Meryt couldn't help but glow with her. "Meryt, I did not know Karl had it in him. He can be so romantic. I was dropping hints, but I didn't think he would really follow through. Meryt, can you believe this!"

"Yes, Cindy, I can believe it. Karl is the luckiest man in the world to have you as a wife, so I'm sure there aren't many things he will ever deny you, except for a divorce," Meryt said as she chucked silently.

Meryt inhaled the new-car smell. She was sitting back, admiring Cindy and her car. Out of nowhere Cindy started bombarding her with questions. "I heard about last night in the emergency room. What happened to you? That's why I came straight to you this morning. People told me you lost it on three tough guys in waiting room, something about two girls who were admitted last night? Meryt, you know we are not God. If God decides it's done, then it's done. It's His will not yours."

"I know, but that's not what happened. Those guys were laughing at the death of a mother and her child, plus they had another girl with them. I'm pretty sure she would have met up with the same fate. I couldn't take it. How could someone laugh at death, especially that of a woman and her child?"

"Okay, judge and jury, that's not your job. You are here to help those in need of medical attention," Cindy replied.

Meryt continued, "Well, who's to say that they were not in special need of my service? Obviously they needed medical help, laughing at death. They were delusional."

"Meryt, I'm just worried about you. You live alone, you are always working or traveling alone, and you have no real male companionship. Wait before you choke me. I know a man does not define you, but there is much to be said about companionship. God created the heaven and earth, and then He created man and woman. If companionship was not important, then why create two humans? Why did Noah have to take two of each animal on the ark? Even animals need companionship."

"Cindy, is the new-car smell getting to you? Noah took two of every kind because they needed to procreate. As for Adam and Eve, wasn't there trouble in the Garden of Eden? I know what you are saying, but I'm fine. You're my friend, so there's my companionship."

Cindy fired off another question: "What about Rene? Why were you two hugging when I walked in the lab?"

"Nothing. You walked in on the closing of a joke."

"So what's the joke?" she questioned.

"You had to be there," Meryt quickly answered.

"I see," she said as the car turned into the driveway of the coffee shop. "I'll tell you what I really see. He could be your companion. I can see he could be your ivory to your ebony, if you just open yourself up and try to be accepting to a real relationship." Then she started humming *Ebony and Ivory* aloud.

"Funny, girl, just order our coffee."

Chapter 16

No calls from Deacon. Rene was friendly, still maintaining his distance. Meryt had a breakthrough on her equations. She finally had a stable reaction. The hemoglobin still took too long to break down, but when it reattached, it was stable. She had a stable synthetic blood. The synthetic hemoglobin (SYN) had to sit for two days before it was stable. Once stable, it behaved like normal blood. It was filled with nutrients and had an equal balance between systemic circulatory and angiotensin receptors. This was crucial in a heart failure patient. The best part of hemoglobin synthetic blood was that it had no side effects. A patient would just have to endure the same process as a dialysis patient, a weekly blood transfusion. In the scheme of things, a heart failure patient might not mind.

It was Friday evening, and the day of the hospital's Annual Spring Charity Ball. Meryt quickly dropped off a few samples of the SYN hemoglobin in the lab. She had sampled Fritz's patient X's blood and started the infusion eighteen hours ago. It required six more hours. She needed to get in and out of the lab quickly or she would be late for the ball.

This year, the hospital was raising money for the pediatrics department. She never looked forward to hospital's balls. Once there, she usually had a good time, but just getting there was so painful.

Meryt grabbed more samples and more needles. She wanted to inject another bag with the hemoglobin to complete the final part of the infusion and start a new sample to see if the hemoglobin would infuse faster and remain stable.

To her surprise, Fritz walked in with his lovely wife, Lolita. Meryt was speechless, admiring them with her mouth wide open like a child caught with its hand in the cookie jar. They were mesmerizing. He had on a black Armani suit with a white tie and she had on a beautiful formfitting red dress that crossed over one shoulder. Her brunette hair was pinned up in a high bun, simply gorgeous. Meryt must have looked silly. She literately froze with one hand on the injection needle and the other on the bag of blood.

Fritz broke the silence by asking, "Shouldn't you be at the ball? Meryt, this work can wait at least one night. And might I add, you are looking stunning this evening."

Meryt had on a black goddess-styled dress with an A-line cut. Each shoulder strap twisted then advanced down her back to form a deep plunge. The front of the dress had thin patent-leather belts crisscrossing around her upper midsection. It was a simple but elegant dress. For a change, she wore her hair down in loose finger curls, nearly reaching down to her waist. Meryt was wearing her most expensive pair of black, strappy Gucci shoes.

"Thank you, and I must say the same about you and your lovely wife. You are right about the ball, but I may have a surprise for you. It's slow, but I think it will work. I took a sample of patient X's blood yesterday, and I'm mixing the final portions with the SYN hemoglobin. So far, it has remainded stable. Plus I'm starting a fresh sample." Meryt placed the bags of blood in the walk-in refrigerator. "You know, I do realize this is probably someone close to you. I don't mind meeting him or her. This would probably work better if I had a fresh sample of the blood."

Lolita smiled. "She is right; don't you think it's time? The three of you are so close, why not arrange a visit."

Fritz did not answer his wife. He just gave her a special glance. He wasn't mad, but he did not want to continue this conversation at that moment.

"Fritz, you don't have to answer me now, but just think about it. I still need to determine the complete timeline on this current fusion," Meryt said as she was locking the door to the refrigerator. She read his expression. He hated an ambush.

Fritz replied like a gentleman, "Agreed, I'll think about it, but for now, let's attend the ball. May I escort you with my wife?" He held out his hand.

"I would be honored." Meryt reached for his hand. They all left the hospital together in his car. Meryt made small talk with Lolita. She enjoyed speaking with her. Lolita rarely came by the hospital, but when she did, it was always a pleasure.

They arrived at the hotel's ballroom; the theme was Casino Royal. The three of them stood at the top of the stairs overlooking the main floor.

Karl and his committee had done a fantastic job transforming the room. Bells were ringing and people were cheering the gamblers. All monies raised would be given to the pediatric department. What a wonderful cause. How could anybody say no? The dice were rolling, and the alcohol was flowing. Fritz escorted the two ladies down the stairs. Meryt on his right side, and Lolita was on his left. They slowly walked down the stairs, making a grand entrance to Casino Royal.

Meryt guessed Rene must have seen them, by the time they made it to the bottom of the stairs he was there waiting with a smile. He looked fabulous. He had on Armani suit as well, but with the European straight-leg cut and a little black bow tie. It fit him in all the right places. All Meryt could think of was her science teacher Mr. O. *Outstanding.* She did not think it was possible to look any better than Fritz did in his tuxedo, but there before her eyes stood the proof, Rene. Meryt's heart started to race. She told herself, *Just remember to breathe. It will be okay. One . . . two . . . three . . .*

"Fritz, why are you so lucky to escort two beautiful ladies tonight while I have none?" Rene said.

"As you stated, brother, I'm just lucky."

Rene returned his attention to Meryt. "Does the lady gamble?"

Meryt breathed slowly. "Why, yes. Blackjack is my sin."

"Blackjack it is, my lady. May I?" He held out his arm, and they were off to the nearest blackjack table.

It wasn't long before Cindy found Meryt with Rene. She sat down in the vacant seat next to them. "Meryt, when did you get here? I've been looking for you. Karl is killing me with all the introductions. I can't drink a glass of anything if I'm constantly shaking hands and giving out friendly hugs. What are you drinking?"

"Champagne," Meryt answered.

"Do you mind?" Cindy asked as she pointed to Meryt's glass.

"No. You can have it."

In one gulp, Cindy drank the entire glass.

"Thanks, girlfriend. That should steady my nerves for a while. Oh, by the way, Ebony and Ivory, you two look great. Steer clear of Darren. He's searching the room for you. I told him not to worry; you would be here in time. Oh and all of you are at the same table, so make nice. Well, gotta go. Karl needs me. You know I'm the official name keeper. All night I get, "What's his name?" or "What department does he work in?" or "Do they have children?" Cindy kissed Meryt and was off, mixing in the crowd, heading toward Karl.

Rene laid out one thousand dollars worth of chips on the table. He placed five hundred in front of Meryt and five hundred in his spot. They placed their bets. The dealer dealt the first set of cards Meryt received an ace, and Rene received a ten. Rene whispered into her ear, "Aren't we a compliment?" The next cards followed, a six and an ace.

"Blackjack for the gentleman," the dealer announced.

Meryt had seventeen. The dealer was showing 12. Meryt didn't take a hit. She stood. Meryt hated getting seventeen. In normal cases, a seventeen never wins, but she couldn't afford to take a chance on a hit. So she had to wait on the dealer to bust. The dealer took a hit; the number two appeared on the card. The dealer took another hit. It was a ten,

"Bust!"

Meryt leaned over to Rene and said, "This is the story of my life. I only win the hard way, and my men always get blackjack." Meryt said it jokingly, yet when their eyes met she had to quickly tell herself, *One . . . two . . . three . . . breathe.*

Rene replied, "The men you've dated were foolish. If they were lucky enough to have you and get blackjack, they should have never let you go."

Meryt felt his thirst for lust in his words. If she didn't know any better, she would have sworn his eyes had flashed red, and she had seen herself naked in them. *One . . . two . . . three . . . breathe,* she told herself again for the third time in a row. At that moment, the bells chimed for seating. *Thank God.*

"Time to join the rest," Meryt said slowly.

The dealer pushed their winning chips over. Meryt pushed her portion over to Rene.

"Thank you for the entertainment," Rene said as he pushed the chips back to the dealer. "It's for charity."

Rene took Meryt's hands and tenderly kissed the back of each, "Thank you for the company and the good luck." He placed his hand on her lower back to direct her to the dinner tables. Chills ran up and down her spine. She felt a little tugging as Rene wrapped a loose curl around his finger.

"I never realize the length and fullness of your hair. It smells so sweet," Rene whispered in her ear. She could feel his breath against her earlobe.

Not here, not now. *One! Two! Three! Breathe. Damn it! How does this man do this every time?* Her nipples began to stand to attention, and she wasn't wearing a bra. Thank God the room was crowded, and people were weaving in and out trying to find their seats.

Meryt no longer resisted. She had to know, so she blurted out, "Are you flirting with me?"

By this time, he was standing close, pushed up against her back. He had to have felt her body warming up to his touch. Rene just smiled.

When they got to the table, Darren was waiting. He greeted Meryt with a hug. He too looked very dashing. He pulled out a chair for Meryt to sit. He exchanged greetings with Rene and asked if he and Meryt were together.

Meryt quickly answered, "No. Let's just sit and not play musical chairs."

Rene sat to her left, Darren to her right. Fritz and Lolita sat next to Rene. On the other side of the table were Dallas and his date Samantha. Next to them were Tab and her husband Richard. Not Rick or Rich, but Richard. He was a no nonsense kind of guy. This completed the table. Cindy and Karl sat at the VIP table closest to the stage. Meryt could see her from the side, and Cindy looked as if she needed another drink. To be honest, so did Meryt.

The dinner went well. No one completely put their foot in their mouth, but how could they? They were extended family. Meryt actually had a pretty good time during dinner. The DJ spun his first record of the night, *The Glamorous* by Fergie. Everybody jumped up except the Danielses and Richard. Darren pulled Meryt's chair out, and they were off to the dance floor. Two songs later, Cindy and Karl joined them. Meryt assumed Cindy must have put her foot down with Karl. It was time for her to have fun too. The DJ was fantastic. The floor was packed. Their little group started a *Soul Train* line dance. Meryt saw Danielses watching from the sidelines. They didn't appear to be the dancing type. Then Meryt's song came on, *Blame It* by Jamie Foxx. Darren and Meryt were a match when it came to dancing. They moved well together. The *Soul Train* line had shifted forward and the two of them were up next for center stage. Meryt started lip-synching the words: "Got you in the zone. Blame it on the a—, a—, a—, a—, alcohol. Blame it on the a—, a—, a—, a—, alcohol. Blame it on the vodka, blame it on the Henny." Darren and Meryt were doing the Snake down the *Soul Train* line. Darren moved his body in a manner that surely confirmed any doubts a woman might have about his gifts in the bedroom. They moved to the groove, to the right, to the left, then down, rising up slowly. Meryt was having an outstanding time. It had been awhile since she had been dancing. Like all good things, the song came to an end. A slow song came on next. Before Darren could wrap his hand around her waist, Rene appeared next to Darren, asking if he could have the next dance. Darren agreed and slowly walked away from the dance floor.

This song was a goodie as well, *Lost Without U* by Robin Thicke. Rene asked, "Can you tango?"

Meryt replied, "Just lead the way, Fred Astaire," and she picked up the end of her full-length dress and held it in her hand that held his hand. *This could be interesting.*

Rene, not being shy, looked directly into her eyes and embraced her waist pulling her up onto her toes with his powerful hand. Then gently he moved his arm while holding her hand into the prefect angle for the start postion in the Tango. Meryt stood with matching perfect posture, holding on and waiting for the ride to begin.

Two steps back. Quick look left, Quick look right, and then center eye to eye.

"Are you ready?" Rene asked.

"Born ready. It does not take all day to recognize sunshine."

Two quick steps, followed by two slow steps. Before they changed direction, Meryt quickly kicked out her leg and swung her hips side to side matching Rene's stance. Again two quick steps followed by one slow step, and he pulled her in close. Their bodies were barely touching. He asked in a voice that only Meryt could hear, "How long did you think I would allow you to dance with another man?"

Meryt raised one leg up to his waist and slowly lowered it down his leg. She replied, "Who knew you cared so much?"

They changed directions again—two steps forward, followed by two quick pelvic turns out and then in. He firmly pulled her close, eye to eye. Again she saw herself naked in his eyes. He eased her in slowly and then pushed her back hard. Meryt dropped backward on her toes toward the floor. He gently grabbed her by the head and slowly pulled her upright, and then spun her back around. They slowly raised and slowly dropped down to the floor eye to eye, each of them with a foot pushed back, slowly turning. They looked like a flower opening and closing.

Finally, Rene answered as they rose to their feet. Now he decisively pulled her in close to his body so that they were cheek-to-cheek, but no body parts touching other than their hands and arms while maintaining prefect posture, he began to sing the song softly in her ear, "I'm lost without you. Can't help myself. How does it feel, to know that I love you?"

He held her even tighter. "I want you if you will have me." At that moment he released her into a spin, only to pull her close again. Now the room was spinning and the audience wasn't. *Where did these words come from? Why now? Why tonight in a room full of people.* Meryt was pretty sure they all were watching. *How often do you see the tango?* These are moments in life she was thankful to be brown skinned. If she were not, everyone in the room would have seen her face turn a deep shade of red from the whirlwind of emotions she was feeling at that exact moment.

Rene continued, "Meryt, are you without words?" He slowly sniffed her neck.

She felt faint again; her heart was pounding faster and faster as the blood rushed through her veins. Meryt kept thinking she wasn't crazy. He had feelings for her. *One . . . two . . . three . . . breathe.*

Meryt finally answered, "Is this sunshine or just the eye of a storm?"

He kissed her ever so softly on her neck, the weak spot, and whispered, "Both."

Meryt could barely hold onto the perfect posture.

The song ended and she responded in a dry whisper, trying to appear normal, "Get me out of here. Please take me home."

The room erupted with cheers, cat whistles, and clapping. Meryt and Rene had not realized several of the couples danced off to the side leaving them on full display for the dance of love, the tango. They smiled and quickly left the ball. Meryt saw Cindy on the way out of the room. She gave Cindy the I'm-sorry-to-be-leaving-you look; Cindy just waved her on and ran interception with Darren.

The ride to her house was quiet. They rode in his car. Meryt's car was still at the hospital. It was extremely unusual for her to leave her car at work. But this was an unusual time. A man, who first avoided her like the Black Plague, confessed he was lost without her. What could she say other than "Why?" Meryt thought better about asking; it might spoil the moment.

During the thirty-minute ride to her house, surprisingly, Rene did not ask for directions. They sat quietly in the car, listening to soft music playing in the background. Each song was beautiful in its own right, all music and no lyrics. Strangely, Meryt began to hum one. Rene had the big-boy Mercedes-Benz, CL65 AMG, 36-valve, V-12 engine. It was black with black sports seats. It had a backseat, but it was clearly for show. This car was meant to hold two in pure unadulterated luxury. Meryt thought her seven with the beefed-up engine and special options was hot, but Rene's car was over the top. The soft lights from the dash, the smell of his cologne, and the music playing softly, if this was his ploy, she was buying all of it with no regrets in the morning. The only problem was, her heart was buying it as well. It had been a long time since her heart had come out to play, but it had been a long time for a lot of things.

He pulled into her driveway and followed it up to the side entrance. "We're here," he said.

Again, her mouth took over without consent. "How did you know where I live?"

He replied, "Don't you know where I live?"

Meryt quickly understood some things were common knowledge. Rene got out the car as smooth as the evening breeze, he was at her door before she secured the keys out of her purse.

"Thank you," Meryt said as he opened the door. She had to admit it was a beautiful night. Meryt had spent one too many nights out in the field, and she knew the time of night by the position of the stars and moon in the night sky. It was clear, which was highly unusual for upstate. The moon was high, appearing as a single large pearl pendant in the night sky. There was a clean, crisp feeling in the air. Meryt knew it was after eleven o'clock, not quite midnight.

Rene must have noticed her looking into the night sky and enjoying the air as she walked to the side door.

"So, do you like the night air?" Rene asked

"I do, sometimes I think it's the best part of the day." By this time Meryt had the house door open. Rene was still standing outside the door entrance. "Are you coming in? Or are you waiting on a personal invitation?"

Rene responded with a devilish smile, "The latter. I never enter where I am not invited."

Meryt turned around, and he was still standing at the doorsill. "My, aren't we a bit old-fashioned?" She took a deep breath and slowly asked, "Dr. Rene Daniels, would you please enter my home?"

As the word *home* fell from her lips they were met with a sweet, tender kiss. It was so quick that she didn't see the kiss happening; she only felt the pressure against her lips.

He picked her up and said, "I thought you would never ask." Rene kissed her again and glanced around the foyer. "Nice." He put her down, and she took off her shoes and entered the main part of the house. They headed down the long hallway, which led around to the main foyer, followed by the grand room and the kitchen.

"Yes, this is nice," Rene, said as Meryt turned on the lights.

"See, I thought you were talking about me, but you're really referring to my home." By this time they were standing inside the front main door of the house. She showed Rene the music room that had a baby grand piano. To the right was the formal dining room, and directly in front of where they were standing was the main staircase, done in black stone marble, which led to the upstairs bedrooms. The master bedroom's double doors were centered with the main staircase. Meryt continued the tour around the staircase to the great room, which was the modern-day family/TV room; the kitchen was next to it. She entered the kitchen heading straight to the refrigerator, searching for a bottle of champagne. Meryt definitely needed the bubbles to lighten her mood before her nerves got the best of her.

"Rene, would you like a glass?"

"No, but what's on the other side of the glass window?" On the opposite side of kitchen was a glass panel covering the length of the wall.

"Oh, I'll hit the light switch. It's an indoor pool. You might say I believe in staying fit. I use it for laps. It's better on my knees."

"You have a lovely home, but I should not expect anything less from such a lovely woman." As Rene spoke, he turned from viewing the pool to face Meryt. "I must ask you one request. Can I smell your hair? All night, I've longed to stand behind you and touch your curls. It smells like you, sweet and warm with fire."

"Sure," Meryt said invitingly as she sipped on champagne.

He strolled over and stood behind her. He lifted her hair with his fingertips to his nose, and then he ran his nose down her neck, embracing both of her arms pulling them into his body. Meryt couldn't help but arch her back. It tickled. Her neck had always been her most sensitive area. Meryt now smelled him, and her mouth began to water for his kisses. Rene ran his hands down the sides of her dress feeling her curves under his touch, while rubbing his face in her hair.

Rene whispered, "Where did you learn to tango?" He was trying to stay in control of his lust as he imagined her naked in his arms. Meryt had a full bottom and round tempting breasts. Rene believed she possessed the true form of a woman's body: long hair, long neck, round full breasts, and hips that dared any man to look twice when she walked by. Rene distasted modern media's displaying stick-figured women as true beauty. Women that skinny would have been considered diseased or penniless in his time.

"I love music and I love to dance. It only seemed natural to learn the dance of love. And yourself?" Meryt hadn't pictured Rene as a dancer.

"Meryt, you would be surprised at the things I know." He turned her around in his arms preparing to kiss her as he had in the woods. The kiss was meaningful and slow but quickly picked up intensity as it continued. Meryt ran her fingers under his dress jacket, sliding it off his shoulders. Fever was running through her entire body. Heated with so much passion, she wondered, *how can he do this with a single kiss?* All she could think was, *Please, don't faint.*

Rene picked her up, still kissing and cradling her in his arms, and carried her upstairs to the master suite. Meryt had to catch her breath when she realized they were standing in front of her bedroom door, "Wait! I mean, please wait a moment. I want to freshen up." Rene just smiled.

The master suite doors opened up to a sitting room; to the left, beyond the wall, was the bed. The bed area was separated from the sitting room by a half wall with a double-sided fireplace mounted within it. To the right was Meryt's favorite part of the whole house, the bathroom. It had it all: a huge soaking tub and a walk-in shower made of a golden orange marble and crystal fixtures. Down the hall from the main shower, were a steam room and a sauna. The end of the hall opened up to a huge closet, where a girl could keep her entire shoe collection.

Meryt left Rene standing at the entrance to the bathroom. "Relax. Sit down on the love seat and I'll return in a few minutes." Meryt promised.

First, she stopped to turn on the shower, and then continued to the closet to hang her evening gown. The bathroom was shadowy from light that filtered in from the sitting room and the closet. She walked naked down the hall, returning to a steamy shower. She stepped into the shower and realized she'd forgotten to put a towel around her hair in all the rush. She didn't want to wet it. She had spent too long getting it done. Plus, Meryt didn't think Rene was ready for the wet, super-curly look. But, it was already too late, her hair was getting wet. So she just leaned back into the warm water enjoying the sensation as it ran down her back. With her eyes closed, she stepped further back in to the water and bumped into Rene. Meryt quickly turned around; there he was, naked in the shower. His body glowed in the dim light; every muscle was chiseled perfectly from God's hand.

"I cannot wait any longer. I've already waited six long months since the first day we met in your office," Rene said in a seductive soft voice. Meryt felt warm at the mere mention of their first meeting. Rene gazed over her body from head to toe and continued speaking, "You are the most beautiful creature I have ever seen." Then he kissed her again, continuing his mission of seduction. Meryt didn't remember leaving the shower, but she remembered every moment afterwards.

Rene laid Meryt down on the bed, studying every line, every curve of her body. He wanted to commit every detail to memory. Rene knew Meryt felt nervous, wondering if he approved, as he ran his hand down her neck and across her shoulders, finally resting along her hips. He more than approved. Meryt was created solely for him and solely for his pleasure. Rene pressed his body against Meryt's leg, desiring the need to be close and wanting to breathe her in. He was growing in size along her leg. Rene saw Meryt close her eyes and he felt her heartbeat rise from anticipation. The next thing she felt was his cool mouth on her breasts. Rene pushed them together, licking each one slowly, making little circles around and around, causing her nipples to stand at attention. It only added to her fever. Slowly he released one hand to continue down her side to her hips, playing a musical tune with his fingers. Each time his fingers touched her skin, she raised her back farther from the bed. Finally his hand stopped between her legs as he continued to play his tune.

Meryt's senses were on fire. The whole damn house could have burned down, surrounding her in flames, and she would not have felt any pain. She only felt desire and lust for him.

Meryt was already in ecstasy before Rene penetrated her, but nothing compared to when he finally did. Meryt's body yearned for him; it invited him in on every level. Her body no longer took orders from her; it was obedient to him. Meryt had never known her body to be a traitor. It had complained in the past, but now her body belonged to Rene. Their bodies were moving as one. Somewhere in all the madness of lust and love she heard him say, "Tonight was the first time I've been jealous in centuries. I forbid any man to be so close to inhale your sweet scent."

She heard another voice that sounded like hers say, "I'll never let another man be as close as you are to me tonight." *Traitor!* The little voice screamed out in her head.

Meryt gazed into Rene's eyes, feeling every inch of his life run through her body. She came with more pure pleasure that she had ever known in her entire forty-two years of life.

Rene felt Meryt shudder with ecstasy. He had role-played this night over and over in his mind. What else was there for him to do since a dark angel never sleeps? In his wildest dreams, he never imagined what happened next. He should have known better. Meryt never did the normal human thing. As he lay on top, admiring her face, wishing she would open her closed eyes, he felt her body slowly surrender to his love. She opened her eyes, and in an unexpected move, rolled him over. With a devilish smile, she said, "Your turn."

Now he was on the bottom, her full weight pressed against his. Her arms stretched the length of his as she sat on top of him. She glowed like hot lava as she slowly began to kiss him down his chest, licking and biting each of his muscle groups. He was stunned to feel her teeth touching his naked skin. It caused his erection to return faster than normal. She must have been aware, because she dug her knees in on each side of him and started raising and lowering herself. It was slow and loving, gradually evolving.

Rene was accustomed to seeing Meryt with long, straight hair and fully dressed. Now she was naked, riding him like a horse with her long ringlets of curly hair bouncing in the air. He didn't have to fantasize anymore. Meryt was right there, on top of him with her damp curly hair hanging down over her shoulders like a bride's veil. She smelled so sweet as she was giving him pleasure that he had only dreamed of for the last six months. He began pulling harder on her hair as the passion grew. Meryt's neck was propped back exposing her main arteries on both sides of her neck. Rene's burning desire was to touch more of her flesh, to be deeper inside of her so he grabbed Meryt's waist, pulling her hips closer and tighter to his body with each motion. He was losing his mind. He was slipping into ecstasy. Now his eyes were closed because he knew the color had changed and he did not want Meryt to see them just yet. His fangs started to emerge. They were on fire calling for blood. Rene bit his tongue, just to fulfill his blood thirst, while still holding her hips and pulling her closer, tighter and faster, until they both screamed.

Chapter 17

The next morning, Meryt woke to Rene sitting in a chair next to the bed already dressed in jeans.

"Good morning," he said.

"Good morning?" Meryt looked over at the alarm clock, holding the covers with one hand and her head with the other hand, thinking that she never slept late. "Why aren't you in bed? Why didn't you wake me up?" Meryt's relaxed state was slowly changing to panic.

"Oh, I had a little cleaning to do. One of your pillows did not survive the night," he said.

"Oh," Meryt replied, still looking around the room trying to get a bearing on the whole situation. "Why do you look so worried over a pillow?" she asked as the knife dug deeper into panic territory, wondering if Rene thought last night was a something, something.

"My brother called this morning; our mother had a bad night. Apparently you offered Lolita your services yesterday to come visit our mother. Well, Lolita would like to take you up on the offer."

Meryt sat up on the edge of the bed. She began to take mental inventory of potential aches and pains, but amazingly, she felt well rested. "Why didn't you wake me earlier? Do you want to leave now?"

"Meryt, they can wait another hour." Rene sat on the bed next to her, rubbing her temples with both of his hands. Meryt's body began to immediately melt against his touch. All of her worries of sleeping too long and wondering how he felt about last night were melting away. She felt selfish, being relieved that his tension was not over her, but over his sick mother, patient X. Now she felt nauseated.

"Meryt, you worry too much. Please, you do not have to worry about me leaving you. It's I who worries about you leaving in the end." He said this as he kissed her forehead. "I'm sorry you awoke with me looking so worried. I've been thinking of a way to tell you about my mother."

"What is it? Tell me, because you are playing havoc with my emotions."

"Meryt, she's dying from an illness that we have never seen." He hesitated, "How do you feel, are you okay? Did you enjoy last night?"

"Yes, it was a perfect evening." Her body started to tingle, recalling images from the night before. "I feel fine."

Meryt stood up barefoot on the carpet, stretching and yawning next to the bed without her sheets. Delayed inventory reports from her lower back finally filtered into command headquarters. Meryt was a little sore, as she stood on her feet. She smiled a little. It's been awhile since she received that report. "I'll get showered and dressed. Call Fritz and tell him we'll be over soon." Meryt walked across the room on her tiptoes reaching for the ceiling, trying to continue stretching her back out. Rene met her at the bathroom entrance. "They can wait. I want to shower with you again, my beautiful brown queen."

The shower reaffirmed her body's loyalty to him. *Traitor.*

Within the hour, they left the house. She explained about the SYN hemoglobin at the hospital and said that they should stop by there first. The shower and hemoglobin mixture seemed to have lifted Rene's spirits, but Meryt sensed something was still wrong. Rene was still a little detached. It was nothing he said or did, quite frankly he was a prefect gentleman, but it was still something there, something a little off.

While at the hospital, she insisted on getting her car. Meryt didn't want to leave it in the hospital parking lot another day. She agreed to follow him home in her car. While following Rene, the cell phone rang. She hoped it wasn't Deacon. It was almost as bad. It was Cindy.

"Girl, I need the scoop!" Cindy screamed into the phone in a high-pitched voice. "I have my coffee in hand, Karl is off at the gym, and I have time to listen, blow by blow. Spill it!"

"Cindy, I have my coffee as well, but I don't have time to spill my guts to you over the phone. I'm following Rene to his house. He wants me to meet his family."

Meryt knew this statement would lead into a flurry of questions and jokes.

"What! He wants you to meet the family? That's the first step in commitment. You do realize that you and Rene were the talk of the ball. I didn't know you could tango!" Cindy did not disappoint Meryt's expectations. Cindy asked and answered almost all of her own questions without a single reply from Meryt. "What happened between you and Rene? I can't believe it! The two of you barely speak. It was like magic watching the two of you dance across the floor. Karl was contemplating charging a fee to onlookers who wanted to get closer to the dance floor. You know he is all about raising money for the hospital. Did you two spend the night together? Well, guess so if you are meeting the family this morning."

Meryt finally got a word in, "Cindy, that's the million-dollar question. I don't know what happened between us. Don't laugh, but there was always something there, but I chose to ignore it. But last night it came out. I didn't plan it. I surely would not have opened Pandora's box in the middle of the dance floor at the Annual Spring Charity Ball."

Cindy rang into the conversation, "Well, Pandora's box is wide open, and the smoke signals you two were sending ignited the whole room. I think everyone went home last night and had a little fun. You two were so hot and steamy. It was contagious."

"I gotta go. I'm pulling into Rene's driveway now. I'll call you when I have a chance." Meryt abruptly ended the call and cut the car off.

Rene parked his car and came over to Meryt's car door. "Who left you smiling on the phone?"

"Cindy. Apparently, we left quite an impression last night at the ball. In Cindy's words, 'I think everyone went home last night and had a little fun. You two were so hot and steamy. It was contagious.' I am sure we will hear more of this on Monday." Meryt grabbed her bag with meds and other supplies. It was an army-olive-green. She threw it over her shoulder, as the bag hung diagonally across her body. It was her go-everywhere, do-everything bag. Meryt wore a pair of jeans with a beige cashmere sweater set and old faithful, a single ponytail. That was all she could do to fix her curly hair with the limited amount of time she had left after the shower activities and dressing exercises.

They walked toward the front entrance. It was a huge home. It looked more like an office building from the outside. It had two rows of tall, wide windows. Meryt assumed the second row was for the upstairs. Once inside, Meryt realized most of the downstairs was wide open. There were no walls defining each room, only the furniture described the purpose of the area. It was beautiful, done in all white: white halls, white carpet, and white furniture. Now it was clear that the second set of windows were not directly for upstairs but rather for the entire house. With the house being decorated in white, the light from the windows gave the house an open, airy feeling. It smelled fresh, almost like a spring day. The second floor sat back toward the rear of the house, more like a loft.

Fritz and Lolita greeted them in the great room. Lolita appeared worried but still beautiful. Meryt assumed that their mother caused her distressed appearance. Lolita made eye contact, giving a brave smile as Meryt approached.

"I'm so happy you came. Thank you for coming on such short notice." She hugged Meryt. Lolita appeared to be slightly relieved.

"No problem. How is she? I picked up the SYN hemoglobin from the lab. I hope it works."

Meryt turned toward Fritz, "So, Mr. Secrets, tell me your mother's symptoms?"

Fritz looked puzzled at his brother. Rene was still standing by the door. Meryt couldn't help but look around the spacious house. She noticed the kitchen was set off to the rear and spotted his niece and her children. They were just standing there motionless. If she had not seen them, Meryt might not have known they were in the room. Meryt gave a warm nervous smile, and they slowly returned the greeting.

Fritz asked his brother, "Rene, you didn't tell her?"

"No, I didn't. I couldn't find the right words. She's the one. I could not stand to witness the possible rejection in her eyes once she knew the truth."

Meryt spun around somewhat concerned. "Tell me what? What's going on here?"

Fritz walked closer to Meryt, and Rene stayed by the door.

Fritz spoke next. "Meryt, we are not as we seem."

By this time Lolita was standing next to her. Meryt's senses were sounding off. Intuition was telling her to get a gun. Yet everything seemed so peaceful and beautiful. What could they possibly tell her that was so wrong?

Meryt asked, "So what are you, if you aren't what I think?"

Fritz continued, slowly yet directly, "We are dark angels, but we are commonly called vampires."

"What!" Meryt said, feeling relieved at the joke. "Stop playing, what is really going on?"

"It's true," Lolita said. "We are not joking." She then flashed her fangs, and her eyes turned blood red. In an instant, her eyes returned back to normal.

Meryt felt as if she were falling down a black hole. Every contact and every conversation Meryt had had with the brothers played back in mind. It all became clear; the flashing eyes, the secrets, and the double-meaning statements. The room began to spin.

"All of you are vampires?"

Fritz answered, "Yes."

Meryt shot a looked at Rene, who had stepped away from the door and was now standing next to her. "You are a vampire?"

Rene could not speak; he just nodded his head in agreement.

Rene knew this would be a disappointing moment. He could not think of a single word to ease the mounting fear he saw in Meryt's eyes. During his sleepless nights, he tried to think of a way to tell Meryt the truth while not invoking fear. In every scenario he had played out in his mind ended with the same fear that Meryt had in her eyes right then.

"You made love to me! You were inside my body!" Meryt started touching herself, rubbing her arms. "You were in my house! I trusted you."

Meryt looked around the room. "And now you bring me to a house full of vampires. Are you trying to kill me?"

Fritz took offense to Meryt's statements. "No, Meryt, no one here will harm you. If anything, we will all protect you against any harm." He reached for her hands.

Meryt pulled away instinctively before Fritz could touch them, and she ran for the door.

Fritz was there in a blink of the eye. "Meryt, don't leave. Let us explain everything."

"What is there to explain? I've been working next to two vampires, and one of them seduced me." Meryt shot a look of anger at Rene. "Who would believe me or any of this?"

Meryt turned back and spoke very evenly to Fritz. "If you mean no harm, then let me go outside, now."

Fritz opened the door, and Meryt walked out. Meryt looked back at the house once she opened the car door. Rene was suddenly standing behind her. "Meryt, please. I understand if we disgust you or even frighten you, but please stay for my mother. She is in dire need of medical attention.

Help her, and then if you want, we will leave. We will all leave the area. Remember you are a doctor. Remember your oath."

Meryt slammed the door as she sat in the seat and turned on the car. She was so disgusted. She didn't have a gun with her, but did it even matter? They were vampires. It would probably just piss them off. But more importantly, she had made love to a vampire. Just thinking the words, made her body melt all over again. *Traitor!* She felt sick thinking about how she could allow her body to melt over something that was not human. She hit the steering wheel as hard as she could, with both hands, screaming, "What the fuck!" That was her go-to word. It always centered her. Meryt was college educated, a world traveler who spoke eight different languages, and "fuck" was her go-to word for expression.

She couldn't leave. Rene was right. For whatever reasons, the Danielses had gone through an awful a lot to gain her trust. All they wanted from the beginning was treatment for their mother. Meryt turned off the car and stepped out. Rene was standing by the front door. Meryt saw the rest of the family peering out the windows. "Rene, promise that neither you nor your family will kill me and that all you want from me is treatment for your mother."

"If that is what you wish, yes, I promise," Rene said with defeated in his voice. He knew this ending. He played out this scenario. Rene had hoped Meryt had enough adoration to help heal his mother, but he did not believe she had enough adoration to love a dark angel.

Meryt felt pressure pulling on her right shoulder. She still had the bag with the meds and the SYN hemoglobin hanging across her chest. Meryt re-entered the house before doubt could change her mind. At the top of the stairs Meryt saw her, the mother.

Chapter 18

The mother was not what Meryt was expecting, but what was Meryt expecting from a vampire family?

"Meryt, please come up. I've been anticipating your visit. My sons believe you can cure my illness." Meryt climbed the stairs never taking her eyes away from the mother. She realized the mother was not talking from her mouth but talking directly to her mind. "Sorry, I don't mean to frighten you. I suppose this is a lot to comprehend," she said, with her arms down by her side. "The weaker I become, the harder it is for me to master small movements." At that moment, Meryt realized she was floating several inches above the floor. She wore an off-white linen dress, which dragged the floor along the back hem. Meryt followed the mother down the hall to her bedroom.

"What is your name? I just know you as their mother."

"My name is NeiNei," said with a slight accent.

Fritz and Rene had followed Meryt into the bedroom.

"What seems be to the problem?" Meryt asked, hoping to maintain her aloofness.

Fritz started to explain, "NeiNei cannot process the nutrients from blood. The more we give her, the less she absorbs."

Meryt was mesmerized by their mother, she couldn't stop staring. It felt like déjà vu, like Meryt knew her. But where she had no idea. Meryt felt instant kindred toward NeiNei. She did not appear to be much older than Meryt. Truth be told, she might look younger. Meryt was confused by her nationality. NeiNei looked like a diaspora of ethnic backgrounds. She could pass for African-American, Indian, Italian, or maybe Egyptian. She had long dark hair, down past her waist. The front of her hair was twisted in an unusual braid. As Meryt studied her features, Meryt noticed weakness beneath her eyelids. Yes, NeiNei was in pain. "NeiNei, do you mind explaining your symptoms? I'm not sure if I can help, but if I can, this is how it must start. I must know the whole truth."

As NeiNei started to undress, Meryt watched in amazement. Her skin, her beautifully shaped breasts, her thighs, and her legs all belonged to Greek goddess statue. Sudden thoughts of Rene flooded her mind; what did Rene see in her flawed body compared to a vampire's body? Was the seduction apart of his ploy? Meryt forced her mind away from such trivial thoughts and focused it on NeiNei's skin as she turned around. Meryt noticed a small scar over her heart. Meryt asked if she had had some type of surgery. NeiNei touched the scar as if she was surprised Meryt noticed the marking.

"No, it's the bite that transformed me to a dark angel."

Meryt shook her head, trying to stay focused on the examination. Meryt had hoped she could find discoloring, a rash, or even lumps to explain the steady change in appetite.

While NeiNei undressed, she told her story. Her feeding problem began a year ago. She had noticed she had to feed twice as much to feel full. Over time, she and her family noticed that she was eating three times as much, but appeared as if she had not fed at all. Meryt could not resist, she had to inquire what the family was feeding on.

Fritz spoke-up, saying they had been bringing blood home from the hospitals, and they also fed from small animals. Dark angels must feed on blood twice a week. They can eat human food, but it offered the same nutritional value as humans eating paper. There was no benefit other than for show, to appear normal. The only human food they could conceivably digest was freshly slaughtered raw meat. That was now how the whole family fed. From time to time, for simple pleasure, they fed from humans, but they did not take enough to kill the humans.

Meryt tried hard not to let her mind wonder past the basic patient and doctor questions,

"Who or what did you feed from before you started to notice any changes?" Meryt asked, running her hands down NeiNei's neck and along her spine. NeiNei's skin felt cool and smooth, like fine china.

"I cannot remember anything unusual. I know my skin feels hard. The longer I go without feeding, the stiffer I become. If I do not find a cure, I will become a living statue inside this hard shell until I can feed properly again."

Stroke victims instantly came to Meryt's mind. She remembered them from residency. Patients lying in bed, unable to move, unable to communicate with the rest of the world, trapped inside their bodies. Meryt knew this was a fate worse than death.

"Fritz, can you give me a fresh sample of her blood?" Fritz took out a needle. It was a 20-gauge needle and drew 10cc. Meryt asked if she could analyze the fresh sample in the lab.

"No, you can spin it here. I have a full lab down stairs."

"Why am I not surprised? Go, and I'll be down in a few minutes," Meryt replied.

Meryt continued the examination with her eyes closed and let her hands and nose examine NeiNei's body. Oddly enough, she didn't see a color change or any markings. Now she hoped there would be an odor change. Meryt opened her eyes after a few moments. She noticed a small odor change, near her kidney area, along her back. Meryt wondered what her renal arteries looked like, but what are normal stats on a vampire?

Meryt asked Rene if he had heard of vampires being diabetic.

Rene frowned. "No."

Meryt grabbed her bag and laid the SYN hemoglobin out on the bed. She had one mixed bag with NeiNei's blood from two days ago. Meryt asked Rene which way was the fastest for NeiNei to ingest the blood: by digesting it or having a transfusion.

"Both are the same," he replied.

"NeiNei, drink this. It's an enriched synthetic blood. It has more nutrients than common everyday blood. It's your blood combined with human blood on steroids." Rene said as he poured the blood into a large drinking glass for NeiNei to sip.

"It tastes terrible," Meryt heard in her head.

"I'm not here to win taste awards. Give it a few minutes and tell me how you feel."

As Meryt turned toward Rene, she asked, "Can you take me to your lab and have Lolita stay with NeiNei?"

Rene escorted Meryt down to the basement, to the lab. Half of the basement was dedicated to the lab. It was bigger than her lab at the hospital. It had better lighting, better countertops, and better computers. Fritz had three laptops and two wall-mounted screens connected to two of the laptops. In the rear of the lab was a wall-to-wall dry-erase board with

NeiNei's timeline and congruent treatments. It was fair to say that Fritz was taking his work home.

Meryt found Fritz in the corner, still processing the blood sample. "Fritz, have you ever processed NeiNei's sample against your own?"

"Yes, but the results were inconclusive."

"You compared the two samples? You must have had a normal/control and a not normal/atypical sample with particular notable variances. While I was examining your mother, I noticed a problem area around her kidneys. I want to examine her renal arteries. Is it possible for a vampire to be diabetic or have renal failure? That would explain why her body can't process nutrients from the blood."

"That's impossible, a vampire does not suffer from human illness."

"Fritz, if it's impossible, then why can't she process her food? She's suffering from something. The impossible is possible, your mother is sick and I believe it starts in her kidneys. Has she ever tried insulin? Let's not forget about the other symptoms in renal failure, like extreme thirst, frequent urination, loss of appetite, and swelling of the lower extremities."

"No. Meryt may be right," Rene started in on the conversation. "She has lost her appetite. We do not urinate, but at first she did have an extreme thirst that has since died down."

A light bulb went off in Rene's head. He said, "I have to go to the hospital and pick up some insulin."

"Bring back the insulin and mix it with the second SYN hemoglobin bag I left in the walk-in refrigerator. I hope we can guess the right combination to return her glucose levels to normal. Maybe this illness is a one-time problem that has never been resolved. Much like pregnant women who become diabetic during pregnancy, something in her history may have been the catalyst, and her body was unable to recover and return to normal."

Within the hour, NeiNei had been given insulin. It was the missing link.

Insulin is a hormone that has extensive effects on metabolism and other body functions. Most importantly, insulin causes cells in the liver, muscle, and fat tissue to take the glucose out of the blood. NeiNei's deficiency in insulin did not allow her body to process her food. It tricked her body into believing she was not eating at all. NeiNei had had this problem for a year.

During the last six months, she basically had been surviving on less than a third of her normal intake.

Eleven hours after NeiNei met Meryt for the first time, she started to regain her full control. Meryt sat with her for the last two hours, just talking as if they were old friends. Meryt couldn't shake the feeling that she knew NeiNei. Why did NeiNei feel so comfortable to her soul, like an old pair of house slippers?

Before long, it was late, just before midnight. Meryt had stayed not only for the good conversation, but she also had wanted to observe NeiNei responding to the new treatment. Meryt had noticed a tremendous change in NeiNei's complexion. She still had an olive-brown skin color, but it no longer had a hint of gray. She now was talking from her mouth and using her hands to gesture while the two women gossiped and giggled together. Meryt loved her job. For a brief moment, she celebrated internally for the gift of healing. It was like witnessing a miracle again.

NeiNei smiled. "You are a healer. That is one of your gifts."

Meryt was surprised. She had forgotten how NeiNei spoke directly to her mind earlier. "Can you read minds? Do you all read minds?"

NeiNei laughed. "We all have gifts from God. Yes, I can read your thoughts, but more than that, I can read your heart. I guess my boys did not tell you very much about our kind."

Meryt responded with a smirk while NeiNei continued, "They did leave things to a minimum. Meryt, I am very old. The older I become, the stronger my powers become. I can read or feel the mindset of a person or a room full of people. I can look into a human's soul at my fullest strength. I can change the mindset of a person. Fritz is a healer and a slave to science. Lolita can sense emotions. She can tell if a person is lying or being truthful. Rene's powers are similar to mine. He can read minds to a limited level; his real gift is his strength. My one grandchild can control the temperatures, and her children can control extreme temperatures. We all have gifts from God, the Creator. A dark angel's gifts are more concentrated."

"If Fritz is a healer, why didn't he heal you?"

"He tried. We still do not have all answers, other than it was something Fritz has never seen before. There isn't a hospital for sick vampires. Normally, we heal. Fritz read day and night. That's when he came across your name. Apparently, you published a small article on hemoglobin, which sparked his attention. This is why we are here in Niagara Falls. Fritz wanted to work with you for a cure."

Meryt sat back in the chair. She had always known Fritz was here for her work, but she wasn't expecting it to be a cure for vampires. Meryt didn't know what to think; yet in the back of her mind she always knew. Meryt knew Fritz was using her to help find his cure, but hearing it aloud did not play well on her emotions.

"Meryt, I'm sorry if I spoke too freely. I sometimes forget my manners. My family means no harm. Fritz is a loving son who wanted to cure his mother. He truly meant no harm."

"What about Rene? What were his plans in all of this?"

"Rene did not believe in you as a human. He definitely wasn't interested in relocating to Niagara Falls. He believed that he and Fritz could solve the problem. When he saw me grow weaker, he was willing to try something new, so we moved here to Niagara Falls. When Rene first met you, he was afraid. He fell in love with you that very day in your office. He'll never admit it, but I knew he was in love. Until that moment, I didn't think my little Rene loved anyone other than his family. Rene tried to keep his distance from you. He did not want to interfere with the progress you and Fritz were making, but love was calling his name." NeiNei smiled and looked off into the distance, recalling an old conversation with Rene. "One night, just before Christmas, Rene was sitting here with me, the way you and I are sitting now. I looked into his heart, and I told him, 'If she is the one, then go after her. Find out if your love is returned. You cannot number my days. My days are numbered not by you but another. Go after her and live your life, as I have lived mine.'"

Rene returned to NeiNei's bedroom. "Are you hungry?" he asked Meryt. "It's been hours since you last ate."

Rene looked different, and Meryt felt different. She was embarrassed by the behavior she had displayed earlier. She wanted to eat, but not now, not here. "I should probably head home. It's late, and my patient needs her rest. I believe you and Fritz can handle things." Meryt smiled while reaching for her bag and keys.

Meryt said her good-byes to the family. It was pushing one o'clock in the morning. It was funny how time marched on regardless if anyone was paying attention to it or not. Meryt had been there since eleven that morning.

Rene walked her to the car. He was a gentleman until the end. She sensed his reluctance to let her go. They studied each other, trying to find the right words, but what words? She did not know what to say or where to begin. And so Meryt got in the car and drove home back to her normal, crazy, strange life. She didn't listen to any music on the way home. Again, what words did she want to hear? There was no song out there about this; there was no "I fell in love with a vampire. And sorry I insulted your family before I saved your mother," kind of song. Meryt rode home in silence.

Chapter 19

The ride was uneventful. No music, no singing, only thoughts of *Maybe*. Meryt pulled into the garage. As she got out of the car, she felt a cool breeze against her cheeks. She hadn't closed the garage. The night sky was clear, two nights in a row. This had to be a new record for Niagara. Last night, Meryt had stood outside in the night air with a man she thought she would share her life with and now she stood alone knowing he was not human. The air felt the same. The night air smelled the same; only she had changed.

As she walked toward the garage door, Rene was standing there with a bag of groceries. Meryt did not jump because she was not afraid. Meryt wanted one more night with Rene. Without a word, they embraced. The traitor from inside her heart came out. Her body was completely on fire. Feelings and emotions she had never felt for another man were alive and running unsupervised throughout her body. They stood inside the garage in the cool breeze of the night, locked in the embrace of something more.

"I'm sorry I didn't tell you earlier, I just didn't know how to tell you," Rene whispered in her ear.

Meryt didn't want to think about it. She wanted to live in the moment. Tonight Rene was just a man, a man she was falling in love with. They went straight to the kitchen. Rene made her a club sandwich. Finally, Meryt broke the silence. "Would you like to stay the night?"

"Yes."

They finished cleaning the kitchen and started up the stairs. Rene followed close behind. Meryt turned on the fireplace in the bedroom to kill the chill that had built up in the empty bedroom and turned on soft music to fill the background. She started to walk toward the bathroom, but Rene stepped in front, blocking her path. He started to undress Meryt piece by piece. First her sweater, followed by the shell. Next came the bra, then her jeans, and lastly her low-rise panties. He pulled each side down her legs slowly, never taking his blue eyes away from hers. Meryt felt as if she was in a dream watching Rene undress her; there was so much intensity with so little effort.

Once Rene finished stripping Meryt's clothes off, he laid her down on the warm carpet in front of the fireplace. Then he took his clothes off while Meryt watched helplessly, listening to the music playing softly. It was Otis Redding singing; "I've been loving you too long." Meryt was so drunk on lust and love that she felt the pain in Redding's voice as he sang his sad song. Meryt watched Rene undress as the flames danced across his pale skin. Meryt began to feel warm all over with anticipation, remembering last night's lovemaking. All she could do was wait for his embrace.

Rene joined her on the floor in front of the fireplace. They snuggled for a moment, enjoying the warmth of their bodies and the heat from the fire. What started as slow soft kisses gradually turned into a powerful, longing, breathtaking kiss. He took his hand, circling one of her nipples with his fingertips. It wasn't long before Meryt's body began to tremble from his touch. All of her fears, all of her worries disappeared, replaced with pure lust. Rene's kisses moved slowly down her neck, while sliding his hands further down her stomach. His lips followed the path of his fingers, causing her to arch her back with every move he made. Meryt couldn't help herself. She reached and grabbed two handfulls of his blond hair and pulled his head up to meet her face. Meryt had to kiss him again. She needed to taste him. She needed to smell him, but most of all, she needed to feel him inside of her. "Please, Rene."

"You will never meet a man that needs, no, that loves you, the way I do. Tell me how I can make you mine. I've placed my trust in you; why can't you put your trust in me?"

Meryt was at a loss for words. Her body yearned for him to continue, but the little voice in her mind demanded Rene to stop and never return to her home again; and her heart, which had come along for the ride, was scared. This was definitely more than a something, something.

"Please, Rene, don't talk. Just make love to me. I want to feel your love. I want to believe this is real," she said as she pulled him closer.

Meryt felt him growing harder on her stomach. Rene slowly raised himself above as she wrapped her legs around his waist. He leaned forward to push himself slowly inside. She moaned. She could feel his love. Meryt saw love in Rene's eyes. He pushed slowly, stronger and deeper while continuously kissing Meryt along her neck. They must have stayed in the same position for what seemed like hours. Meryt shuddered so many times she lost count. Each time, he drove a little deeper. She wanted to hold on and wait for him to climax, but she was struggling not to lose herself in another world. Meryt didn't want any more dreams. She wanted to stay here in this world with Rene. She was sweating from head to toe. No matter the position, if he was sitting up or leaning over kissing her neck, he would not stop gazing into her eyes. For the first time, she saw his eyes change from blue to black and then red. Unlike before, they flashed, but this time they remained red. Meryt noticed he had started sweating. Faint pink drops of sweat rolled down his face. The light from the fireplace made his body glisten. They were both hot and sweaty, breathing in the same rhythm. With each stroke, Meryt was falling in love with Rene.

He increased his speed. Rene reached for a pillow behind Meryt on the sofa and placed it beneath her head. His rate picked up faster and so did their breathing. He dropped down, burying his face in the pillow. At that moment, Meryt felt every muscle in his body tighten, as they became one. She felt his love. Meryt moaned at the power moving from his body into hers when he released a growl. Meryt could no longer hold on. She was lost to ecstasy.

Chapter 20

In the morning, Meryt awoke to find a beautiful diamond pendant necklace around her neck. When she rolled over, the pendant fell down off the pillow, making a thumping sound as it hit the bed. Her eyes followed the path of the noise to find two small holes and what appeared to be blood stains on the pillow. Before she could ask why, Rene began to explain. "It's not your blood. It's mine. I had to taste blood last night, so I bit myself. It's not important." He rubbed his blond hair back off his face.

"I don't know how you feel about us," he continued, "but I do know how I feel about you. I want you to have the necklace no matter how we end. I love you." Rene explained that the diamond pendant was a replica of his family crest that he had had placed on a white-gold chain. "Please wear it. It's a gift from me. It signifies you are a member of my family." He kissed the pendant and kissed her cheek.

"Thank you, I will wear it." Meryt wanted to say something more, but what? What are the conditions of a vampire and a human dating? What were her conditions for dating a vampire, as she looked back at the bloodstains and the two small holes? And why did he need to taste blood? She wondered if she needed to be a vampire. Meryt accepted the fact that one day she would die, but she wasn't ready to die any time soon. Crazy thoughts ran around loose in her mind, but at that moment, her heart belonged to Rene. Meryt felt the tears swelling behind her eyes as she held back the tears. She knew she wasn't a pretty crier. As she began to speak, Meryt realized she had morning breath. *Yuck.*

Saved by the bell: her cell phone rang. She looked at the number, it was Deacon. Meryt knew exactly what the call meant.

"Hello. Okay. I'm moving. How long? Okay. Moving." Deacon needed her in Virginia, as soon as possible. The jet would be at the airport in thirty minutes. She knew she'd be gone for a minimum of five days. Talk about timing. That was the story of her life.

"Rene, I have to leave town for a few days, well, more like a week. Believe me this has nothing to do with you or your family, but everything to do with my promise to help an old friend in trouble."

Rene moved the covers back and said, "I can come with you. I can help. I'm sure Fritz can handle mother from this point."

"No, you can't come. I don't know enough about you, and it could be dangerous to you and your family." Meryt placed his hands in hers. "I can't explain who or what you are to anyone. Its best you wait here until I return."

Rene watched Meryt get out of bed and head to the bathroom. He wondered if this was how rejection felt, a sharp pain of the knife slowly cutting his dead heart out. So, she wasn't ready to accept him as a dark angel. He felt certain that last night she had felt his genuine love for her. She must have, because he felt her love. He took his time pleasuring her. He wanted every single moment committed to memory.

Rene felt his heart break. Why couldn't she accept him for being different, when everything she did was so unusual and different? Rene started regretting that he ever opened his heart. He bit down, flexing his jawline. He knew she was his life, his love. Rene would never leave her side. Then he remembered NeiNei's comments: "Show her your love and wait for her to return it." He was immortal, so he had time to wait, but for now he would cherish each moment with Meryt.

Meryt got up to brush her teeth. Rene stood behind her waiting. "Do you brush your teeth? I have an extra toothbrush." She threw one over to him.

Graceful as always, he caught the toothbrush in midflight. He smiled. "Yes, I do brush my teeth and fangs." He protracted his extra set of teeth and brushed them all.

They showered in quietness except for the soft music playing in the background. Meryt threw on a pair of navy dress slacks and a silk sweater. She loved the way the silk blends felt against her skin. Meryt figured she might as well enjoy it while she could, because she knew in her gut this was going to be a rough mission.

Meryt called Cindy to tell her she had to take emergency leave. She planned on being absent for a week or more. Cindy had a ton of questions, starting with Rene. Was he taking her somewhere? Were they eloping? Meryt busted out laughing while Rene sat patiently beside her.

"No, Cindy, we are not running off to Mexico to get married. No, we are not eloping. Most likely you will see Rene and his brother at work tomorrow. Just let your husband know. Thanks."

Rene had to smile, listening to Cindy carry on. "Is she always so personal?" he inquired.

"Yes! Yes! Oh, did I say, yes? It's her duty to know all the gossip, especially mine."

Meryt finished packing. She usually didn't pack a ton of clothes. It was mostly personal hygiene items. She ran to the basement to a secret, secure room to retrieve one of her special bags that always remained packed for rapid departures. It included all of her party starters: two 9mm's, a few hand grenades, tracking devices, smoke bombs, a few of her favorite various-shaped knives, passports, and fifty grand, half in American dollars and half in euros.

When Meryt returned upstairs, Rene saw the bag and offered to carry it. "Do you have the kitchen sink in here?"

"Nope, just my travel things. A girl's gotta have things for the road." Meryt giggled and kissed him on the cheek.

She locked the house up, looked back from the car window and gave it a mental good-bye. Rene drove her to the airport. The jet was waiting as Deacon had promised. It still looked sexy, but this time Meryt was not excited about leaving. They kissed one last time. Rene saw the sadness tugging on Meryt expression as she exited the car.

He asked once more, "Are you sure you don't want me to come, my love?"

Grabbing her two bags she replied swiftly, "Very sure," as she got out of the car and boarded the jet.

From the plane, Meryt saw Rene's car leaving the parking lot. She wondered for a brief moment if she would ever see him again.

Chapter 21

"We found the mole. He was in the president's own bodyguard detail. I can't believe he got that close. A few of my agents were compromised, but you were not because you're on the outer loop. We didn't figure it out until it was too late." Deacon paused on those words and took another sip from his white Russian. Meryt couldn't help but wonder, *Too late? Too late for what?*

Deacon continued, "They have taken the president's daughter Iman. They, meaning the United African Front (UAF), took her from the White House. She was sleeping next to her sister less than five hours ago. We found one of the president's detail dead on the grounds. No one else died. He was the informant. We believe he must have taken her and was murdered when he turned Iman over to the UAF. We have gone through his personal effects. That's how we found out his affiliation to the UAF out of Sudan. This group is known for a number of illegal profiteering schemes, but they are most notorious for drugs and the slave trade."

Two Secret Service men entered Deacon's office with the president. Deacon and Meryt immediately stood to attention. The two service men stepped aside as President John Lee walked toward them by the desk. If Meryt did not know any better, she would have bet the president was insulted by her presence. "Is this the operative you plan to send to return my daughter?"

Deacon replied, "Yes, President Lee, please meet Special Agent Meryt Brownstone. We have a long history together. She served ten years on active duty in the United States Army. She was a medical officer assigned to Speacial Operations. She proved her self to be more than a doctor, so they crossed trained her in counter intel. We served together for the last four years in human intel and light tactics. Naturally, I recruited her when I went into business. During the last six years, since she has departed from active duty she's completed quiet, discreet missions for me directly. This was the primary reason her identity was not compromised during this past invasion. I use her only for highly classified missions, and I keep no records of her name on file. She is an excellent candidate for this mission. You must understand, this is Meryt's specialty. She has dealt with the UAF before. She understands their mode of operation, and better yet, she is highly skilled at getting in and out undetected."

It had been a long time since Meryt had heard her military résumé said aloud. She wanted to look around the room for this person Deacon had described. Yet, Meryt sensed the president was not impressed.

President Lee spoke with more determination. "This is the soldier you are sending to get my daughter? One soldier? One female soldier?"

Now Deacon spoke with authority, "This mission needs to be done discreetly. If we come in with full metal jacket and activate any number of units, you will cause a war. But more importantly to you, Sir, they will kill your daughter at any sign of retaliation. Our first mission is to get Iman back as quickly as possible. Time is of the utmost importance, before Iman changes hands. During normal abduction cases, forty-eight hours is the maximum amount of time before the likelihood of finding a child drops dramatically and the trail grows cold. Sir, we need to secure Iman, without the UAF knowing we have her back."

The president sat down, rubbing his face. He was the first elected African-American President of the United States in history. If asked, Meryt had never thought it possible in her lifetime. President Lee had only been in office for six months and now this: his ten-year-old daughter had been abducted from the most secure home in America, the White House. He was going through a personal hell. With so much tension in the room, Meryt had not noticed his wife's presence. Her face was swollen from tears. She had their twelve-year-old daughter, Collette, by her side. If Meryt were a betting woman, she'd bet the child had not left her mother's side since the nightmare began.

His wife, Rhona, came over to the president's side and spoke with a voice of near death. "Honey, let Deacon do what he is paid to do."

Then she turned to Meryt and said, in the same voice, "I order you to please bring my baby back home."

What could Meryt say? Tears were swelling in her eyes. "Yes, ma'am. That is my mission." Meryt looked down at her daughter. Collette had started to cry, holding on tightly to her mother's waist. It was an overload of heart-aching emotions taking over. Something had to be done to change the spirit of room. This was a suicide mission. They already looked defeated before Meryt even attempted to take on this daunting assignment, which included her life. For if she failed, she would lose her own life in the mission. Truth be told, the last time she was in Sudan she had no fond feelings for returning without anything less than a nuclear weapon.

She studied them all slowly and chose her words carefully. "I have dealt with this group before. Deacon is absolutely correct. This mission will need to be done discreetly if we want your daughter back alive. I will immediately prepare and depart for Khartoum, her last know location. We have forty-three hours before she is moved again, so speed and discretion is of the utmost importance."

Meryt looked over to the president's daughter with tears rolling down her plump cheeks. Meryt motioned for her to come over by her side. Collette reluctantly came over. Meryt squatted down to her level and said, "I need your help."

Collette continued crying. "How can I help you?"

Meryt dried her tears with the edge of her sleeve. "I know you are the big sister, and I know you two must have secrets. When I find her, and I will, she will be terrified because I'll be yet another stranger. I may have only moments to grab her and go. Tell me something or give me something that she will know it came from you, so she will immediately know I'm there to save her and bring her home. I want her to know that you sent me."

The little girl thought for a few moments and reached around her neck and took off a gold necklace with a beautiful tiny pink pearl. "My mother gave me this for my birthday. Iman always wanted my necklace, so I know she will recognize it."

Meryt took the necklace and placed it around her own neck. "Great, I will give this to her when I see her." When Meryt touched the pearl, she also felt the diamond pendant Rene had given her earlier. A spark of hope twinkled in Meryt's eyes. She took off the diamond necklace and placed it around Collette's neck and whispered in her ear, "Listen, I may still need your help again. Let's switch necklaces. I will make you a promise that when I return, we will switch necklaces back."

Meryt leaned in little closer to whisper softly in her ear so no one but Collette could hear the conditions of the promise. "Keep the diamond pendant inside your shirt. If I am not back in two days with your sister, wear the diamond necklace on the outside of your shirt for the world to see. A man may show up at night. Don't be afraid because he is my friend and tell him everything you know. He will find me with your sister and bring us both back home. Can this be our secret mission?"

Collette held the pendant under her shirt and nodded her head in agreement.

Meryt kissed the child's forehead, stood up, and sent her back to her mother.

Her mother smiled, maybe for the first time in the past six hours. Meryt hoped and prayed it would not the last.

"Let's get this mission moving. Mr. President and Deacon, I will start the briefing and my preparations. When does the flight leave?"

Chapter 22

Within three hours Meryt was en route to Khartoum. She had received the brief. It was believed that the child had been kept in a suitcase while in transit, locked to the hand of Lord Atken, a wealthy realtor who had strong ties to the Sudan government. He was a jack-of-all-trades when it came to the black market. Name it, and he named a price and it was done. Anything in the drug, diamond, oil, and the sex-trade markets he had his fingers in. He was connected to most of the illegal trafficking done worldwide.

Meryt had tangled with this organization before. It had ended pretty badly the last time. She had a hunch it was going to be pretty bad this time too. Atken led with money, and if he couldn't buy a person, he erased the person from existence. His mode of operation created a line of loyalty, which could infiltrate any organization. His loyalty was until death do you part. Hence, the reason why the Secret Service man in the president's detail was found dead, as well as six members of Meryt's team the last time she tangled with the UAF. That was the beginning story of how Meryt ended up in SERE school, which led her to Deacon. It was funny how life had turned full circle.

Meryt tried to rest her body while her mind ran through the mission. She planned to check into the Meridian Hotel in Khartoum. She would need to set up a series of checkpoints all over town after meeting with the informant. Once Meryt was on the run, she would not be able to return to the hotel. Extraction was going to be difficult at best. Once she had the girl, and the UAF noticed her missing, they would totally lock down the city. No aircraft and no vehicle would be able to depart without inspection. Meryt would have to get Iman out of the city before they noticed she was gone. Impossible.

Meryt was going in as an entertainer. Atken was having a party in fifteen hours. She was assigned as a back-up singer for the band preforming at his home as her cover. When she was not on stage, she would search the house for Iman's location. She had less than three hours once the party started to retrieve the package and meet at the rendezvous site thirty miles outside of the city limits.

Intel had Iman located upstairs in the master suite, under the bed in a body case, a human suitcase used to store sex slaves under the bed of the owner. The thought of the child being confined in a body case made her blood run cold, all the better for this mission. Meryt demanded the killer within her be released. She was heading into battle, and she couldn't afford to hesitate. The problem was not going to be locating Iman in the house but extracting Iman from the house. She knew in her heart, the extraction was the deal breaker. Once they realized Iman was missing, all of Sudan would be in lock down mode. Atken's payroll reached that far, if not beyond.

Khartoum, the capital of Sudan was hot, just as she remembered. The city itself was torn between new money and plain poverty. A country with such a rich history should have been more stable. The country was plagued by constant war with its own people. It was the largest country in Africa and had had strong influence on the Arab world since its birth. Sudan was bordered on the north by Egypt. Meryt planned on exiting through Egypt if the initial exit plan fell apart. Interestingly enough, Sudan was the only country that ever ruled over Egypt during the Pharaonic period.

Sudan had one of the fastest growing economies in the world, mainly because it was rich in petroleum and crude oil, otherwise known as black gold. Yet like every country, it was a country of haves and have-nothings. Its have-nothings were painfully obvious. Instead of the country being known for its rich history, the birthplace of mankind, and the home of temples and pyramids, it was known for tribal warfare. The most recent terror headline was from Darfur.

Meryt checked into the hotel and immediately left to rendezvous with the informant on the ground. They planned to meet at an outdoor teashop. Meryt couldn't image drinking hot tea in this weather. Midmorning in Khartoum was already one hundred degrees. She left early for the rendezvous. Meryt wanted to recon the area before she met any informant. More important, she wanted to people watch. Meryt needed to get a feel for the city. She'd never forget the last visit to Khartoum. It was burned into her flesh. Meryt turned her arm over to see the bullet wound. Atken had bought an informant on her squad.

Meryt hung around the perimeter, observing, as the informant, Will Jenkins, approached the teashop. They had worked together before. She watched him for twenty minutes before making contact. Finally, she felt at ease and walked over to his table. They exchanged greetings and immediately the waitress moved in with hot tea shots. Great.

"Tonight the party starts at 9:00 p.m. with cocktails, followed by the band performing at 10:30. Atken is expecting over four hundred guests. At any given time ten to fifteen guests will be arriving or departing. There is a valet service with twelve men working; a minimum of four will be at the door all night. Atken keeps ten men patrolling the grounds, plus cameras throughout the house." Will passed Meryt an invite. "Security will be expecting you around 4:00 p.m. for practice. The group should be fine without you but stick around during practice. Then return to the party later." Meryt was listening to Will unfold the story of how it should go, but this was a mission, not a story. Stories were for children. Missions were constantly unfolding, and redeveloping at every turn. A mission could only hold one form and that form would not be complete until the mission was over. Then a storyteller could recite the story.

The whole time Meryt could not stop wondering how Will drank hot tea in scorching weather. He was on his second cup, while Merty struggled to drink her first. Will was a young guy; he appeared as the techie type but a little smoother. Will kept a short, combed-back haircut. His face and hair were a little shiny due to the heat, but it helped him to blend in. It was an ordinary day: two people, who were talking about potential business at a local teashop.

Will was still unraveling the story; "Atken's maid service for the upper rooms noticed a large case under Atken's bed yesterday. Every six hours, Atken or his top security guard took food into the bedroom. The maid believed that this is where our package is located. The maid placed a vase of yellow and purple flowers by the door to this room. It is the master suite down the main hall, upstairs to the right. There are four windows and one main balcony facing the north side of the house in the suite. Directly beneath are Atken's personal garages that lead around to the front valet. Do you have any questions?"

Meryt answered, "Just one, how long have you been in country?"

"I've been here for three weeks. I was assigned to his son, who's trying to sell stolen oil. The more important question is, when am I leaving? If you no longer need my assistance, as soon as this conversation is over, I'm out." Will hesitated for a moment and then continued, "Meryt, what are you doing taking this mission? I thought you were done with jobs like this."

"I know, but a friend called and a promise was made. Dare I say anymore?" Meryt looked away from him, and then around the small tea café. She had planned to be out of this country in less than two hours after being at the party. "I don't require your services from this point. Oh, and you are right. Leave town as soon as the party starts. If I see you again, I'll consider you to be an informant."

Will stood up and threw money onto the table, not sure how to take Meryt's comments. He hestaited for a moment, and then said, "Good luck."

Will quickly disappeared into the crowd. She waited another thirty minutes before leaving. After supplying the checkpoints around town with cash pots, IDs, food, and a change of clothes, Meryt returned to the hotel. She did a mental drill of the plan.

The evening came quick, and before Meryt knew it, she was at rehearsal. So far it was uneventful, other than the lead singer wanting to hook-up after the party. The lead singer made her desires known to Meryt in the restroom. It was crazy, considering that Meryt was on a mission and that the lead singer was a female. Meryt touched the pearl pendant on her neck to remind her of the true purpose. The band agreed to meet back at the house by 8:30 p.m., two hours before the show. This left Meryt with one hour to get dressed and finish her preparations.

While dressing, Meryt thought about the security layout. A guard stayed with the group and three rotated through the room. The rest must be rovers. She was able to go to the restroom unescorted with her new girlfriend. Meryt saw five cameras. Surprisingly, one was in the restroom. Freaks! But there were no guards in the halls or staircase. She wondered where the rest of the guards were positioned. Atken's security was more for show, than for being expert at their jobs. There was no doubt that Meryt could get around in house and get out of the house with the little girl. Getting to the helicopter located thirty minutes away would be another mission. She continued dressing, feeling her blood get a little cooler as time moved on, humming to herself, *Oh What A Night.*

Chapter 23

The party was jumping. If Meryt weren't working, this would be an awesome event other than the female lead singer kept constantly touching Meryt. People were smiling, drinking, flirting, and maybe a few something, somethings were being discussed in the crowd. Who knew the president of the free world's daughter was upstairs in a body case under the homeowner's bed? The guests had no clue that the only thing keeping the president from raining missiles on this home and possibly causing World War III was the idea of saving his daughter. To be honest, Meryt thought they were all on borrowed time. There was still a strong possibility that it could start raining missiles right now. The moment the president believed Meryt had failed the mission, it would be all over, the drinks, the laughs, and the booty calls.

Meryt made her way around the room, sizing up the situation. She had met up with the band members and promised to help stir up the crowd during their session. Meryt explained that if she went missing from the dance floor to check the bar and the restroom. Meryt gave a special wink to her new girlfriend to ensure she maintained her cover. She mingled for a few moments and then was off upstairs, searching for the master suite. As she walked down the hall, Meryt came across one of the security guards from earlier.

Before she could say word, he smiled and began to speak. "I knew you would be up here tonight. Nettles could not keep his eyes off you at rehearsal. I knew he'd ask you upstairs. You are looking for the room down at the end of the hall. It's a good thing the chief is leaving tonight. I'll tell Nettles you are waiting," he said, showing off his white toothy smile.

Meryt smiled back and continued to walk in the same direction, wondering, what the guard was talking about. Meryt located the flowers in the vase placed outside the master suite. Once in the room, she closed the door behind herself wondering what the guard's comments meant, "The chief is gone. Tonight?" Meryt quickly scanned the room for the master bed. She found it up on a platform. Images of a small child trapped under the bed flashed through her mind as she ran over to rescue Iman. Meryt tapped along the sides of the platform bed hoping to hear any response while searching for the handle. She found the hidden door to the body case and opened it immediately. The body case was empty.

This was where the mission started to develop and the story began to fall apart.

Meryt's mind began to race through possible scenarios. Where could Iman be? She had just seen Atken downstairs. He couldn't be gone yet, or at least, he could not have gone far. Meryt ran over to the balcony. They were standing by his Rolls Royce: two bodyguards, a female, and Atken with a large suitcase attached to his arm. They were moving Iman already. Where? Meryt had no idea. This could be the last known coordinates. Slowly she climbed over the balcony and lowered herself onto the rooftop of the garage. Meryt unhooked the full-length skirt from the dress and pulled out her 9mm with the silencer that was attached to her inner thigh. *One . . . two . . . three . . . breathe . . . and release.* She fired four shots. They all fell where they stood. Meryt scanned the area to see if anyone had heard the shots fired. Everything was clear, so she jumped down from the garage roof to the ground.

Meryt tugged at the suitcase attached to Atken's hand. It was locked. She turned the case on its side and shot the lock off. There was her package: a scared ten-year-old little girl. Iman stared off into space past Meryt with swollen, glassy eyes. The child's hundred-yard stare was so convincing that Meryt looked over her shoulder, fearing the child saw someone coming. There was nothing. Meryt shook the child's shoulders trying to snap her attention to the present.

"Iman, your sister, Collette, sent me." Meryt showed her the necklace.

Iman's hundred-yard stare immediately turned into a death hug around Meryt's neck. She stood up and swung the child's tight hug around to her back. Meryt was thankful she still trained with a weighted rucksack.

Another car was parked ten feet away. Meryt peeked into the window. They were in luck; the keys were in the ignition. Meryt breathed in a sigh of relief as she started the car, because she had heard shouts and people running toward the garage area. Meryt hit the gas. She felt like screaming out of the window, "Elvis has left the building. Good night, all."

As they pulled off the property, Meryt heard someone shout, "That's my car!"

That was the starting bell for the chase to give way. Two cars pulled out behind Meryt. She had a ten-second head start. She banked a hard left around the first corner. The hijacked car was a Maserati. Meryt was fully prepared to push that car to its capacity.

The house was located in the heart of the city. The streets were narrow until the main drive. Meryt had hoped to pick up some speed once she was on the wider streets. Another hard left; she was one block away from the main drag. She only saw one car behind her but that was not a good sign. Meryt knew she had to make it to the first checkpoint to dump the car and change clothes. As much as she loved the Maserati for the speed and handling ability, it was too easy to track, by sight and also by satellite. Ivy Boulevard was the main drag. She made one more turn before she banked hard into a makeshift garage.

"Honey, we gotta get out of this car. We need to change clothes quickly." Iman still looked stunned.

"No! Don't stop; keep driving."

"No, Iman. They can track this car. I have another car with money stashed away. Come on. We don't have much time." Meryt found the black trash bag that she left hours ago. She removed the rest of her dress in one swift motion and pulled out a long, dirty white linen dress and dirty red dress for Iman out of the bag.

"Honey, stop crying. We need to stay quiet and calm. If anyone speaks to you don't talk. I'll tell them you can't speak. Keep your face covered with this scarf."

In a matter of seconds they had changed and picked up two more bags. Meryt backed out of the garage in their new, old and rusted-out car. It was so old and rusty that Meryt couldn't tell what make it was. There would be no tracking this vehicle. They slowly crept down the street. Meryt was looking for a sleeping drunk male. For phase two of the exit plan, she needed to add cover.

Yes! She spotted an old man on the right, sleeping under a box. She got out of the car with the 9mm under her dress. Meryt woke the sleeping man up and asked if he knew how to drive a car. "Excuse me mister, Can you drive? I need you to drive to the next town because I can't drive. Could you please drive me and my baby?"

The old man slowly started moving. Meryt could have sworn he called her *mama*. Perfect, he was drunk.

When he got into the tiny rusted car, he brought in his body odors. He smelled as if he'd been drunk and had not bathed in over a week. Iman pushed herself farther into the corner of the backseat. Meryt, who sat in the back with her, told her, "It's okay, just be quiet."

The man, her cover, began to drive the car down the street. Meryt asked him to head to Al Quradat. At this rate they could make it to the helicopter that was thirty miles outside of the city limits.

Second step was complete. Meryt had started running through the next phase, she took her cell phone out to send a text on their estimated arrival when suddenly bright lights were shined into the car. A police officer ordered the cover to pull over.

Moments later, the officer stood outside the stopped car and flashed his shining light into the cover's face. "Sir, where are you going tonight?" he inquired.

The cover looked back at the officer as if no words had been spoken. The officer asked again, and this time another officer came over to the passenger-side window. Meryt released the cell phone and pushed it between the seat cushions and slide her hand under her dress for the 9mm. She was prepared to quiet the police officer, if he asked the wrong questions.

The cover slowly spoke. "I am taking my mama home!"

The officer asked where was "home" as he continued to flash the bright light into the backseat where Iman and Meryt were sitting quietly.

As the officer was about to speak, the cover pulled out a knife and spoke. "Who wants to know?"

The officers no longer concerned themselves with the Meryt and Iman but were on the cover. He was quickly pulled from the car and beaten.

Another officer was walking over to the car as Meryt and Iman began to gather their things quickly to get out of the car. He picked up speed, as he got closer. "Get out of the car!" he shouted. Iman began to cry. Meryt grabbed the two bags. She had to leave the cellphone pushed between the seats because the officer was standing right over them in the car.

"Hush," Meryt whispered.

The officer continued, "Get out of the car. We are keeping it. Now, walk away, and don't look back. And if I were you, I'd get off the streets tonight. It's not safe!" Meryt grabbed her two bags and pulled Iman closer, and the two girls walked quickly away. By the time they turned the corner at end of the street, Meryt heard gunfire. There went her cover, the wino.

The new dilemma, Meryt wondered how could she get them thirty miles outside of the city in less than an hour. Plus, the officer was right. It was not safe for them to walk the streets. The girls continued walking down the block as police officers ran past them swarming like bees over a beehive on the new kill. Meryt was stuck. She couldn't call anyone. Not now. She left her secure phone in the car. Any call she made would be open to being traced.

"Honey, keep walking. We've got to blend in." Meryt kept playing over and over in her mind, *where can we go?*

More officers were running pass. Meryt assumed they were checking on the gunfire. Meryt and Iman walked two more blocks. She thought she might backtrack to the teashop. They could sleep there for the night and get transportation to the border in the morning.

Meryt was looking up at the street signs, trying to determine her location, when she saw an old bus coming down the street. She flagged down the driver and told him it was not safe for her and her daughter. She asked would he provide transportation to the next city.

The driver looked stressed from all the chaos in the city. "We are going to Sayyidna. You got money!" he asked. Meryt pulled out ten euros. "Get in."

Meryt was grateful to be in motion leaving Khartoum. Unfortunately it was in the opposite direction, but at this point she didn't care. They had new cover transporting them out of the city limits. Wherever they were going, Meryt could arrange for new transportation from there.

Chapter 24

Four hours later, they were still riding. Iman was fast asleep. Meryt laid the child's head down in her lap and leaned her head against the windowsill. The cool night air felt great on her face. It was her favorite time, evening, twilight, and the wind was blowing on her cheeks as the bus drove down the dusty highway. Meryt compared her life over the last three nights: romantic tango, lovemaking, and now running for her life. Each night was different, so different from the next. The moon had risen, and the stars were out, creating a luminous night. This was the third night in a row she had seen the stars out.

The driver continued on until dawn. Just as dawn broke, Meryt heard the old bus give out a loud grinding noise.

It sounded like the engine. The driver got out and opened the hood. Smoke poured out onto the desert sand.

Meryt woke Iman. The little girl stretched and yawned. Meryt gave her the signal to follow her off the bus. They walked around to see the driver leaning over the engine, trying not to get burned. He was pouring water into the truck. Meryt assumed it had overheated. She noticed others getting off the bus, taking care of body functions. She figured this was a good time for a potty break. She grabbed the bags off the bus and walked about fifty feet away.

Meryt provided protective cover with a large blanket she pulled from the black trash bag while Iman squatted first. Then Iman held the blanket while Meryt started to go next. At that moment, the girls heard the engine turn over. Meryt looked back, squatting with her panties down around her legs, and saw the bus departing without them. There was no way she could make it to the bus in this sand while carrying Iman.

Chapter 25

Meryt watched the bus pull off and took a deep breath. *Another change to the story.* She had six one-liter water bottles, six protein bars, two small arms, two bombs, knives, money and no phone. Great. This was all Meryt had to get the president's daughter to safety from being in the middle of the Nubian Desert.

"Honey, let's start walking. We need to make it to the next city." Meryt looked over to Iman's questioning eyes and pretended as if it was a part of the master plan to walk sixty miles in the hot, dusty, brown desert. "Keep your head and face covered." Meryt couldn't decide which was worse: walking in the sand off the main road or walking on the main road. Someone might stop along the road and recognize them as foreigners. She felt it was better to be cautious, so she and Iman started walking about two hundred feet off the main road.

At least it was still morning. It was only in the eighties. Iman could easily tolerate this temperature. The sun had not fully risen in the sky. Perhaps when the sun reached its full height, they would pitch camp to rest and then continue walking at dusk when the temperature started to fall again.

"Are you hungry?" Meryt asked.

"Not really," Iman replied. "I just want to go home."

"I know. So do I."

As they started their long hike to the next city, Iman got in step. Meryt was surprised. Iman was a little trooper. Meryt supposed being the daughter of a politician wasn't an easy task. She definitely had experience in walking through uncomfortable situations.

"You never told me how you got here? Did my father send you? Why are you alone? What's your name?"

"I see you must be feeling better. I'll first start with my name; it's Meryt. Yes, your father sent me. Yes, I am alone. It was a delicate mission to return you home. We were afraid that if they knew when and where we were coming, they would hide you again. So it was decided, it was better to send one person to creep in to get you. Do you have any idea where you are now?"

The little girl just looked around. All she saw was miles of flat desert. No mountains, no rolling hills, just flat, hard, dusty brown sand. It looked as if the sky had reached down and touched the surface of the desert. And the sun was only a few hundred feet in the sky. It smelled the way it looked, dry. Iman looked around more and kicked the hard sand under her feet. "We are in a desert."

"Okay, Einstein, but do you know which desert? We are in Sudan on the east coast of Africa. North of us is the Nile and east of us is the Dead Sea. Your kidnapper really took you far away."

"How long do we have to walk?" Iman asked.

"Until we get to where we have to go. I would like us to make it to Egypt, but I know we will have to find a town or a small village to get more supplies before we make it there."

"Egypt? How far is that?"

"You don't want to know. Keep walking. And when you feel tired let me know. I'll give you some water and a Power Bar."

Iman turned her face up at the menu, but Meryt knew in less than an hour, it would be the best water and Power Bar she had ever tasted.

The wind was light. It felt as if they were walking in an oven with a draft. The wind picked up sand every time it blew. Within an hour, Meryt felt gritty and dry. "Are you okay? Do you want a drink of water?"

"Yes," she responded. Meryt gave her a bottle. Together they drank one bottle.

"Let's keep moving."

They walked for three hours. They talked about everything under the sun. Meryt told her about the necklace and then she placed it around Iman's neck. Meryt held the tiny pearl in her hand, reminding Iman that they had to give it back to Collette. Iman agreed.

Meryt was amazed at how well the ten-year-old little girl was holding up. "Do you know I've trained soldiers that would be complaining right now? You're doing great!"

"You are in the army? You don't look like a soldier."

"Yes, I was in the army. I loved it so much that I still do little jobs on the side. I know I don't look like a soldier. I get that comment a lot. But I did look great in my uniform, if I say so myself."

"Why did you join the army? It was the army, right?"

"Yeah, it was the army. I joined to pay for medical school."

"You're a doctor and a soldier?" Iman turned her face up as if to say, "Why?"

"I told you, I was special. At the time it seemed like good idea. No college loans to pay back. Plus, I was young, and I wanted to explore the world."

They talked about Meryt's early days of training. Meryt began to think of the countless soldiers she had trained and how every step and every mission supported the next in her military career. She wondered if this was her life, mission after mission? Would she ever settle down and have the house with the picket fence in the front yard? That made her think of Rene. How could she settle down with a vampire? She could be committed to an insane asylum for just thinking those crazy thoughts. *Settling down with a vampire.* She felt loneliness tug at her heart.

Meryt's mind jumped from images of Rene to wondering if he would visit her old comrade, Deacon. She prayed that Rene and Deacon would be able to put the pieces together and find them in Nubian Desert before things got dire. They walked another hour in a calm hush.

"Iman, are you feeling well? We haven't talked for a while." Meryt looked down at the little girl. Meryt saw Iman squinting her eyes and breathing through her mouth. Meryt touched her skin along her arms and forehead. Iman felt warm with a slight body sweat. That's a good sign. At least her body still had enough water to make sweat.

"Let's stop here to take a break, and we'll continue walking when the sun starts to set." Iman gave a sigh of relief.

The first twenty-four hours in the desert were uneventful. The second twenty-four hours, a little more painful than the first. Their supplies were getting low.

Their problems started on the third day in the Nubian Desert with no signs of civilization.

Chapter 26

It was day two back in Washington D.C. By the evening, Collette began to realize that her sister would not be coming home tonight. She touched the necklace under her nightgown. She knew what had to be done. Tomorrow, she would force her mother to do a public appearance or convince her mother to let her go with her father for the whole day.

Since her sister's kidnapping, her mother never gave her a minute alone, nor ever under anyone's supervision other than her own.

"I know mom will not let me go with dad. I've got to get her out of the house," Collette thought aloud to herself. Trying to give herself the courage to force her mother out of the house. As if mind reading, her mother returned to the room and found Collette standing in front of her bedroom mirror.

"Collette, are you ready for bed? It's been a long day and still no . . . Well, let's just say our prayers, go to bed, and start a new day tomorrow. Agreed?"

Collette started her scheme, "Agreed . . . Mom, is it possible for us to go to the Hank's Famous Just Like Mom's Ice Cream Parlor tomorrow? It's been a while since we've left the house. I would like a little change of scenery. I want to get beyond these gates. Please, Mom. Please." Collette knew it would be tricky, so she had changed her tone to a more submissive one than she ususally used.

Before she could continue, her mother began. "I don't know. Your father doesn't think it's safe, and what will people say when we don't have Iman?" Collette felt her mom on the brink of another meltdown, so she placed her arms around her mother's neck, cheek to cheek.

Collette whispered, "Mom, we can say Iman is with Grandma. Please, oh please, can we go somewhere tomorrow? I can't take staying inside with all my sister's things. I just keep thinking, 'Why her? Why not me?'"

Collette used her final weapon. She started to cry.

"Okay, baby, you're right; maybe we can go out for a few minutes. Perhaps a change of scenery will do us both some good."

Collette felt a weight lift from her chest. *Hurray, we're going out*, she gave in to a mental cheer. But soon her thoughts returned to the reality of the moment: Iman wasn't here, her mom was an empty shell stressed over the kidnapping, and her father refused to come home and face the loss with his family. Collette said a silent prayer asking God to return things to the way they had been, a happy family of two girls, a mom, and a dad.

The First Lady and Collette made several appearances in public. Once the First Lady agreed to make an appearance, the White House PR staff ran with it. On point, the news cameras and the paparazzi were always present. For there was a visit to the burn unit at Walter Reed Hospital, followed by lunch, gardening, and finally the ice cream parlor. Collette managed to get her mother out of the house for two days straight and still no visitor appeared in the night as Meryt had promised. The weight that once was lifted was slowly returning.

Maybe dad was right. It was wrong to send one soldier to get my sister, she thought. Collette lay in the bed next to her mother wondering. It had been four days since Meryt made her promise and almost five days since her sister had been taken. She rolled over, holding Meryt's diamond pendant in her hand, praying for some kind of miracle. When she rolled back, facing out from the bed, her eyes met Rene's. Collette jumped.

Rene spoke in a voice that only Collette could hear, "Where did you get that necklace?" Collette was uncertain if she was afraid or glad that someone was there in darkness. How could someone sneak into the White House without being caught a second time? How could he move so quietly? Collette decided to speak, after convincing herself, *whatever it takes to get my sister back, I am committed to do.*

"Meryt gave me this necklace," she whispered. "She told me to wear it outside my shirt and a friend would come."

Rene, still quiet and motionless, asked, "Do you know where Meryt is?"

Collette scooted a little closer to the edge of the bed. "Yes, she went to Khartoum to find my sister. My sister was taken five days ago, and Meryt was sent to bring her back. She told me if she was not back in two days to wear the necklace outside of my shirt in public and you would come. She promised me you would find her and my sister. No matter what, she said you would bring them back."

Rene slowly sat back, resting against the wall. He was thinking, *what kind of trouble is Meryt in? Why is she searching for the president's daughter? Is this her friend she had to help?*

"Did she go alone?" he asked.

Collette replied, "Yes."

Rene asked one last question: "Where did you last see Meryt?"

"I last saw her with my parents at a special operations office. She was with a man named . . . Jed Deacon. She told me to tell you to go to him. His office isn't far. I haven't been there before but it was near the Virginia state line, about forty minutes away."

There was silence for a moment, and then Collette asked one last question: "Do you want the necklace back?"

Before Rene responded he looked into the little girl's eyes. He saw the pain and the puffiness surrounding her eyes. She most likely hadn't slept in the last five days.

"I will take it back when you see me again." Rene placed his hand on the little girl's face. "Now rest, my dearest."

Collette enjoyed his cool hand against her cheeks. She slowly closed her eyes, and for a brief moment, she felt free from the pain that she carried in her heart for the last few days. When she closed her eyes, it felt as if it was the first time in the past five days. Gratitude filled her heart when she learned she could keep the necklace. It meant hope was still alive.

When she opened her eyes again, Rene was gone.

Chapter 27

It was day four. Iman was not doing well, and Meryt began to worry. *We are literally going from the frying pan into the fire,* Meryt thought. At least Iman was better off now than being held captive, waiting for her execution day in a suitcase, not sure when or if death would come. But if they continued walking in the desert with no food and water, death would come. Iman was old enough to know that if they didn't find civilization soon, they would die from dehydration. Iman was just coming out of the shock of being kidnapped, and now she faced being stranded in the desert.

Meryt haven't seen any vehicles or animals to kill for food. The midday sun was at its highest with 110-degree temperatures. Their supplies were getting low. Meryt was down to one bottle of water and one protein bar. By this time tomorrow, if they didn't find food and water, they would die in the desert. Meryt couldn't travel fast enough to cover the great distance with Iman nor would she leave her behind. The mission always deviated from the plan.

For once, couldn't things go as planned? Meryt pondered. First, get in country; second, rescue the girl; third, they get out of country; and fourth, return to Niagara Falls in less than forty-eight hours of being gone. This mission was playing out totally different: first, get in the country; second, rescue the girl and walk around in the desert trying to locate food, water, and a working phone, then die of dehydration.

Meryt didn't have poles to make a tent. She used the blanket and placed it over both of them as they sat next to one another, drank half a bottle of water, and took two bites out of the last bar. They spoke a little longer, and soon Iman fell asleep in Meryt's lap. She rubbed Iman's back as she slept. Meryt knew the little girl was tired. She was handling this like a champ. She had been kidnapped, rescued, and now was stranded. Meryt knew this was better than being kept in a suitcase alone in the dark, but the little girl had been through a lot. Meryt wondered how much more could she take. Meryt looked up to the heavens and began to pray that they would find civilization before it was too late.

Iman woke up two hours later. She was ready to walk again. They took a few sips of water and began their travels. The girls repeated the ritual of resting, taking a few sips of water, and then walking three hours for the rest of the day. The top temperatures were well in the 100s. Meryt could tell that this last stretch had gotten to Iman. She wasn't talking as much, and she was moving even slower.

"Let's break again."

Iman started with her questions again. "Are you married? Do you have kids?"

Meryt responded quickly, "No, and no. Being in medical school and the army didn't leave much room for being in love or raising a family." How clever. A little girl knew Meryt was lonely. When Meryt was young it didn't seem to be that important, not having a family of her own. But these past few months after watching the Daniels and even observing Cindy and Karl she started to become interested in the idea of a family.

Iman exhaled. "You must live a boring life."

"Not really. I don't think traveling to Sudan and rescuing the president's daughter is so boring." Meryt gave her a little hug as they sat in the sand. The heat was getting to her too. Meryt's throat was starting to feel scratchy. The long dress was not cooling; it felt more like a hot sauna wrapped around her lower waist. Fatigue was starting to settle in. Her body had begun to complain, wanting to resist commands. Meryt's knees were leading the revolt. They wanted to collapse on the desert floor for a long rest.

"Tell you what, why don't you get on my back? I'll give you a break. Just hold my dress up between you and my back?" Meryt swung her makeshift backpack, from the black plastic bags to the front. Iman jumped up on her back, and they began to travel north again.

Meryt walked about another four hours until dusk. She was completely exhausted as she dropped down to her knees. This time the sand was a little softer. Iman stumbled off her back onto the ground. Meryt's dress was wet, hot, and stuck to her back. She stood up again to shake the dress down. By this time Iman had already opened the bag for the half bottle of water that remained. This was the last drop of water they had left. Meryt was starting the second phase of dehydration. She felt her legs and arms tingling. Meryt had to rest and come up with a plan that contained water.

She bent down on one knee to touch Iman's skin. It was dry to the touch and she had not used the bathroom in the last ten hours. "How are you feeling?" Meryt asked.

"I'm sleepy and my head hurts."

"I know, baby. Is it in the front? My head hurts too. Let's rest for a while until our strength returns. Lay your head in my lap."

Iman lay down and was asleep in less than five minutes after asking a few questions. Meryt looked around. There was nothing but sand combined with dirt surrounding their makeshift camp. *What camp?* She thought. It was just the two of them laid out in the sand. There appeared to be a low mountain range about ten miles away, but Meryt wasn't sure. A sandy desert was just like being on the water, land appears closer than it really is. Sand plays the same trick. It was now crucial for Meryt to have a good sense of direction and distance in this desert. There was no more room for mistakes. It was a matter of life and death. That's why Saddam Hussein never thought that US troops would cross the desert to reach Iraq. There were no landmarks. It all looked the same, and when the sun was high in the sky, a person couldn't tell if they were walking into or away from the sun.

Peculiar feelings started happening as Meryt began to get sleepy thinking about their next move. She should be stressed out because she knew they wouldn't make it to the next city without more water, yet she felt comfort, like this was meant to be. Like she knew this place. She wondered if this was how death felt when it was near. It felt like an old friend. Meryt always thought death would leave a chill all over her body forcing the hairs on her neck and arms to rise to attention. But instead, it felt natural. She felt at ease, but none of this made sense. If they died, here in the middle of nowhere, who would find them? Would Iman's family ever have closure? How could the president not command revenge for the death of his youngest child?

Before Iman fell asleep, she mentioned her mother and sister, wondering how they were doing. Meryt sat brushing her fingers through Iman's hair hoping it offered some reassurance even though she was sleep. Meryt allowed herself a momentary thought of Rene. She wondered what he was doing tonight as she looked up into the same sky Rene stood under, only thousands of miles away.

She hoped Rene would be able to follow the leads, but she knew there were no leads. Meryt never meant for anyone to trace her steps in hostile territory. To be honest, she really thought Deacon would have sent aircraft searching the desert floor for them. Meryt never thought they would be out there in the elements for so long. But she had gotten turned around. She had no idea where the search party would start and where she and Iman were positioned to it. For all she knew they could have walked in circles for the past five days. Meryt looked down at Iman and started to rub Collette's tiny pearl on the necklace repeating one single word *Please*.

Chapter 28

Later that same night, Rene appeared in Deacon's office. Deacon was sitting at his desk going over the reports coming out of Khartoum for the hundredth time. The day before, he had opened his reach to any reports from the whole country of Sudan. He was looking for any signal from Meryt that she was alive. The only thing he knew for sure was that Atken was dead and no child was found in his house or near his dead body. One hour after Lord Atken's death the country shut it doors and airspace. Nothing moved inside or outside of the country as officals tried to pinpoint the killer within its territory. Based on the reports coming in, Sudan government was treating the investigation as an internal contract. US government was relieved, but Deacon was not. He knew the Sudanese were searching for Meryt just like he was. It was a race to determine who would find her first.

"I know you have the girl, but where are you?" Deacon said aloud alone in his office.

At that moment, Deacon felt a presence in the room. His office had dark corners, full of shadows from his awards. At night, he preferred to use only the light on his desk. He focused better in the dark with the one reading light. Deacon pulled his reading glasses down onto his nose to get a better look around, and his eyes came into focus as Rene walked into the light.

Rene asked, "Where did you send Meryt?"

Deacon stood up. "Who are you? How did you get in here?"

Rene repeated his question without making any recognition of Deacon's questions. In Rene's mind, it was only a waste of precious time. Rene felt it in his bones. He felt it the morning he had put Meryt on the plane. Something wasn't right about the way she was leaving, but more importantly, Meryt was hiding something. Between her discovering the truth about his family and his own admission of his true feelings, his judgment had been clouded during her departure. Rene had gone home feeling confident and prepared to wait for Meryt to return his love. But as the hours turned into days, he received no calls, and her voicemail immediately responded to all his calls as if her phone was turned off. Even if she wished not to speak to him, she would have never turned her phone off. Anxiety began to settle in, pushing confidence out. When he saw his necklace on the president's daughter during the ten o'clock news, it confirmed his gut feelings. Now, he was two feet away from the man who sent his love into danger under the pretense of helping a friend.

He continued the questioning. "Where in Khartoum did you send Meryt? Has she been there for the last five days?"

Deacon, being from the old school of interrogations, would not be shaken by the stranger's words. Not when it came to Meryt, who was more like a daughter than a soldier. He stood his ground.

"How do you know Meryt and who are you?" Deacon demanded.

"Listen, old man, my patience is running short. I have been asked to find her, and you were the one who sent her on this suicide mission. So answer my questions now, or you will suffer my full vengeance."

Deacon sat back down and took a sip of his drink, with a slight smile on his face. It was more a sigh of relief. He briefly thought the situation might have called for hand-to-hand combat. It had been a while since he participated in such activities, especially in his office.

"I know who you are now," he said. "You're the doctor she recently met. Sit down, and I'll tell you what I know."

They talked for an hour. Deacon explained how the president's security was compromised, which resulted in the president's daughter being kidnapped. Meryt had been sent in less than seven hours after the kidnapping to Khartoum to retrieve the president's daughter in a quiet manner. Deacon continued, explaining that he had lost contact after Meryt was believed to have the package, Iman. Deacon showed him satellite photos of Meryt's last known location, Lord Atken's house. Deacon ended the conversation with this is not to be repeated.

Within the next hour, Rene was on a private jet to Khartoum. He had his own connection into the country. During the flight he was on the phone coordinating his search.

Chapter 29

"Mr. Deacon, it's been five days and no word from your soldier. I knew sending one soldier wasn't the correct action."

The president sat on the opposite side of the desk, staring down at Deacon, feeling disgusted at the situation, but mostly disgusted with himself. How could he face his wife with this information? She had never wanted him to run for president in the first place.

"America isn't ready for an African-American president," she would constantly say. And every hurdle and every election he passed and won had proved her wrong. Yes, America was ready. Ready for a change. Now this! This proved her to be right. What kind of person would sneak into a man's home at night and steal his child away? A coward from a country that was not ready for change. The president thought of his sweet, sweet Iman in the hands of a coward who dared not face him but rather inflicted pain on his daughter. Thinking of his daughter's pain turned his sorrow and disgust of the whole situation to pure anger. Someone or some country must pay.

"Mr. President, Lord Atken is dead. I have confirmed reports. I can't prove it, but I know Meryt has your daughter. Your daughter is not alone."

"Damn it! Then where is she? She's not here in your office, nor is she home with her family." He stood up and walked toward the door. "She's somewhere out there, in some other country, with a coward who means her harm."

"Mr. President, please calm down, I know this is difficult to stomach. I have a soldier who's like a daughter to me out there! I have not slept in five days. Every asset I have is dedicated to bringing them home. All my Intel reports lead me to believe Meryt has your daughter. The problem is getting them out of Sudan or wherever they maybe. I've sent another person in to locate Meryt and your daughter. Please give me twenty-four more hours before you consider other operations."

"Twenty-four hours?" The president rubbed his head with both palms, wiping away the built-up perspiration. He took a deep breath. "Twenty-four more hours you have. After that, I will send troops in to destroy everyone believed to have had any part in my daughter's kidnapping." The president stood up and headed for the door. "I've got to get out of this office. I need fresh air."

At the door, he turned back to say in a pleading voice, "Deacon, I'm trying hard to do it your way, but I can't hold back the demons that demand retribution for my daughter's death. Help me. Get my daughter home alive."

Chapter 30

Rene hit the ground running. He had a local contact, Kyndle, who knew of the excitement at Lord Atken's home, which happened five days ago. He had been living and feeding in Khartoum for several hundred years, taking delight in humans slaying one another. When the humans went on a killing spree, he could help himself more freely. Who would miss a few extra bodies?

Kyndle pulled up to the airport's arrival terminal in a blood-red, hardtop Porsche.

"Get in. I'll take you by the late Atken's mansion. I don't know if your friend was there, but the person who went there was a professional. He or she killed four people, Atken being one of the four. Atken was running one of the biggest transatlantic slave trades in the world. He had it coming. I knew that one day he would kidnap the wrong girl."

"He did kidnap the wrong girl. My friend, Meryt, was sent to retrieve the little girl, but no one has heard from them since that night. I need to go there to see if I can pick up her scent."

"Sit back. Don't take your shades off. We'll be there in less than ten minutes, bro."

Pulling up to the house, Rene saw the wide tire skid marks on the driveway leading to the street. His thoughts ran back to the night he and Meryt were chasing Mr. Tuswang. She loved to drive.

Kyndle drove past the house, "We'll park down the street and walk back to the property."

Within thirty minutes of being in the country, Rene was walking down the very same halls Meryt had walked five days ago. Rene followed her scent right to the master suite. From there Rene touched the window, the same window Meryt looked out when she caught Atken leaving with the package. Rene felt a small breeze from the open window. He looked up over to the garage. In one step he was there on the rooftop. Kyndle met him on top of the garage.

Rene spoke. "She was here," and he picked up a piece of Meryt's dress. "Now the next question is where did she go?"

Kyndle asked, "Can't you sense your friend's location? Maybe she's not in Khartoum anymore."

Rene held his head down, a little embarrassed. "No, I've never tasted her blood," Rene said as he turned away, indicating the subject was closed.

"Fine. We'll handle this the new way with technology," Kyndle said as reached for the garment and tore it in half.

He sniffed the garment and flipped open his phone. "I'll call a few friends to help in the search, if that meets your approval."

Rene agreed with a head nod.

He searched the house for an hour, but there were no more clues. No one was talking about the killings from five days ago. No one in the house had seen the killer. They only knew the killer left in a stolen car. He could still smell blood in the air, but one good thing, none of it smelled of Meryt's blood. Her blood did not spill here.

Rene repeatedly asked himself, *Where did she go since, she never made it to the helicopter outside of town?*

He felt the urgency stir in his gut. Time was getting short. A human's life was fragile. It could only endure so much.

Chapter 31

For a moment in time, Meryt no longer resisted sleep. She closed her tired eyes and began dreaming of her last night with Rene: on the rug, in front of her fireplace; the kisses that led to her total surrendering of emotions; his strong hands, holding her by the small of the back; the way he held her total weight so effortlessly. Another wave of passion ran through her body. *I must remember: one . . . two . . . three . . . breathe.*

Meryt opened her eyes. There was no sunlight from the desert blinding her sight. Instead, there was a soft yellow light from a fireplace.

Am I dreaming? Where's Rene? She strained to focus and began to sit up. She was stopped in midaction; her arms and legs were chained down to a table. Correction, she was chained down to the table.

"Who? What the?" Meryt spoke as she began to assess the situation while scanning the room for Iman. It was all coming back to her. Meryt had been dreaming, but this was no dream. Her soft carpet was replaced with a stone table. The sweet smell of her bedroom was replaced with the smell of oldness. The only thing pleasant was the coolness in the air compared to the 100-plus-degree days she'd been exposed to for the last five days. Meryt was definitely being held captive, and she couldn't see Iman anywhere in the room.

Two black men rushed into the room and surrounded the table. She began to pull with all her might to test the strength of the chains. They wouldn't give. While tugging at the chains, Meryt started rattling off questions, "Who are you? Where am I? And where is the little girl?" The chains did not give a single inch.

In all this madness, she heard voices in her head, but she could not understand. She tried speaking in Sudanese Arabic. No response. They spoke a language she had never heard before. She could not comprehend their conversation completely. The language sounded familiar with a different dialect. It was close to Coptic, yet not exactly.

She studied her abductors a little closer. They were African men dressed solely in kilts or were they wraps? Meryt was African-American. She understood dark complexions, but she had never seen this shade of black on any African. It was black without any luster. It was almost as if they were so dark they turned into shadows. She could sense the voices in her head were coming from them, but their mouths weren't moving. As she examined them closer, she saw it. They had fangs!

Meryt began to pull fiercely at the chains again. "What the fuck! Where are these vampires coming from?" she screamed. Up until a few days ago, Meryt never thought for a second that vampires existed outside of fictional stories.

The chanting in her head and the chains rattling against the stone table made Meryt's head spin. It all sounded like chaos. It was too loud and too fast to make any sense.

Meryt screamed over the chants, "Where is Iman? Did you kill her?" Meryt wondered, *did Iman suffer? Did they scare the living crap out of a little girl?* Iman had been through so much already. If she had to die, couldn't her passing have been peaceful in Meryt's lap, not alone with monsters? Meryt felt so much anger and resentment run through her body. Her blood began to run cold. She felt her strength return.

Meryt began to pray, "Father, please give me the strength and the courage to bring the same pain to those who harmed Iman." It was a miracle. Meryt began to feel the chains give a little. She felt the chains growing longer with each pull. She was winning the tug of war against the chains. It inspired her to pull harder and harder. The chains were slowly being pulled loose from the ground.

She began to cry out adding to the noises running wild in her head. "How could you hurt her? What savages are you? Vampires!" The chains gave way again. "Who should I kill first?"

"Stop!" Everything went quiet. A woman walked into the room. Meryt felt her presence before her eyes made contact. The woman circled the chained table and brushed Meryt's body with her fingertips as she slowly walked by. Her fingers were as cold as ice. She had long curly black hair. Her skin was olive brown, and she had an unusually long neck and jet black eyes. Yet, in all of this, she was beautiful. She was dressed in white linen, a wraparound top and a long skirt with long slits up the sides held together by a belt of gold. She wore a gold necklace and matching bangles on her arms. Meryt had only seen this type of jewelry in museums surrounding King Tut and his buried treasure. The woman turned toward the others and spoke in the same unknown language. Meryt spoke eight different languages and twenty different dialects. Meryt complained to herself, *how do I not know this one?*

The woman turned to Meryt and said, "Calm down before you injure yourself. I apologize for your treatment. We seldom have"—she looked back at her soldiers and then back at Meryt—"guests. I will remove the shackles, but you must promise no warring."

"Before I make any promises, tell me if the little girl is still alive."

"The girl you call Iman is fine. She is safe." The strange woman turned and spoke to the others.

She looked back at Meryt and began to speak in a regal voice. "They are bringing her to you now. Again, I must apologize. We have not had guests in some time." She removed the chains.

Meryt rubbed her wrists, while looking around the room. Two more men entered the room, Meryt assumed they must all be vampires. Meryt was assessing the room, trying to identify an escape route.

"Where am I, and who are you?" Meryt asked.

"My name is Queen Hatshepsut, and you are in my home."

Iman came into the room with two more guards, and ran directly to Meryt's side. "Are you okay?" Meryt asked, hugging her tight.

Iman replied, "Yes."

Hatshepsut stood uncomfortably close while observing the two girls embrace. "I have a question. What were you doing in the desert with this child? She is not your daughter."

"She was taken from her parents. Her father asked me to return her home," Meryt quickly stated.

Hatshepsut responded, "Clearly, the desert is not her home. Why were you walking around in the desert?"

Meryt continued her story. "My exit plan fell apart. I was traveling to the next city in hopes of getting back to Egypt."

Queen Hatshepsut smiled when Meryt mentioned Egypt and quickly dropped her own questions in. "Were you thinking of staying in Egypt? Who is the child's father?"

As she was asking questions, Meryt could feel Hatshepsut's voice and thoughts inside her head. It felt as if she was searching for something, yet

Meryt could feel she was pleased. "I think you know the child's father, therefore you must understand how important it is for me to return her home at once."

"You are correct. I do know the father of this child. You must travel back and visit again, Meryt." This time Queen Hatshepsut stopped directly in front of Meryt's face, slowly inching her face closer, and constantly stroking Meryt's cheeks with her icy fingers. "You are a warrior indeed," she said.

Meryt refuse to move. She felt compelled to stand her ground as this stranger violated her personal space, but Meryt wanted a closer look as well. Who was she? How did she know her name? *Probably the same way she knew Iman's father. Perhaps she can read minds.* As Meryt determined this conclusion, Queen Hatshepsut smiled.

Queen Hatshepsut knew Meryt knew her little trick. What Meryt was not expecting, was what happened next, a kiss.

At first Meryt fought the kiss, but the Queen was too strong. And within seconds, Meryt encouraged it.

Chapter 32

Meryt began to dream one of her oldest dreams. It was a dream she had grown accustomed to, she had had this exact dream before. The dream altered ever so slightly each time, but she always knew it was the same dream. Meryt drifted back in time, a time she'd grown to miss, but something was different. It normally felt as if the dream was happening to someone else, like she was watching a movie unfold, but this time it felt real. It felt like it was her life unfolding.

She was the main character, Queen Nitocris. Meryt opened her eyes to a dead man lying next to her on the bed. She sprang from the bed and cautiously looked around the room. The room was beautiful, made of pale white stone and golden columns with huge open windows and long white panel curtains blowing in the wind. As she tuned back to the dead body, she knew instantly that he was her lover, and pain started burning deep in her chest. Meryt couldn't breathe. She tried to listen for his heartbeat while feeling the temperature of his body to measure how long he had been dead. Her heart exploded as reality settled in; he was truly gone. She fell to her knees with tears running down her face. Immediately, she tore her clothes in anguish and lay down next to his body. She lay there crying and cursing for hours asking over and over, "How could you leave me? You promised you would never leave me."

Pliny returned. "My Queen, it is time. The soldiers await your command." Queen Nitocris looked back at the Pliny, pushing the hurt back, allowing anger to come forward. She wiped away the tears and stood up from the low-lying bed, naked for all to behold. The passion she held for Atum was replaced with revenge. There was nothing left to hide, there were no more secrets, her one true love was gone. Two nursemaids, noticing her nudity, quickly dressed her in fine white silks.

"No, I will not wear white!" The queen tore the clothes from her body. "I want to wear black. I want my people and my enemy to know; I have nothing but blackness in my heart. If it is war they want, then death I will bring."

Chapter 33

War came to Nubia just as the Oracle and Hatshepsut had prophesied. Queen Nitocris united her Nubian army with the Egyptian forces. Pharaoh and Queen Nefertiti held Egypt proper, all territories surrounding Amarna, the new capital, and the old capital in Giza. Atem and Nitocris engaged the Babylonian's along the Nile and fought them back deep into Egypt's eastern border, back to the Great Sea. At this point, Queen Nitocris received orders to separate the forces from Smenkhkara, the pharaoh's right hand. The pharaoh ordered Atem to continue to push the enemy into The Great Sea, the Mediterranean, while Nitocris took the remaining force and turned her attention to the Mountains of Jeb, the last place Atum had fought and lost his life. She wanted revenge on the land and on the people who spilled her love's blood. Nitocris knew the Mountains of Jeb held the truth to all her questions about the war and about Atum's death. Without hesitation, she accepted the orders. She was eager to start the campaign.

As the weeks passed, Nitocris conquered each village, expelling the Babylonians and pushing them further back to their homeland. She placed a bounty on the cowards who killed Atum. She promised a reward for any information that could lead her to Atum's killers. Her army defeated city after city; Gaza, Beersheba, and Hormah. The morale of the troops grew as they prepared to defeat Edom. As they defeated each city, she interrogated the locals for any evidence that could lead her to the truth; surprisingly, there was none. No one knew of any Egyptian's fighting in the mountains prior to her arrival.

A few of the villagers had seen Atum and his men come through the mountains, but they had not heard of any fighting. Nitocris didn't know what to believe. The villagers had first been captured by the Babylonians and were now freed by her army all within the last sixty days. The depressed villagers had experienced so much bloodshed and were so terrified that they barely knew their own names.

What truth could she find in their fear?

Chapter 34

The new capital of Amarna had been completed in record time. Some would say that the Creator willed it to be done because he knew war was coming to its homeland. Amarna's beauty was matched only by its decadence in gold and precious jewels. Pharaoh had taken on new architects. It was rumored his new wife, Queen Nefertiti, had brought her architects from Nubia. The new architects built the outer walls to the new city higher than earlier structures found in Egypt. In addition, they strategically placed corner towers and hidden fighting positions within the walls and towers. The pharaoh's home possessed similar features, which made it impossible to scale and easy to defend.

Once the war had officially began, Pharaoh ordered his entire family, closest friends, and priests to remain within the walls of his home. Smenkhkara first disagreed with all key leaders being in one location, but he eventually gave in to the pharaoh's will. Remarking, it was a brilliant plan with the limited soldiers remaining to defend the area. Everything was on a strict schedule. Atem left detailed orders to the remaining soldiers guarding the royal family and the new capital. Atem was confident in their ability and the safeness of the new capital. If he didn't feel comfortable, he would have never left the pharaoh's side to fight with the armies pushing the Babylonian's back to the sea.

On this particular night, the guard shift changed with no unusual reports. Still, everyone was tense, jumping at shadows lurking in the darkness. Atem had a habit of appearing out of the darkness with a surprise attack, testing the integrity of the defense. On this night, it was quiet. The pharaoh had left the queen's quarters and retired into his own. Sitting in his favorite chair, reviewing written scrolls from the front line, he had become so engrossed in reading the success of the two armies, that he had not heard his uninvited guest moving in the shadows toward his chair. Atem had reported that all Babylon's army in his range were at sea, and Nitocris had already passed through the Mountains of Jeb and was preparing to attack Moab. The war was moving faster than the pharaoh had hoped. The good news gave him a moment to breathe deeply and release the tension he held in all day. The pharaoh desired an end would come sooner than expected. As he breathed deeply and exhaled a second time, allowing the scrolls to fall free from his hand, his guest positioned for attacked.

A ten-foot king cobra coiled its body and lifted his head four feet into the air, hovering at the same height as the seated pharaoh. The pharaoh opened his eyes to the waving twin-forked tongue of the snake. Fear seized him as he gazed at the massive bulky hood and the distinctive yellow *V* marking on the cobra's underbelly. He closed his eyes as a flashback of his dead brother, the one should have been the pharaoh, appeared in his mind. It had been a family secret, but a snake cut short his older brother's life. At that moment, he felt his brother's fear; he felt his brother's heavy breathing as panic took over his body. With closed eyes, the pharaoh willed himself to open them. He would not die a coward. He would not die with closed eyes while his enemy gorged upon his flesh sending poison throughout his body. Pharaoh opened his eyes just in time to see the cobra's unswerving attack to his face. Natural instinct took over. He grabbed the snake's head, but it was too strong. The cobra continued to slither from his grasp, biting the pharaoh along his forearm. The bites immediately stung, causing excruciating pain as the venom rapidly broke down his flesh and muscles spreading pain beyond the wound site.

Then he remembered: he was Akhenaten, the Pharaoh, the ruler of Egypt. His father was a pharaoh and his father before him was a pharaoh. He had the blood of the Creator running in his veins. He decided that the snake would never taste another drop of royal blood again. Akhenaten refused to die a coward.

While the cobra continued biting the pharaoh's arm trying to free itself, he reached with his free hand to grab anything to kill the snake. His fingers found a scroll with its metal core. The king cobra had bitten him three more times, climbing along his arm trying to break free. Pharaoh immediately gripped the scroll and swung it down on the cobra's head repeatedly. A new thought emgered in his head, *who sent this snake to my chamber, the same person who released the snake to murder my brother?* It did not matter now; the pharaoh knew it was too late for him because no one survives the deadly bite of a king cobra. So he fought through the pain in his arm. He fought back the fear in his heart. He fought for his brother's life. He promised himself that that snake would not kill another from his bloodline. The pharaoh swung the metal scroll down on the snake's head until they both lay dead on the floor.

The following morning the guards came into the pharaoh's chambers and found him and the remains of the once ten-foot cobra's blood spattered all over the marble tile. It was obvious that the cobra had killed the pharaoh, but no one had ever seen a cobra killed by its intended victim. Once word had gotten to Queen Nefertiti, she ran to the pharaoh's quarters to confirm its truth. Upon seeing the sight on the floor, she screamed in horror. She had seen death; she had come from a family of warriors, so amputations and assaults were a common site but not this. The pharaoh's bitten arm had become so inflamed from the venom that it actually tore open at the wound sites. His hand was totally unrecognizable, and his face and neck were grotesquely disfigured. The pharaoh's blood poured out of the wounds. The king cobra's blood mixed in with Pharaoh's pooling beneath both victims.

Queen Nefertiti went into shock. She refused to leave her quarters during the burial ceremony. Egypt was at war. It needed a pharaoh. Queen Nefertiti was shaken to the core and refused the crown. Queen Nitocris had the Nubian army deep in Babylon territory and was unable to return to Egypt.

It only made sense for Smenkhkara to be named Pharaoh.

Chapter 35

Meryt awoke to a new noise, the sound of cars racing down the desert highway. She recognized this place. They were in Cairo. Iman lay in her arms, still asleep.

"How did we make it?" Meryt scrambled to remember her last thoughts. She remembered falling asleep. She remembered dreaming about a war. Everything else was a blank. She looked around trying to determine the time of day or any fimilar signs hoping to regain some type of bearing. She peeked down her dress to ensure she was intact, that was always a personal fear of hers, losing a limb or being fatally cut. Other than being dirty, she was okay. Meryt couldn't make heads or tails of it. *We must have gotten a ride, and I can't remember due to dehydration,* she thought to herself. Meryt made a mental note to ask Deacon to run blood test to ensure she wasn't drugged when she returned home.

Meryt didn't have a cell phone, but at least she was now within a true walking distance of a phone. She looked down at Iman. Meryt tapped gently on her back to wake her up. When Iman opened her eyes, they were as big as golf balls.

"How did we get here?" she inquired as she looked around.

"Honey, I don't know, but I'm thankful we are here. Let's get moving." Meryt gave her a big hug and whispered in her ear, "And you thought my job was boring."

Dirty and tired when they reached the first working phone, Meryt called Deacon.

The operator connected her through. Deacon answered, "This better not be a joke. Who is this?" Meryt answered in a dry, scratchy voice, "It's me. I've got your package, and I need a ride home."

Deacon just held the phone to his chest and said a silent prayer.

Meryt asked, "When did you start praying? Just get me out of here."

"Don't worry, Honey, your friend is around the corner. Let me call him on the other line." Deacon called Rene.

"What friend?" Meryt asked as an image of Rene on her rug flashed followed by a quick image of a full-shaped, curly-haired woman appeared in her mind, Queen Hatshepsut. Meryt shook her head trying to remain focused.

"Rene, we got her, and she's got the girl. They are in Cairo, Egypt. How fast can you be there? I can have a flight ready in thirty minutes for them to come home. Hold on and I'll give you the exact address." Deacon punched a code into his computer to trace Meryt's call.

Deacon returned to Meryt's conversation, "Hey, move over two and your friend, the doctor, will be there in one hour with all of your paperwork. Just be there, and stay safe." Deacon paused for a moment, and then in an apologetic voice continued, "All I can say is thank you."

Meryt couldn't help but reply, "Well, let's just hope I'm around long enough for you to return the favor."

Meryt left the hotel and moved two blocks south. That was always their code when talking on an unsecured line. "Iman, we are going home. We've only need to walk two more blocks."

Clockwork. Rene was there on time. He turned the corner driving a black Range Rover with tinted windows. Meryt stood off the main street at a bus stop. They were still dressed in the same dirty clothes with head wraps from six days ago. Rene rolled the window down and drove slowly down the street searching for Meryt's scent. As he passed by, they walked toward the truck. He smelled her and slammed on the brakes. He jumped out of the truck and grabbed them both.

Meryt felt like a teenager excited to see her boyfriend. He held them tight in his arms, enjoying a few stolen moments before releasing them from his bear hug. Iman and Meryt jumped into the backseat, and they were off to the airport. Meryt thought it was premature to call the mission complete until she delivered the package safety to the White House, but at this moment it felt mighty close.

Six days and ten hours and it was over. Meryt stood in Deacon's office in the same outfit, slacks and a silk sweater. Meryt was ten pounds lighter and twelve shades darker, plus sunburned in a few areas, but the package was intact. Iman lost six pounds, sunburned and dehydrated. None of that mattered; she was safe back home in the states. They had finished the final debriefing, as well as blood tests. Everything came back normal.

Naturally, Meryt left Rene on the plane. She told him they would fly back together once she finished with debriefing. Rene had a ton of questions, but Meryt was so exhausted from the previous mission that she was left speechless.

The president and his family fought the Secret Servicemen to pass through the door. Actually, the First Lady won the battle. She shot past security to catch Iman running into her arms. This was yet another treasure Meryt was allowed to enjoy. Reuniting a family. A simple miracle.

Deacon cleared his throat to get the president's attention, "Mr. President, the mission is complete." The president came over and shook Deacon's hand. Deacon continued, "We've done all of our tests to ensure your daughter is healthy. You may want to follow up yourself. It appears she suffered stress and is recovering from mild dehydration."

The president gave Deacon a hardy handshake and said, "Thank you for keeping the demons away."

"You are welcome, Mr. President. No problem at all, sir." Deacon responded as if all went according to plan.

President Lee then turned to Meryt and gave her a bear hug. He whispered in Meryt's ear, "I can never repay you for this. I owe you my life. Thank you for retuning my baby and my life back home safely."

"You are welcome, sir." Meryt replied, but before she could finish, Collette and Iman made their way over. Meryt pulled them over to the side and squatted down to their level. "I guess it's time for us to exchange our necklaces. I want to thank you for being brave and sending my friend."

Collette replied as she gave back the necklace, "*Thank you* for bringing my sister home."

Meryt kissed both girls on their foreheads and shot a quick comment to Iman. "Who says my life is boring?" Both girls giggled.

Finally, the First Lady came over to join her daughters with tears in her eyes and whispered, "Thank you very much."

This was more than Meryt could take. Expressing emotions was not her strong suit. Meryt headed for the door. She gave Deacon the call-me sign as she left the office.

All Meryt wanted to be was homeward bound.

Chapter 36

Rene and Meryt finally spoke of the events that took place in Sudan on the plane ride home.

"Why didn't you tell me you still worked for the military?" Rene asked.

Meryt shot Rene a look of sarcasm. "Why didn't you tell me you were a vampire?" Meryt turned in her sit to be a little closer to Rene. "Do you recall that night in the car, when I chased those men into the woods? Remember when I said, 'You aren't the only one with secrets.' Why else would you live in upstate, unless you were born here or you want to live under the radar? Technically, I don't work for the military. I do occasional jobs for a contractor. Where else would I have gotten my toys from that night?" Meryt closed her eyes. "Please, can we finish this discussion at home? I'm tired which is making me a little short. I can't stop thinking. I wasn't worried about my death about my death, as much as, I worried about what my death meant to you or even Iman's death meant to the world. Does this sound weird? For a moment, when we were lost out in the Nubian Desert, I thought we wouldn't make it back. All I thought about was how do I get her home to prevent a war from coming. To be quite honest, I'm not sure how we made it out. On all accounts, Iman and I should be dead."

Rene kissed her forehead. "Okay, my love, you are safe, just rest. We will be home soon."

An hour and a half later, Rene pulled into her driveway. It was nighttime Meryt was finally home. She was torn between being elated and exhausted all at the same time seeing her home after six days of the blinding sun and stinking hot temperatures.

"Are you staying the night?" Meryt asked in an apologetic manner.

"Yes, do you want me to carry you over the threshold, or do you think you can make it in the house, sleepyhead?"

"I can make it. I'm not that old, but I will be heading straight for the bathtub."

Within the hour, they were soaking in the tub. Meryt lay back onto Rene's chest, enjoying the combination of the steaming hot water and Rene's cool skin.

Rene asked, "Is there more I should know?"

"Well, let's see. I practice medicine; I do occasional contract jobs for my friend. How else do you think I pay for all of this? Have you seen the reimbursement up here for medicine?" Meryt ran the bath cloth down her arm. "Plus, I think I'm falling for a vampire, no I mean a dark angel. What else do you want to know? My shoe size? A girl's gotta keep some things private."

Rene smiled. "What am I to do with you? Somehow I think you may be the final death of me." He was happy she'd returned home. Now he was prepared to wait for Meryt to return his love.

Silence took over the room. All that could be heard was Meryt's breathing and night gusts of wind against the bathroom windows. Meryt sank even further into Rene's chest, thinking this was a far cry from the conditions she was in forty-eight hours earlier.

Meryt finally broke the silence. "Tell me about yourself. Where do you come from? What are your restrictions? It's obvious you can go out in the sun. Are any of the myths true about vampires?"

"I come from what is now Germany. I was a Goth soldier when I was made in 1386. My restrictions? There are some, and only a few of the myths are true. I can take direct sunlight, but living on the beach would not be my choice of a lifestyle. Any long periods of exposure to the sun are not good for my kind. The older I become the longer I can stay out in the sun. I'm ten times stronger than a man my size. I can move faster than the human eye can follow. My five-senses are more in tune than in humans. I can feel emotions or maybe a flash image of what they are thinking and sometimes I can even change their mindset, but not as well as my mother. As you know, I cannot enter a home while a human is present unless I'm invited."

"How often do you feed?"

"About twice a week. I usually drink stored blood from blood banks or from animals. Most dark angels feed from humans without killing them. The idea is not to attract attention to the dark angel race. Oh, and I rarely sleep."

"How many vampires are there, considering I never thought they existed?"

"I don't know, maybe twenty thousand or so. There aren't that many. One of the main rules is to stay 'off the radar' as you put it. But we usually don't stay together or form groups larger than five or six."

"How do you work? I mean, do you feel the same as humans do? Do you lust for or love humans?" Meryt said. "What I mean is, how do 'we' work? I know I have feelings for you. I'm physically attracted to you. The way you look, the way you smell, the way you command my attention when you enter a room. Is that you or some special vampire scent or mind power? Is this some kind of ploy to lure your meals? Do I look like your favorite food?"

Rene started to chuckle. "Yeah, you're my favorite dish, *Meryt a la mode*. Yes, dark angels have the capacity to have emotions. I hoped that I have proven I'm extremely attracted to you. I can't speak for all vampires, just like you can't speak on courtship of all humans. From the first day I met you, I had a strong connection to you. I've never felt this bond for any angel or human. I can feel. I love you." Rene lifted his arms out of the water. He showed Meryt the little hairs standing up on his arm from the temperature change. Then he wrapped his arms around her waist. "I do not think of you as food. You are my love. I can sense your blood running through your veins. I can feel your blood flow, so I can easily tell when you are excited. Unfortunately or fortunately, it excites me too. I often wonder what you taste like, meaning your blood, but I will not take from you what you have not offered. I know you are B negative, which I might add has always been my favorite."

"If you bite me does it convert me to a dark angel?"

"It takes more than a bite. It takes mixing dark angel's blood with the host's blood. Not in all cases can a vampire create another. A tremendous amount of things have to happen in order, similar to the compound you created for my mother. There has to be a modular break down and rebuild in a timely matter. In most cases, the person gets flu-like symptoms and recovers in three to four weeks. The dark angel has to deliver enough blood to convert the host. It has to be enough blood to kill the host's immune system, yet not so much that it completely kills the host. Some dark angels can have 100 percent success rate while others are unable to convert a single person."

"Have you ever made a vampire?"

"No. I've never found the need to give this curse to anyone. Why? Are you thinking about a lifestyle change?" Rene asked in an entirely different voice. A spark of hope was lit. *Perhaps I'll have more than a mortal's lifetime with Meryt.* He thought to himself.

"No. I like my human life. I just wanted to know about yours. I need to be sure that if I drink after you, I wouldn't catch your bug," Meryt said, laughing.

Rene did not laugh. They got out of the soaking tub and began to dry off.

"Meryt, I have an important question to ask of you. If you are planning to continue this line of work, traveling the world on military missions, would you allow me taste your blood. Allowing me to taste your blood creates a bond between us. It gives me the ability to track you easier. As an dark angel, my sense of smell is more powerful than a human's." Rene paused for a moment, trying to convey his true emotions without anger, "Meryt, you never asked me how I felt when I saw the necklace I gave you on another. If it weren't a child, I don't think I would have had the patience not to kill. Make no mistake, I cannot lose you again. I have no idea how to handle your death. The bond I feel for you is beyond love. It's as if I've waited for you all my life. I felt this strongly from the first day we met."

Rene held her up by her arms, so he could look directly into her eyes. Meryt's tiptoes barely grazed the bathroom floor tile as he held her tightly while he stared into her eyes searching for reassurance. She dropped her towel, returning his stare.

The only light in the room came from the flames dancing in the double-sided fireplace. Meryt saw the same flames reflecting in his blue eyes. She felt the mental pull, the longing to be one with him. They began kissing. She wrapped her legs around his waist. He pulled her close and moved his hands from her arms to cradle her bottom. He held her weight against his. Rene never answered the question about whether he had a special scent to seduce women, but at that moment, Meryt really don't care. He carried her into the bedroom and laid her gently across the bed.

After sleeping on the desert ground for the last week, it felt like heaven, and between wanting him and being on a soft bed, Meryt would have sold her soul in an instant.

They continued kissing, and Meryt was slowly drifting farther into heaven, getting lost in the clouds surrounding her body. It was his body and hands touching her aching muscles and kissing her neck. Meryt started to tingle all over. In a soft voice Rene asked, "Meryt, can I taste your blood? I promise I will only take a small amount." Meryt couldn't tell the direction of Rene's voice. It was in her head; it was on her lips. His voice surrounded her spirit.

"Will it hurt?"

Rene replied softly, "No."

By this point, her breathing had started becoming deeper. Meryt was losing her voice. "Yes," she repeatedly said.

Meryt felt Rene's lips on her shoulder, slowly moving up her neck. It tickled not the kid tickle, but the adult tickle. The kind that gives goose bumps up and down the spine. Her back arched against his weight as he held her down with his body on top of hers and his arms wrapped around to her back. Meryt felt the first bite on her neck. For a split second it burned, afterward it felt like an orgasm, one continuous flow. She was lost in another world. His mouth felt so warm, so robust. Meryt could feel his life force pulling her closer and closer. It was a huge ball of red fire rotating. She wanted to touch it. Meryt opened her eyes to verify her vision. When she opened them the rotating fire ball was gone.

Meryt felt Rene kissing her body, moving on past her neck. He was slowly sucking her nipples, taking turns from left to right. He started to move his hands lower, down to her special area. She felt wet all over. Meryt was pulling his body closer to hers. She wanted to make love. She wanted him inside of her body. Rene kept kissing her hands, pushing them away during his descent to her stomach that ended on her upper thigh. Rene bit Meryt on her inner thigh. Meryt screamed in a painful delight. Her body shook. Another massive wave of continuous pleasure hit her body. She refused to faint, so she pulled his head up as hard as she could trying to make him stop until she saw the red ball of fire. Meryt let go of his head and started moving toward the fire. She went to reach for the light. It was gone, but when she opened her eyes, Rene was inside of her rocking slowly in a seated position. She was holding on to him, and he was holding her in his arms like a baby, cradling her head.

Heaven.

Chapter 37

The heavy fog cleared. The morning sun continued to burn off the remaining light fog as the sun moved higher into the sky. It was a beautiful sight to behold. The Creator was good. He sent clouds from the heavens so they could admire their natural, pure beauty. "Good morning, my love. Tell me again, why should I let you travel alone?" Queen Nitocris asked.

"I won't be alone. I'm bringing a contubernium. I have eight of my best men. I will go and return before I am even missed. Besides, you need to ready the army for war."

Queen Nitocris walked over, feeling torn between doing what was right for her country, preparing them for war, and mad with jealousy because she want to go and fight along Atum's side. Nitocris was so delighted Atum had decided to return home with her to Nubia, when she left Egypt. She had been home for one month and in that time Atum had stolen her heart. There weren't enough hours in the day or night, in which they could spend together. Atum was correct. She must stay behind to prepare her people. "You do know that it is punishable by death to give orders to your Queen."

He grabbed her arms. "Now if you order my death, who will be left to love the Queen?"

Nitocris answered smartly, "My people."

She walked away and changed the subject. "I do not understand why this war is coming here. We are warriors, but there is no need to fight. I know the Oracle said war is coming, but it makes no sense. The water is plentiful and food is in abundance. Yet there is a war coming to our land over petty raids? Why? I consulted with Hatshepsut, my cousin; she has the gift of vision, and she agrees with the Oracle. War is coming to our land. Is it that man needs to fight to know he exists? My father taught me when I was a small child, 'You know a thing is real when it has weight or can be counted or when it becomes a burden to carry.'"

Nitocris would protest and say to her father there were things in the world that were real that did not fit his criteria. She would tell him life was real. "You can't count life, it has no weight, and surely it can't be a burden to live." Her father would correct her, "Life can be counted in days or even years. And it has a weight," he would add as he squeezed her cheeks. "But most of all, life is a heavy burden, for you to live and see the following morning sunrise, someone must die."

"My father," Queen Nitocris whispered. "This war does not rest well in my soul. Give me direction." Nitocris returned to the window to see the last of the clouds disappearing into the horizon.

Father, who must die for our people to live free? She said to herself, and then turned her attention to Atum as she walked toward him.

"Do as Atem, and Smenkhkara have asked, locate the Babylonian rebels and end these raids. You must discover the truth behind this war before it becomes blood thirsty requiring deaths of thousands to quench its thirst."

They kissed. Afterward, Atum fell to one knee, holding her hands in his. "My love, I will return before the moon is full again, and I will have your truth."

Chapter 38

"Is it morning?" Meryt woke up looking for her clock. It read 10:31 a.m. She had been dreaming and had overslept. She felt well rested, yet still sore from the desert. Rene was lying awake next to her.

"Good morning, lover boy." Meryt said while trying to pull the covers over her naked body. The bed was a complete mess. The sheets were pulled from their corners. Rene lay naked with the soft light pouring over his body. Meryt guessed if one had a body like that, why cover it?

Rene responded, "Good morning, how are you feeling? I didn't mean for all of that to happen last night. I wanted to wait and give you a few days to recover, but you" he touched her face "I can't get enough of you."

"Somehow your words sound romantic, but your expression says concern. What is it now?"

Rene was concerned. He was a seasoned dark angel, behaving like a newborn. He had fed earlier in the day. He had no reason to be concerned about his own thirst. Rene merely wanted to sample Meryt's blood to store it in his memory bank.

But this time, it was different. Rene had bit into Meryt's main artery along her neck, and it was delicious. It was the perfect temperature, perfect texture, and perfect taste. He literally fought with himself to release from the first bite, but as he began to kiss her body, passion started to rise and his fangs began to burn. He yearned for more. Rene had to take another bite.

There was no doubt; he was in love with Meryt. He knew this relationship was dangerous. She was human. Human lives were fragile. He had worked in hospitals for the past hundred years. Rene had seen death come over and over. Death was a part of a human's world. Rene knew two things for certain: death would come for Meryt, and on that day, death would take him as well. After tasting love, Rene refused to live in a world without it, without Meryt.

"I love your blood. I only meant to bite you once. I pulled away, but I had to taste you again. It was hell trying to stop."

Meryt touched her neck, and then she quickly pulled the covers down revealing her inner thigh. At first, she didn't see anything. She ran her fingers past where she thought the bite happened. She had too many crazy dreams. Meryt was trying to remember what was real. She found it. Right there were two small holes on her inner thigh. If she weren't looking for it, she would not have found it. It was silly of her to think that. Of course, she wouldn't find something, if she were not looking for it; but even though she was looking for it, it was hard to find just two little circular scars.

Meryt ran to the bathroom mirror to find the marks on her neck. "I won't turn into a vampire? Will I?"

"No, Meryt, my blood did not cross over."

Meryt's smart wit blurted out, "Talk about unprotected sex."

They both started laughing.

Rene came toward her with arms open wide. "You are my special blend."

As the next three months passed, she had never been so happy in her entire life. Meryt was in a loving relationship with a dark angel.

February, happy.

March, happy.

April, happy.

Chapter 39

The past three months had been a beautiful dream.

Rene and Meryt were coming along nicely. No missions from Deacon only questions from him on Rene's background. Also, Deacon was still working the angles behind the president's daughter's kidnapping. It bothered Deacon that no ransom was ever submitted. Lord Atken had no real motive to take the president's daughter.

This was the first time Meryt had been in any type of relationship that didn't include a debriefing from Deacon. She wished he would leave well enough alone. Deacon insisted on running a background check. Meryt fought back trying to explain the *who* and the *what* of Dr. Rene Daniels to Deacon. She had never lied to Deacon, and she was not prepared to start. Meryt only wanted to enjoy the few precious moments she had with Rene and not look to the future. She did not want to think about long-term commitments or of what was going to happen as she continued to age and Rene remained the same. She thought to herself, *time, will reveal the truth and direction.*

There was an early scent of spring in the air, even though the groundhog didn't spot his shadow back in February. Everyone in upstate knew that spring didn't start until June. But what is a cloud-free, sunshiny day in the mid-50s in April? Hope. Meryt would take it. It worked for her. It beat their normal 35-degree, cloudy, overcast day.

Rene and Meryt made plans for dinner and a play in Buffalo that night. Meryt finished her rounds and headed home to shower to wash away the hospital smell and put on a cute dress she had purchased online. It had been a busy week. Three auto injuries, three heart attacks, and one psych ward admit.

As night fell onto the Falls, so did the temperature. The scent of spring was quickly erased. Winter was still here. Goose bumps ran up Meryt's legs beneath her dress when Rene opened the car door. She asked herself, *what was I thinking, coming out in the night air without a heavier coat?*

"My love, are you cold?" Rene asked as she got out of the car.

"Yes, but I'm sure a cocktail at the bar will warm me up," Meryt said as she ran on her tiptoes in high-heels into Blackmen's Steak House.

Rene was there to open the door. As soon as he did, the heat greeted her legs and face. Blackmen's was one of Meryt's favorite restaurants. The food was pretty good, but it was the decor that she loved. An enormous dark wood bar took up most of the first floor. There were a few small dinner tables scattered about for overflow and a hostess stand by the door. The seating on the main floor was way too close for comfort. Meryt remembered about a year ago, sitting next to a couple listening to their breakup. By the end of the conversation, the girl was crying, and Meryt was trying to be supportive, while not making eye contact.

Most of the seating was upstairs on the two upper levels, but the prime seating was on the middle level. On that level the main floor could be easily observed from above, and guests could still admire the pictures and lighting that were arranged perfectly among all three levels. Meryt couldn't forget to give extra credit to the lighting. There was enough light to read the menu, yet just enough light to make a girl's makeup look flawless. What more could a girl want?

Dinner for two, great wine, and great company Meryt couldn't ask for much more.

They had just finished with ordering when Rene started talking about the study. "Do you want to publish your finding on the new synthetic hemoglobin? Fritz is currently working on a clean version, which can be published. Thankfully, my mother was patient X, so there is no name or detailed description in the trial on her; plus you had additional patients during the trial with human blood, so it isn't going to be hard to compile the true raw data."

"Well, I never thought it would get this far or have this much ground-breaking information; I would rather submit it anonymously to Cleveland Clinic or Saint Jude Children's Hospital. Then they can complete the work with no question-and-answer phase."

Meryt took another sip of wine. "Is this the reason we are at dinner to discuss your brother's work? Rene, I like the way things are now. I like our life the way it is. I know I can't control everything, but I know living under the radar beats living in the limelight every time."

Rene responded, "You see, there lies the problem. Everything changes, Meryt. You can't live in the shadows of life. We can't publish this report in fear of questions that may rise. We could save thousands of lives."

"Rene, I agree. Publish the report, but I don't want my name on it. It's not only your life that is put on display; it's mine as well. I don't want my face thrown around the media. I would never be able work again for the government. I'd become too hot."

"Meryt, you mean you are still willing to take more jobs, especially after the last job? You almost lost your life."

"Yes, but I saved my country from going to war."

Rene snapped back, "I almost lost you."

"Rene, what are we talking about? This makes no sense. Are we talking about the trial or are we talking about my lifestyle or yours? I'm confused."

"Meryt, I'm saying things will change. You are changing every day. I don't change. I have to make changes happen to survive. If not, I will literally go crazy."

What on earth was he talking about? Are we breaking up because I don't want to be mentioned in the trial? Is this some kind of mind game? I knew it. I can't be happy and in love. I can't settle down with a normal person nor can I settle down with the undead. Meryt had the whole conversation in her head. The mounting fear of a broken heart started to take root. She was judge and jury. Rene was found guilty.

"Rene, I'm not understanding this conversation. I don't speak 'crazy.' Tell me like you would talk to a two-year-old. What is going on?" All her good feelings for the evening were quickly escaping, leaving fear and anger in their place.

Rene was slow to speak. She had never seen him look so stern, and so withdrawn. She took that back. Meryt had seen this look, two weeks after they had met it was the "I can't stand to be in the same room as you" look. Fear and nausea took over, and anger was on its way out of the door. If timing could be any more in tune, Meryt's phone rang.

Only Deacon had that kind of timing but when she looked at the phone, it wasn't Deacon. The caller ID showed it was Karl. What could he want at this hour that he wouldn't have Cindy call?

"Hello. What's up? You're kidding me. Oh my God. Okay, I'm on my way." Meryt ended the call, still frozen by the conversation.

"Meryt, what's wrong?"

"Karl called. He thinks Cindy had a heart attack while driving. She slammed her car into their house. He performed CPR until the ambulance came. Cindy is still unconscious and on her way to the hospital. Karl is a mess. He wants me at the hospital."

Rene clutched Meryt's hand in his hand. "It's going to be all right. Let's go."

How could Cindy have a heart attack? She was too young. She had no prior history. And Karl, a grown man, was breaking down on the phone like a little baby. He sounded as if he couldn't believe it was true. Cindy was his world. Karl would no longer exist without her at his side. She had to be all right for all of their sakes.

Rene and Meryt rode in silence to the hospital. Meryt's thoughts were no longer on dinner's conversation, but rather on finding the strength to be a support mechanism for Karl.

By the time they arrived, Cindy was in surgery. Meryt found Karl sitting in the waiting room alone and weeping. Everyone in the hospital knew him, but no one dared to sit next to him. It was shocking to see this normally giant force of a man broken. What words of comfort could anyone offer? Especially when he was a doctor. He knew the facts. The brain could not function without oxygen. Brain cells were destroyed after four to six minutes without oxygen. A person goes unconscious when the brain has had no oxygen after ten seconds. The brain is a mass of soft electrically charged tissue, which cannot withstand any environmental changes from the normal. But when the brain is working properly, it has no limitations. It is better than any computer man could ever build. Meryt quickly thought of the one limitation that tops the list. Time. No one knows for sure how much time Cindy went without air.

"Hey . . . umm, Rene, I had better handle this alone. I'll call you when I have news."

Rene's distant look from earlier was gone, replaced with massive concern and regret. "Call me when you are ready to go home or if you need to talk." He kissed her forehead, turned, and walked away.

Meryt entered the hospital to find Karl. *One . . . two . . . three . . . breathe.*

"Karl, your wartime consular is here." Meryt had her arms open to embrace this broken man. He eagerly fell into them and clung tightly to her. The initial embrace took the wind from her lungs. "It's fine. She is a fighter. She knows better than to leave us alone. She knows there's no telling what troubles we will get into."

His weeping only grew stronger. His pain seeped through her skin and wrapped its jellyfish tentacles arounded her heart. He was drowning in pain and panic. As much as Meryt told herself not cry, she felt tears rolling down her face. Karl's head hung so low that he could bury his burning tears into her neck.

She returned his hug. "Let it all out now. You don't want her to see you like this when she is out of surgery." They stood in the middle of the room, not caring who witnessed this mental breakdown. It was their private moment and their private pain.

Meryt prayed two prayers. First, that Cindy would be fine. The second prayer was to help unburden Karl's pain. He loved Cindy the way she wanted to be loved. And what was there not to love about Cindy? She was an angel. She always had the right words for the right moment. She knew what a person needed before they knew. She was Meryt's only female friend. She never questioned her strange, crazy ways. She just laughed. Not a laugh at Meryt, but rather a laugh of joy. She knew how to handle Meryt's stubbornness. If she was this good for her, Meryt could only imagine how Karl must have felt. He can't lose her, not now.

They waited, and it seemed like an eternity. For some reason Melondi Jacobs came to Meryt's mind. This must be how her family had felt, waiting and wondering. Wondering if they lost both Melondi and the life she carried in her belly. That's how Meryt felt about Cindy. *Will I lose her and the spirit of joy she carries? God, please don't take them from us.*

Karl and Meryt continued to wait. Sometimes no news is good news.

Finally the double doors opened from the surgery bay. Dr. Puente walked out. They stood up and walked toward him. Meryt tried to read his body language before he spoke. She wanted a warning before he delivered any news. All Meryt could determine was he looked spent. "Karl, Meryt, she is recovering. She had a small clot on the left lower ventricular wall. It is confirmed that Cindy had a heart attack. We were able to stent the vessel, but as you know, she sustained other injuries to the head and chest from the car accident. We were able to drain and relieve pressure from her brain. She sustained three broken ribs. We were able to lock them back in place, but it will be a while before she comes around. From what I can tell, she has brain activity, but she is still unconscious. When she wakes up we will know more. We have done all we can. Now it's up to her. Cindy has to heal herself. From what I know of her, I'm sure she will."

Karl looked weakened from the news. Once this tall, strawberry-blond man, had stood over six foot three; he now appeared two inches shorter, and he had aged ten years during the wait.

Karl asked, in a dry whisper, "Can I see her?"

"Yes, she's in Recovery. She will stay there for another hour, and then they will move her to a private suite." Karl moved past Dr. Puente, through the double doors.

Meryt remained with Dr. Puente. "Puente, what are the chances for a full recovery?"

"Meryt, I meant what I said. We did everything and more. It's all up to her. Is she a fighter or not? Those are her chances for a full recovery."

Meryt said with a smile, "Good, because any friend of mine is a fighter."

She then followed Karl's path through the recovery room. Meryt peeked between the curtain to the recovery bay and found Karl had already gotten his chair. He was sitting facing Cindy, holding her hand in his. Viewing Karl and his wife together from behind the curtain Meryt could feel their love, the passion and intimacy. Some things are solely between a husband and wife. This was that moment. Meryt closed her eyes, and then closed the curtain, and left them to their moment.

Meryt stood outside in the night air in the wee hours of Saturday morning. Several hours ago she was singing, "It's Friday night, just got paid, time to get down," excited about her date with Rene; to this. That's life. She took in a deep breath of the night air. She thought about calling Rene. Instead she called a cab to take her home. She didn't know if she was being a coward or just plain tired, but she knew she was incapable of dealing with any more stress.

Chapter 40

Meryt woke up Saturday, still feeling the same emptiness. She located her cell phone. No missed calls, no messages. She called the hospital to check Cindy and Karl's status. Both were the same. Cindy had not opened her eyes, and Karl had not left her bedside. Meryt called Karl on his cell phone. He did not answer. She wasn't surprised. Still tired, Meryt got up and tried to workout. But she, too, was in a holding pattern waiting for a response. She felt as if her heart was on the brink of a nuclear meltdown. Meryt was no good. She knew what had to be done, so she picked up the phone to make the dreaded call.

If it's the end, let it be done, so I can move on. I can't stay in this middle place, this holding pattern, looking down at the ground at what could be or what might be, Meryt thought to herself while remembering the tense feelings from dinner with Rene. *Let's get this party started.*

The phone rang. It was Rene.

"Hey you, what's up? Cindy is in a holding pat—, no, I mean she is still recovering. We won't know her complete recovery timeline for sure until she wakes up. You want to come by? Sure? No problem." Meryt hung the phone up. *One . . . two . . . three . . . breathe.* "That definitely sounded like a break-up call. Hold it together, girl."

Fifteen minutes passed, and Rene was at her door. She had decided she would not allow him to come in the house. Meryt wanted a place to escape to when the conversation went bad. She figured outside was better than inside. If he were in the house he might not want to leave, saying some craziness like, "You need to calm down. Don't cry." She didn't want to give him the privilege of seeing her break down. Plus, his smell would linger inside her home. That would not be good for the home team, trying to be strong getting past a breakup. Meryt opened the door and stepped outside.

"Hey, what's going on?" she asked in a shaky yet upbeat voice.

Rene looked around and asked, "Don't you want to go inside. It's a little chilly out."

"No, I'd rather walk around in the backyard. I want to get some fresh air and see what kind of mole damage I might have from the winter." Rene, looking unsure, agreed.

They started walking toward the backyard.

"Meryt, I want to apologize for my behavior last night," Rene began. "Is that why you didn't call me for a ride home?"

Meryt never looked up. "I was completely exhausted last night. I didn't know where our conversation was going before I got the call at dinner. I felt that I needed to go home and get some rest first."

Meryt looked up from her half-truth and half-lie to see if it was believable.

This time Rene turned away and then looked back. "Meryt, I know no other way to explain this: my maker is in town. She normally doesn't make me feel uneasy, but things have changed. I've met you, and I'm not so certain she will be accepting of our relationship. I know this isn't the proper time with Cindy in the hospital, but could we, just for a while, not be together? It might be better if I leave town with her for a few days."

"What are you talking about? Are we breaking up? Are you ashamed of me, or is it both?"

Rene saw the fear building up in Meryt. She pulled her hand away from his as he tried to reassure her.

Meryt started backing up. This was it, the break-up.

"I knew it!" Elizabeth said as she stood next to Rene. A beautiful, fiery, redheaded woman had suddenly appeared in the yard. "Is this the business you had to handle last night?"

Meryt stood in amazement. "Who is this woman?" As she spun around and added, "Where did she come from?" Meryt started to realize that being outside was not a good idea after all.

Meryt heard three car doors slam from the front of the house and saw three shadows dart across her yard. Fritz, Lolita, and NeiNei were all standing in her backyard. Meryt definitely did not imagine her breakup to be a family matter.

Meryt asked in a stern voice, "Rene, what is going on?"

"Meryt, this is my maker, Elizabeth. She and I have a special bond."

"What is a maker?" Meryt fired back.

"My maker is the person who made me a dark angel. Every dark angel has a maker. You must display a certain level of loyalty and obedience to your maker."

"Rene, what does this have to do with you and me?"

The last thing Meryt heard was NeiNei scream, "Stop!"

Chapter 41

Meryt woke up two hours later on the sofa at the Danielses' house. Her head was pounding. She scanned the room for Rene. He wasn't there. Now her last memories began to populate her mind. Elizabeth had been in her backyard, and now she found herself lying on a sofa, rubbing her head.

NeiNei answered in her head, "They aren't here." Meryt rubbed her forehead in pain. NeiNei spoke aloud, using her voice this time: "Sorry." NeiNei began to rub her cool fingers across Meryt's head.

After a few moments, Meryt finally spoke. "Where are they?"

NeiNei looked remorseful. "I am not certain, but I can assure you they are not in the state of New York." NeiNei began to fill in Meryt's two lost hours.

Apparently, Elizabeth, the maker, was not accustomed to sharing. She and Rene had been having a relationship, and she considered Meryt to be the other woman. Elizabeth, having an explosive, jealous personality, went on the attack. Evidently, she literally held Meryt responsible for the affair and she had held Meryt by the neck trying to break her skull against her own house. At least this explained the burning throat and pounding headache Meryt had. NeiNei, being the senior vampire, demanded Elizabeth to cease her attack and leave the area.

Immediately, Rene and Elizabeth left. No good byes, no explanations, just gone. That was a hell of a breakup story. Meryt had no idea how to even begin to explain this to anyone. "This sucks," she said aloud, quickly regretting it, because her voice rang in her head.

Meryt grabbed her head in pain as the story finally settled in her mind leaving her with the understanding the relationship was over. *It had to end sometime. Why not now?* Meryt thought to herself. She gently pushed NeiNei's hands away. "Enough, it's done."

"Meryt, he loves you."

"Yeah, I see how much he loves me. If he loved me any more I might be dead."

NeiNei pushed on, "It broke his heart to leave."

Meryt interrupted NeiNei before she could say any more. "And what about my neck almost breaking?" Meryt stood up to continue, "Okay, I understand, NeiNei. He cheated on his wife, lover, or maker, whatever you want to call it. He got caught. He's hurt because she wanted to kill me, but he loves me so much he left town." Meryt stopped and shook her head. "I don't mean to be disrespectful, but in the human world it sounds like he got caught cheating, and I got played. I don't want to talk about this anymore, I just want a ride home so I can clean myself up and go to the hospital and see my human friends." The once vibrant house stood cold and empty.

The niece came out. She drove Meryt home.

Meryt no longer flew in a holding pattern. Her plane had landed in Broken Heart Central. She started to understand how Cindy's heart attack must have felt. The squeezing pressure began to build up in her chest the closer she got to home. By the time, Meryt entered her house and locked the door; she doubled over in pain and fell down onto the floor. It felt as if someone was squeezing the life out of her chest. She could hardly breathe. She tried counting hoping to distract herself from the pain. Nope. The pain still remained and grew with each swallow breath she took. Meryt felt for her pulse to be sure it was emotional pain versus a real heart attack. Meryt tried to think of something other the pain. All she could manage to muster was a scream.

Finally tears came to her eyes and oxygen filled her lungs. Meryt cried the same broken-hearted tears that Karl had cried the night before, but harder. At least, he had hope. He had friends by his side, telling him it would be all right. Not Meryt, she was alone, on the cold tile floor in the dark, crying. There was no hope. It wouldn't be all right.

Rene was gone.

Chapter 42

The war left a cold mark on the city of Amarna. What once stood as a pulsating, thriving capital made of gold now stood still full of shadows, doubts, and sorrows. Egypt and Nubia were caught in the mist of war, but they saw no enemy. There were no major attacks on the cities' capitals only raids on the outter most villiages positioned on the borders and along the great sea. The true battles were fought deep in Babylon's countryside. News had traveled fast from the army's front lines, that victory was close, which meant an end to the mysterious war would come soon. Yet, Eygpt and Nubia were still torn apart with despair and uncertainty because the war had claimed their leadership in less than two months. The cities were mourning the loss of their beloved queens, Nefertiti and Nitocris, and yet it had gained a new pharaoh, Smenkhara. Hushed whispers in both countries about the future of their union and the status of the war grew louder every day.

Atem, who normally stood in the shadows with his brother as a protector, now stood lifeless and alone. Lifeless was a new emotion. He had already lived a century, but it had been good. He had his brother, he had a mission and he had love. Now his brother was truly dead, and he had failed in his mission to protect. Everyone he vowed to protect Atem, Akhenaten the Pharaoh, Queen Nefertiti, and Queen Nitocris were all dead. What hurt him most, more than the loss of his brother, was the loss of Queen Nefertiti.

Atem came back to Amarna on the night Queen Nefertiti's and Queen Nitocris's bodies were being prepared for burial. He had come back to check on the guards. Atem was worried about Queen Nefertiti. She had not been well since finding her husband dead on the floor. Emotionally she was a shaken to the core, but at least she was safe under the sanctuary of the royal guards.

Atem was not expecting the news of their deaths. He was told that Nefertiti had left the compounds in Amarna searching for Nitocris. When Nitocris received word that Nefertiti had left home looking for her, she broke ranks, retreating to the rear, searching for her sister. In the mist of the chaos, the Babylonians had captured and tortured them both. He wished over and over that he could take back time. He would reconsider his decisions to be on the battlefield. He would have remained by Queen Nefertiti's side protecting her from harm. No, but that was not what he had done. Instead, he had let revenge and anger fill his heart and cloud his better judgment. He was all too happy to follow Nitocris into battle and to help uncover the mystery that surrounded Atem's death.

One by one, he had left them all unprotected. He left his one true love unprotected. He left his brother unprotected, and finally Nitocris. They all paid for his mistake with their lives.

Upon hearing the news, Atem rushed over to the burial chambers. He first found Nitocris's body. She had been decapitated. He could not fix her, but Nefertiti maybe. He found her lying on a stone table. She was beaten beyond recognition; her lower jaw was broken, along with both arms and her right leg. Atem's anger grew toward Babylonians as he thought of how they tortured Nefertiti. As he sat alone in the burial chamber, the silence was broken by a faint heartbeat. With his dark angel powers, he could hear her breathing. It was shallow and slow, but it was there. Nefertiti was still alived.

The priests had not started preparation on Nefertiti's body. They had spent the entire afternoon preparing Nitocris. Nefertiti lay still on the stone table. No human hear could hear her shallow breathing, but Atem did. Atem looked around the small room to ensure he was still alone. Atem picked up Nefertiti's broken body and carried her to an abandoned servant's quarters a half mile away. He required privacy. Atem hoped it wouldn't be too late. He wanted to give Nefertiti the gift of life from his blood. He prayed to the Creator that it wasn't too late, and she had the strength to survive the transformation.

Once in the secure quarters, he started the process. Atem first bit Nefertiti on the neck. He only took a small amount of her blood and then bit his tongue pushing his blood forward. He required a direct artery to Nefertiti's heart if this was going to work. Atem waited. No change in Nefertiti's condition. Atem tried the femoral artery on the inside of her leg. Again he waited. Nefertiti pulse just grew weaker. He pushed more of his blood into the wounds in hopes that it wasn't too late. Pink tears began to fall from his eyes as he waited, and still she did not respond.

On his final bite, in desperation, he decided to bite Nefertiti directly in the heart, tearing through her skin and chest cavity. He wanted to place his blood directly in her heart. Atem reopened his wound on his tongue releasing fresh blood into her heart. Atem was not concerned with the wound on her chest either she would survive the transformation and the wound would heal or she would die anyway. There were only a few precious moments remaining before death was permanent for Nefertiti.

Atem waited two hours. He held back his tears. He sat holding Nefertiti's hand, regretting he had never done this small action of love before, holding her hand, while she was alive. He sat in silence listening for her heart to grow stronger. He waited and waited on each heartbeat and with each heartbeat the next came slower until the last. Atem sat with Nefertiti, holding her hand until her last human heartbeat passed. Silence. Atem released her hand and walked away for the last time from his one true love.

Later he ordered soldiers to the area to recover the body. The soldiers returned empty handed. Atem figured the locals buried the body.

It made no difference; Queen Nefertiti would never live again.

Chapter 43

In Egypt the burial ceremonies were more important than birth. If a person was loved everyone made an appearance for the main burial ceremonial event. Based on the family's wealth, sometimes others were buried alive with the departed loved one for help during the crossing to the spiritual world. Upon arrival to Amarna, Hatshepsut and Senunmut went directly to the burial chambers. They wanted to pay their last respects to their family members before the procession began. Once in the chamber, they found Nitocris's body, but not Nefertiti's. Nitocris's body already started to show signs of decay. Hatshepsut saw the stitching marks along Nitocris neck where the decapitated head was reattached. Her organs were already separated and placed into golden vessels with ivory detail marking on the outside. The priests had started the mummification process.

Hatshepsut excused the priests and servants from the chamber. Senunmut ensured everyone understood it was not a request, but more of an order, while Hatshepsut completed her final prayers. Once the room was cleared, she started the sacred chants of death and purification. As she sprinkled the sacred powder of purification, it sizzled as it fell to Nitocris's skin. Hatshepsut stopped in her footsteps. Hatshepsut wondered aloud, "Why does the purification powder burn? Queen Nitocris's soul is not prepared to cross over." She sprinkled the powder one last time. It burned as it touched Queen Nitocris's skin then it left faint smoke streams disappearing into the air.

Hatshepsut turned to a vacant table behind her and spread out her scrolls for a new prayer. She was searching for the prayer of return. It was clear Nitocris' spirit was not prepared to cross over, so Hatshepsut began preparations for her return.

Hatshepsut found the correct prayer and studied the words carefully. She slipped her side knife from beneath her dress and cut a few strands of Nitocris's hair and placed them in a cloth. Then she pushed Nitocris's hand down from the table and placed a small silver vessel on the floor below Nitocris's hanging fingers. Hatshepsut cuts a small hole in Nitocris third finger allowing the blood to drain into the vessel. Hatshepsut started a new chant, the chant of rebirth and new life.

Chapter 44

What was the expression? "Hours turned into days, and days turned into weeks, and in time all things heal?" Not true. Hours turned into hours and days were just days and weeks were a living hell. Time did not heal Meryt; it taunted and teased her all day long. The only thing that stopped Meryt from putting a bullet to her head was Cindy. Time did heal her. Meryt made it her personal mission to be there for Cindy and Karl. It took three days before Cindy opened her eyes. For Karl and Meryt, those were the longest three days ever. The days passed in a vacuum of silence, and the two refused to allow any outside noise in while they meditated. Finally, Cindy opened her eyes. She brought back joy, hope, and her angelic spirit.

Meryt's recovery was helping Cindy to recover. They took long walks together. They joked about their broken hearts. They shopped. When Meryt wasn't at the hospital, she was at their home cooking dinner or having red wine. Meryt hated returning home to her empty house. It held too many memories, especially in her bedroom. She started sleeping in the guest room down the hall, but that didn't work because she would start to beat herself up by asking why she was not sleeping in her own bed. The floodgates opened and memories stormed her mind again when she returned to her own room. The lovemaking and their conversations would take turns replaying themselves over in her head. There was one statement that remained constant: "You'll leave me before I'll ever think of leaving you." Lie.

After Cindy had full recovered, Meryt begged Deacon for any kind of job the dirtier the job, the better. At first he threw her a few jobs, but when he got wind that she was on a suicide mission, then he refused to send her any more work. He insisted Meryt take a vacation.

Her response to the whole thing was, "This is my vacation!"

Deacon did not dignify her statement. He simply responded, "Don't call me; I'll call you," and hung up the phone.

May, suicidal

June, agonizing

July, agonizing

August, manageable

Chapter 45

After the deaths of Nefertiti, Nitocris, and his brother, Atum, Atem promised he would commit his life of servitude to Smenkhkara. Atem was a dark angel who had spent his life as a protector, and he failed the very people who relied on him the most. He would not make the same mistake again. He decided to dedicate his life in protecting the new pharaoh. He would pledge his loyalty to Smenkhkara.

Atem found the pharaoh in his main quarters in a meeting with the elite guards. Upon seeing Atem, the pharaoh dismissed the guards.

"Atem, you look worried. We will find the ones guilty of killing Nefertiti and Nitocris. These Babylonians are treacherous. I cannot believe that they killed so many of my best soldiers that accompanied Nefertiti. She took a few of my private elite guards, and they were all found dead. I went searching for Nefertiti and when I located them, I was attacked. I barely escaped. My remaining elite guards insisted that we return to Amarna."

Atem agreed. It was best that the pharaoh had returned and not chased after Queen Nefertiti. He didn't want to imagine another pharaoh succumbing to enemy hands. This story made him think; perhaps he should make the pharaoh a dark angel. Atem knew there would be more moments when he would not be by the pharaoh side to protect him, but that measure would allow the pharaoh to defend himself during this time of war.

Atem offered his gift of life to the pharaoh. Surprisingly, the pharaoh accepted the idea and wanted to be transformed instantly. The pharaoh, in all his delight, started to ramble on about partnering together and rebuilding the greatness of Egypt.

For the second time that day, Atem extended his fangs. He bit Smenkhkara on the neck. He had taken a small amount of the pharaoh's blood and transferred his dark angel blood into the pharaoh's vein. After a few moments, the transaction started. The pharaoh collapsed into Atem's arms. He placed his new brother on his throne. "Rest my new brother. When you awaken, you will be as I, a dark angel."

Atem left the room to check the security of the main temple.

Chapter 46

Hatshepsut could not dispel the image of Nitocris's body being burned by the powder of purification. She had questions. She had to speak to the pharaoh and to Nitocris's soldiers to find out her last words.

Hatshepsut had never married because she was in line to be the Queen of Nubia. As the Queen she could not have a mate, because she would be married to the people of Nubia, but the law did not make her unappealing to men. She, like her cousin Nefertiti, was a sight of beauty to behold. She possessed thick, black, curly hair, which hung down to her waist. She had a slender build, a long neck, and a curvy, inviting bottom. When she walked, she carried herself with such regal authority that it dared any man to turn away. Hatshepsut possessed natural beauty and the power of persuasion when she spoke. If those gifts did not covert her subjects to agree, then perhaps her third gift, the gift of magical chants would work.

Hatshepsut found Smenkhkara resting in the royal quarters. She requested an audience with him as the new pharaoh to Egypt.

She walked in with the same royal authority. The pharaoh had just woken from his nap and greeted her with a warm smile, like most men with eyes did, in hope of something more to come. He inquired about the accommodations and the timeline for the burial ceremony for Queen Nefertiti and Queen Nitocris. Just hearing the names aloud sent chills down her back. Hatshepsut had not quite accepted their deaths, in one clean sweep, Nubian leadership was gone and Nefertiti child was too young to reign.

Hatshepsut inquired, "Pharaoh, I would like to speak to Nitocris's soldiers or anyone who may have seen her last. I'm curious of how she died. And I could not find Nefertiti's body. Do you know where she is being kept?"

"Queen Nefertiti was not there beside her sister? I will talk to the priests about that matter. But as you may know, Queen Nitocris was decapitated. I assumed you've been to the burial chambers," the pharaoh said, trying to show concern.

"I know, but I was more concerned about her mental state. I wondered, what were her last words?" Hatshepsut said turning away; she didn't feel comfortable talking about the matter with the new pharaoh.

Pharaoh's smile slide off of his face and stillness replaced it. He knew Queen Nitocris's last words and he did not feel compelled to repeat them to Hatshepsut. "Why worry about the past? Queen Nitocris is gone. We have lost yet another of our great warriors. We don't have time to dwell in the past. You and I must look to the future and continue to build an alliance to protect our people from the enemy." The pharaoh reached his hands around Hatshepsut shoulders. He was extremely attracted to her beauty. Now being so close, hearing her heartbeat, he could almost hear her blood coursing through her veins. His gums started to burn. His mind was spinning back and forth between desire for her blood and for her body. Perhaps it was desire for killing her for trying to expose what took him years to put in action. He was now the rightful pharaoh and no one could take that from him.

Still with her back turned, Hatshepsut tried to speak without insulting the pharaoh. "I know we must look to the future, but I cannot move on until the past is completely settled. Is it not true that you must learn from your past? There may be a lesson in the past that is crucial for the future's success."

The pharaoh tightened his grip around Hatshepsut's shoulders. He could no longer ignore his desires. He wanted her blood, he wanted her body, and afterward he would take her life to ensure she kept her mouth closed. All of his needs would be satisfied.

"There is nothing but death in our past." He whispered the words in her ear before taking his first bite.

Out of the shadows, Senunmut charged across the room with a spear. He had heard enough. Senunmut pierced the pharaoh's back, nearly penetrating the arrow's head through the chest; Pharaoh bit into his own cheek and Hatshepsut's neck from the force of the blow, causing him to fall forward onto the floor. In one quick move, Senunmut picked Hatshepsut up off the floor and kept heading for the door on the other side of the room.

Atem returned to the pharaoh's quarters, believing the pharaoh would still be resting while the transformation was taking place. To his surprise he found the pharaoh on the floor, dying. Atem quickly ran to the Pharaoh's side and bit into his own arm, releasing more of his own dark angel's blood. Within moments, the pharaoh regained consciousness. Before Atem could inquire who did this to him, the pharaoh announced they had to leave Egypt at once.

For the first time, Smenkhkara felt he had told one too many lies. He knew that it would not be long before others would ask similar questions and his deceit would be discovered. Smenkhkara thought it best to leave with the only one, who still believed in him, Atem. He decided quickly, he would convince Atem to leave and form a new brotherhood in a new land.

Smenkhkara would wait and develop a new plan for world power.

Chapter 47

Another long day at work, but not a bad day Meryt hadn't thought about killing herself today. Oh, too late, the thought crossed her mind as she walked to her car in the hospital parking lot. When she got home, she planned to go for a swim. Perhaps a few laps would clear her mind as she reminded herself to stay busy.

"Meryt!"

She looked around; Darren was calling her.

"We're heading to The Joint. Do you want to come?"

"No, I'm good. I've got some things I still need to do. Thanks. Maybe next time."

She watched Darren get into his car and pull away. *Will he never give up? Maybe I should go by the Joint. It's not like I've got any real plans. What do I have to lose other than time alone? Maybe, I'll—Fuck! There's that word: maybe!* She had another mental conversation; there were words and phrases she was not allowed to say. Meryt got into the car and slammed the door. Not even the comfort of her BMW made her feel better. She pushed the start button and put it into gear, while looking into her rearview mirror feeling disgusted wondering when the pain would subside.

Suddenly Meryt heard a tapping sound at her window. She looked around, expecting to see Darren being his persistent self. "What?"

To her surprise and heartache it was not.

She let the window down. "What do you want?"

"Meryt, can we talk?"

"Not here." Meryt put the window up and drove off. What could they possibly want now? It had been months, and now they show up at the hospital, asking, "Can we talk?" She wondered what they wanted to talk about. "Let's talk about breaking my heart." "Let's talk about the whole family up and leaving without a single word." "Or we could talk about almost blowing my cover from all the publicity and medical journals contacting me regarding the synthetic hemoglobin."

Seeing Fritz and Lolita after three months turned her blood ice cold. Meryt's hands became clammy while touching the steering wheel. She felt physically ill in her stomach. She wanted to throw up. Meryt drove home in silence, listening to her heart run a marathon. "How could they just reappear like that? No e-mails, no explanations, no "thank you, but sorry I gotta go," and out of nowhere just reappear with a, "Can we talk?" *Hell, no!* Again, Meryt was rambling to herself. She became the judge and jury. The Danielses were found guilty.

Meryt turned into the driveway. She pulled up to the garage door and waited for it to open. She drove the car in and sat for a few moments, hesitating to leave the smallness of her car. Finally she reached for her purse and got out of the car still feeling queasy from seeing Fritz and Lolita. *One . . . two . . . three . . . breathe.*

Crap! They were standing by the garage door, waiting to enter the house. Meryt walked past them, unlocking the door as if they did not exist. Maybe they would understand the hint and go away. Fritz held the door open from the outside. "May we enter?" Meryt looked up from setting her purse down on the table. "Sure you can come inside. What is there left for you to take that you haven't already taken?" On that note, she continued walking into the house. She went upstairs and changed into a swimsuit. A few minutes later she came back down, only to find the Danielses in the kitchen. She went straight to the mini bar and grabbed a bottle of vodka and short glass. Meryt paid no attention to her company and continued on to the indoor pool next to the kitchen.

Meryt sat the bottle with the glass down at one end of the pool and dove in. It felt as pure as a baptism. The cool refreshing water tingled as it covered her entire body. She could feel the rest of her body now, not just her heart aching in her chest. She felt small again. Meryt realized her place in the world. She was one person surrounded by countless of other people and things. She was a part of a billion, trillion things that exist in this world. After the initial dive, she began to swim for distance. Quickly, she realized she was swimming for her sanity. She swam to control her body. She swam to control her thoughts. Meryt swam until she could swim no more. Forty minutes passed. She returned to the wall where the bottle and the drinking glass sat. Meryt pulled herself out of the water with one exhausted pull and sat next to the bottle of vodka. She wiped the excess water from her face and hair. She grabbed the towel next to her and dried off the rest. Her chest was still heaving from the swim.

Meryt eyed the Danielses, now standing next to her glass. Again, she felt the emotions grow beyond her body. Her body no longer hurt from the swim, but from her own heart—the broken heart with no love from Rene.

Instantly, Meryt filled the glass with vodka and swallowed it down in one gulp. It burned, but at least it was a different pain, a pain she had caused, one she could control.

"So what do you want to talk about?"

Lolita spoke first. "You look good. How have you been?"

Meryt followed with, "Thank you, and somewhat suicidal. I try to take one day at a time."

Meryt poured another glass filled to the rim and swallowed it all. The same burning sensation ran down her throat. She spoke with a choking cough. "What about you, Fritz? What do you want to talk about?"

"Meryt, Rene is dying. We need your help."

"Wake-up call to Fritz. We are all dying. I'm dying a painful death at this very moment. That's life. Deal with it. You don't see me asking for help. But then again, who would I ask, and who would care?" Finally, she felt the vodka relieving the pressure in her chest. She could breathe again. Meryt took one more glass filled to the rim to ensure the effect would last awhile.

"Meryt, stop drinking. This stuff will kill you," Lolita said as she bent over to take the bottle.

"No." Meryt placed her hand on the bottle. "You searched for me. You tricked me into helping you find a cure for your mother, which I would have done if you just asked. I let you into my world. You let me into your world. I accepted you as family. I fell in love with your brother. I believed he loved me. I believed you all loved me. To my surprise, he has another woman who tries to kill me. And what does Rene do? He leaves. And you? You know my life. I'm no dark angel, but I have my own secrets, and you go public on our cure and leave me with tons of press conferences and explanations as to how I found this cure. You almost blew my cover. None of that matters. Why? Because you all left! No good-byes. You left. You used me. When you were done, you left me." Meryt poured another glass and swallowed the vodka, this time it took two gulps. "I don't know who I detest more, you and your brother for leaving me here with a broken heart, or myself, for allowing it to happen."

The pain felt pure. It was not clouded by civility. The alcohol stopped working. The pain ran through her entire body. She could no longer breathe or see. Pure pain and rage were thundering around her head, leaving her paralyzed with hate. Meryt threw the glass she was holding against the wall. The noise echoed throughout the room. It broke the paralyzing pain for a moment. Meryt could see again.

Fritz watched the glass break into a thousand pieces and then he turned to speak, "Meryt, he loves you. That is why he left. Elizabeth vowed to kill you if he stayed. She does not take well to competition. Rene left for you. We all left for you. If she knew how important you were to us, she would have killed you on that principle alone. We needed her to leave the area. So we all left. Meryt, Rene feels the same about you. He's refusing to eat. He wants to take his own life. He doesn't want to live without you. Please help us. Help Rene."

Meryt pressed her hands tightly together, forming a knot, and took a deep breath. "What do you want from me? If he wants me, he knows where I live. Rene could come back."

"Meryt, he can't come back. He went to our coven with Elizabeth. If he returned, Elizabeth would return." Fritz bent down next to Meryt. "Please go with me to the coven. Let him see you one time. Give him the strength to live. I will plead with the coven's masters to set him free. I do not know if they will release him, but I know he needs to see you."

"What about Elizabeth? Will I see her?"

"Yes, but she will be on her best behavior in front of the coven's masters."

"Where are we going and when do you want to leave?"

"As soon as you are able. I have a private jet waiting to take us to Naples, Italy. The coven is south of the city. In nine hours, we should be standing within the coven's halls. It will only be you and I. Lolita cannot come. I do not want to send the wrong message with too many of my family members present. The coven may feel threatened."

"I'll be ready in an hour," Meryt told Fritz as she stood up, still wet from the swim. She felt numb, but anything was better than the pain that coursed in her veins a few moments ago. She walked past them into the main house. Meryt needed to prepare for this trip.

In the back of her mind, Meryt knew she had a pledge to fulfill.

Chapter 48

Jet engines roared as they sped down the runway, growing more intense as the plane began to lift from the ground. Meryt watched their ascent, trying to locate familiar landmarks like office buildings or main streets. It helped her to get a bearing, so she always maintained direction. This time, as she scanned the area, she felt a tinge of sadness as she rose above the foggy layers of haze, which sat over the city. It felt like the end of a good book. The jet continued to climb above the fog into the sun, the true light. Good-bye, Niagara Falls.

The flight was uneventful. Meryt felt numb, similar to the calm before the storm. She was war-gaming different scenarios that could possibly play out in the coven. None of them played out without bloodshed. She wondered if Fritz surmised the same conclusion. He too was quiet.

They landed. Meryt reached for her travel bag, which carried a few of her favorite toys and SYN hemoglobin. She figured Rene might be in need. Instinct told her to treat this as a mission. Meryt had planned for this day. She was prepared for however the mission unfolded before taking its true form, a story to be repeated. Waiting outside the plane was the bright morning sun and a black limo with tinted windows.

Meryt hadn't been to Naples in six years. She would have never guessed her return trip to Naples would have been to a vampire coven. They drove for forty minutes, snaking their way down alleys and narrow side streets, trying to avoid the morning rush hour traffic. Normally, Meryt enjoyed Italy with its old and new intertwined, making it one immense piece of artwork. But, this morning she was focused at the task at hand, the mission.

The limo pulled up to an old double garage door. The doors automatically swung open to a long underground driveway. It had a gradual decline that took them under the city. Meryt couldn't image how hard it must have been to build the tunnel considering Naples sat proudly on rocks and cliffs. They drove about a mile down the tunnel before the limo came to a stop.

When Meryt got out of the car, it reminded her of old photos she had seen of the underground subway entrance to a hotel in New York, which in its heyday was used as a secret passage for the president. This passageway was colored in with rusty dull colors to verify its age, but the door looked new. Not brand-new, but new compared to its surroundings. Everything else remained covered with a light, sandy-brown dust. Once they were close enough to the door, it opened. The opened door gave way to a whole new set of colors. Soft shades of blue leaped forward into view. White lights were placed behind blue glass, which gave the room a savoir-faire touch. The room reminded Meryt of an ice castle. Everything was done in glass, minus a few pieces of artwork and throw rugs. It felt cooler than outside, but not freezing cold. There was a faint cloud of smoke that constantly billowed across the floor. Meryt was fully expecting to see a dry ice machine in the corner. Promptly, two vampires rose to escort them to the main hall.

Fritz grabbed Meryt's arm and pulled her deeper into the compound. It smelled of lavender and mint. The place seemed to have a special glow. They passed a few more rooms where people and/or vampires were lounging.

Finally, at the end of the long hall, they came to wooden double doors. The escort stepped aside and told Fritz and Meryt to enter. Fritz pushed the doors open slowly. Meryt wasn't sure if Fritz pushed the doors open slowly for permission or because they required all of his vampire strength to open. The doors gave way to an open room done in dark tapestries and furs. It was a complete contrast to the entrance and the corridors. While the entrance appeared to be modern, this room was purely done in medieval style. In the back end of the room on a small platform sat two male vampires in Louis XIV style chairs. It was obvious they were in command. There were a dozen or so vampires mingling in the room. All came to a standstill as Fritz and Meryt entered.

"So you are the infamous Meryt Brownstone that everyone is chattering over?" the coven master, Smenkhkara, inquired. "Fritz, why do you bring this human here?" The two brethren sat above, on the platform overseeing the room, as the judge and jury to all occupants.

Fritz responded, "My brother is dying. I wanted to speak to him before he makes his decision final. Meryt is a doctor, and she knows how to treat vampires. She wanted to come of her own free will."

"A human of free will enters my coven of dark angels? So explain, why do you bring her here, to this secret location? Can she be trusted?" Before he answered, two large wrought-iron doors opened at the opposite far end of the room. Elizabeth sauntered in, glowing like a queen of the night. She was dressed in a skintight, dark red dress that matched her bouncing red hair perfectly. Had Meryt not loathed the ground she walked on, Meryt might have understood what Smenkhkara meant. No human had free will in the presence of a vampire. Elizabeth was breathtaking, and all Meryt could think of was taking Elizabeth's last breath away. Meryt's stomach immediately turned sour at the next sight: Rene. He walked in three feet behind Elizabeth, in a simple black robe, but his skin appeared cracked. As he got closer, Meryt observed deep gashes in his skin. He had aged over forty years. Rene had dark circles surrounding his eyes. The more Meryt's eyes came into focus, the more she noticed that his once beautiful blue eyes, in which she saw nothing but waves of lust and love, were now a dull red. Rene looked like the walking dead.

As many times as Meryt told herself that she was not in love with Rene, it failed. Every emotion, from lust to love, rushed over Meryt's body. It all came back, like one huge tsunami wave. Every cell in her body called to him, even in his current condition, Meryt loved him. She loved being in his presence. Meryt ran over to Rene and held up his face. "What did you do to yourself?" She looked over to Fritz. "What did they do to him? How can a vampire appear this way?" As Fritz explained, instinctively Meryt ran her hands over Rene's' face, neck, and body. He felt as hard as a rock. Meryt was looking for some color or smell, like his mother, but Rene only smelled of death. There was no color.

"Meryt, he's been beaten with salt water and silver mixture, and it appears he refused to feed." Fritz, too, began to examine his brother. While Fritz looked him over Meryt reached into her travel bag. She took two bags of the synthetic blood out. "Fritz, please feed him the blood." Then Meryt turned to face the two brethren. "My lords, what are his crimes for him to receive this treatment?"

Smenkhkara replied, "We did not order punishment. This treatment is between Rene and his maker, Elizabeth."

Elizabeth added, "I punished him for his insolence. He would have healed by now but he refuses to feed, which causes me to punish him all over. It's a sadistic game we play. I think it's pathetic. I'm growing bored. I wish he would end his own pathetic life." Elizabeth's tone echoed the sentiment of her words. She obviously thought of this as a game and had grown tired of it. How interesting for someone who treasured life so much that she became an immortal, yet cared so little about others. Selfish.

Meryt looked back to Rene and found him sipping the SYN hemoglobin. "Is this the life you want? You want to die by the hands of this egotistical witch?" On that word, Elizabeth hovered over Meryt's head, showing her fangs. Fritz said, "Elizabeth, need I remind you of NeiNei's promise?"

"She's not here now!" she snarled.

"Yes, but the brethren are, and they will enforce her will." Elizabeth slowly pulled away and returned across the room with the same behavior as if all of this was beneath her.

Meryt stood over Rene as he finished off the second bag of SYN hemoglobin. Meryt bent down on her knees by Rene's head. The anger changed to concern in her voice. "If you think you are doing this for me, you are pathetic. You're torturing yourself in vain. Why are you slowly killing yourself? For pity? The one fact, I know for sure, I will die. My life will be over. I will be dust in a blink of your eye, which makes this time, this current time, precious. The only thing that matters to me is your love while I still live and breathe. Without it, I'm not whole. If I can put my trust in you, why can't you put your trust in me? Please trust in me. Tell me you want to live. Confess it now!"

Immediately the blood started working, and his color began to return. Before her eyes, the scars and the age lines began to disappear.

Rene responded in a dry voice, "Yes, I want to live, and I never stopped loving you."

Meryt had to remind herself, *One . . . two . . . three . . . breathe.*

She stood up to confront the brethren. Meryt summoned every ounce of courage in her body and said, "My lords, how do I free Rene from his maker?"

The spirit in the room began to lighten up, as if she had told a joke.

Smenkhkara said, "Dark angels can only be freed from their maker when their maker is dead. Makers cannot denounce their angel. We made this rule so that dark angels would train their young."

Elizabeth was standing across the room, pretending this was completely a bore. "This is a useless conversation. Her very life is protected by NeiNei; how long shall she be allowed to insult me and take up precious time from this coven?"

"My lord, can I request that NeiNei's promise be removed from Elizabeth? I wish to fight to the death, the maker of Rene Daniels." The room fell silent.

Fritz ran over to Meryt. "Are you crazy? If the brethren allow this, Elizabeth will kill you."

Meryt plainly responded, "People die every day; that is a fact of life. Right now, I'm dying as we speak." Meryt walked closer to the brethren. "If it pleases you, I wish no harm to come to the coven. I only want to fight Elizabeth, Rene's maker, for his freedom." Meryt noticed the other brother now staring at her, as if he knew her.

Smenkhkara ordered, "As you wish. Elizabeth, you have been called to the floor. Prepare to defend your angel."

Elizabeth walked slowly over, looking as if victory was already hers. Meryt turned to face Elizabeth and pulled two extended cobra knives from her bag. The knives were her favorite choice of weapon other than a gun. They were twenty-one inches long, slightly curved with spikes along the outer grip. The curve made them easier to pull out of a carcass and even easier to move through the air during combat. The spikes along the grip prevented her opponents from knocking it free from her hand.

"This is like a baby pulling out her play toy to fight," Elizabeth said, laughing.

"Elizabeth, let me be the first to tell you, today is your last living day here on earth."

Elizabeth was still laughing. "You would die over him?"

"My silly child, old age must be affecting your mind. This has nothing to do with Rene, but everything to do with you. Did you really think I would allow you to live after you tried to kill me? Let me tell you a little secret. You should have killed me then; letting me live only started your final countdown."

Apparently, Elizabeth had missed the lesson on "Sticks and stones will break my bones, but words will never hurt me." Meryt had gotten under her skin with one comment. Elizabeth came in close and fast. Meryt barely saw her coming toward her before Meryt did a slight side-step turn, barely allowing Elizabeth's sharp fingernails to rip through Meryt's black shirt.

Meryt continued in motion, spinning around, swinging the two knives, cutting through Elizabeth's flesh on her back. The sheer force caused Meryt to take two more steps from the momentum. Elizabeth screamed, "What the hell is this?" as blood poured from her back onto the marble floor.

"My dear, stupid Elizabeth, if I can save vampires with an elicitor, why can't I kill a vampire with an elicitor? I soaked all of my blades in it. The elicitor causes you to bleed out. Your body can't heal from my cuts. I thought you might like things to be fair. I can't heal right away from cuts, so why should you? Had I known you were this slow, I would have come sooner to kill you."

The fight had begun. Meryt used Elizabeth's speed as a weapon against her. Meryt's strategy was to remain still until the last possible moment and then sidestep from Elizabeth's reach. She came at Meryt again. Meryt repeated the sidestep, causing more destruction to Elizabeth's back. Elizabeth abruptly turned and pushed Meryt across the room. Meryt fell hard on her back, hitting the marble floor. Elizabeth yanked Meryt's foot and dragged her back to the middle of the room. Meryt took the other foot, clicked the blade out from the tip, and roundhouse kicked Elizabeth in the face. Blood poured from her forehead down to her cheek. She cried out in pain. This time Elizabeth moved suddenly, and Meryt didn't see her until it was too late. Elizabeth snatched Meryt's entire body and threw her onto the floor like a child tired of playing with a rag doll. Pain shot through Meryt's back. She had hoped her vest would hold, giving her back additional support. Meryt fought to regain her vision. She rolled over, shaking her head. A few drops of blood started streaming down the side of her face. Before Meryt regained her strength, Elizabeth grabbed her again, throwing her against a wall. Meryt wasn't ready for it to be over so soon. But most importantly, Meryt didn't want to be unconscious when the end came.

Elizabeth held Meryt by the neck, four inches off the ground. "You're right, I should have killed you then, but I won't make the same mistake twice." Elizabeth pulled Meryt's neck close to her mouth. Meryt felt Elizabeth's fangs puncturing her skin and hot blood flowing out. At that moment, Meryt clicked her metal vest and three twenty-inch-long spears punctured Elizabeth's chest straight through to her back. With what little strength Meryt had left, she embraced Elizabeth, pulling her farther onto the spears shafts, and two more knives popped from her wristbands. Meryt slit Elizabeth underneath her arms down both sides. Elizabeth cried out in pain as she pushed off from Meryt's deadly hug. Once they were apart, the spears collapsed back into the vest. Elizabeth stared in disbelief.

Meryt spoke in a calm but lethal voice. "I knew our last embrace would take your breath away." Then Meryt touched her neck, "Didn't you mother teach you it was impolite to bite?"

Elizabeth took a step forward and almost fell. It was working. Blood was pouring from her chest, sides, and now from her mouth.

"What did you do? I'll kill you." Elizabeth stumbled over to another vampire. "Please let me feed from you, so I can finish her off," Elizabeth pleaded.

"Excuse me, I think feeding to heal is cheating, but I don't make the rules here. I do know if anyone feeds from you, they will bleed out. The elicitor is active in your system and is easily transferable." Meryt wiped the blood from her neck, trying to assess the damage. "You see, my blood has the same chemical that my knives have. It causes me no harm. It's like taking an aspirin. But for you, it causes your platelets to become confused, which in turn will cause you to bleed out uncontrollably."

The other vampires pulled away from her. Elizabeth fell to the ground in a pile of dark red almost black blood. "You bitch, you knew," Elizabeth coughed out more blood, trying to hold onto her last breath.

"Elizabeth, the only thing I knew for sure is you should have never tried to kill me." With Meryt's last words, she picked up her cobra knife, pulled Elizabeth's blood soaked hair back and cut her head off in one clean swoop. For a brief moment, as the air stirred, Meryt felt as if this moment was déjà vu.

Meryt heard a hiss in the room. It focused her back to the task at hand. She approached the brethren, "I now lay claim to Rene Daniels. His maker is dead by my hand."

She threw Elizabeth's head down next to her body.

The brethren asked aloud, "Are there any takers who disagree and want to take claim of Rene?" The room fell silent.

Meryt turned to the brethren, she couldn't escape the feeling of fight or flight, "I apologize for the mess; if there is nothing more you wish of me, I prefer to leave with Rene and Fritz."

Smenkhkara spoke first, "No apologies needed. You were only following our law. You may leave. Rene and Fritz will follow. I must have a few words alone with them." Smenkhkara raised his hand, "Clean this mess, dispose of the body. Return Ms. Brownstone to the vehicle. No harm should come of her during her departure. Elizabeth knew the law. Elizabeth agreed to this battle."

Brethren departed from the main hall to a side room. Fritz and Rene, who had fully recovered, followed.

Once the door closed, Smenkhkara asked, "Who is she?" slamming his hand down on the table. "Have any of you seen a human, a human female kill an elder dark angel? This woman had no fear in her eyes."

Fritz answered, "We elicited her help when NeiNei fell ill. I thought we were close to losing her. Meryt helped us save her life."

"I know that story. I want to know Meryt's history. Who is she? I have never witnessed such a phenomenon. She is not welcome to return to this coven. I fear for her life. What will the other dark angels think of a human being so bold?"

Atem said, "Brother, we have seen this woman before. Think back in time, when we lived in the desert." Atem then turned from his brother Smenkhkara to Rene. "Do you love this woman?"

Atem paused for a moment in front of Rene, searching for an answer in his expression, realizing it was there the whole time, right in front of him. Atem had never noticed it before, but now he saw it. "You both must depart at once and return Ms. Brownstone home. She is never to enter this coven's doors again." Atem dismissed Rene and Fritz.

"Dear Brother, you are right, she is not welcome to return, but we will see her again. I do remember," Smenkhkara said, drinking fresh blood from a crystal wine glass.

"I see fate has dealt her the same hand, a losing one."

Chapter 49

Meryt waited by the limo with her escort, a vampire of few words. Talk about tall, dark, and mysterious. He had on a black suit, with an open white-collar shirt. He only spoke four words to Meryt: "Please, walk this way."

Meryt and her silent escort sat in front of the limo for ten quiet minutes before she saw Rene and Fritz reappear in the dusty tunnel. The limo was prepared to exit facing in the same direction they entered.

Meryt's escort quietly walked away, acknowledging Rene and Fritz with a nod. The two of them did not appear pleased or displeased. They appeared troubled and nervous. It was amazing to see Rene completely recovered. Less than two hours ago he was near death.

"Are we ready to go?" she asked. "Because I think we've done enough here today, and I've got an odd feeling that Smenkhkara does not consider me a friend to the vampire world. I need not cross his path anytime soon."

The brothers remained silent. Meryt got into the limo first, followed by Rene and then Fritz. "Okay, is it safe to go to the airport?" Meryt asked the brothers.

Fritz finally spoke. "Yes, we should leave immediately."

"That sounds like a plan," Meryt chimed in quickly.

The limo was quiet with the same stillness they had when they first drove to the coven. At that time, Meryt was traveling to the unknown, mentally prepping for battle. Fritz was tense, worrying if they would be too late to save his brother's life. Meryt was tense wondering if they were too late, if she could she stand the pain of losing Rene a second time. The pain she felt the first time was now stored in the back corner of her heart, out of the way, but it could easily be pulled out to the front. She had wondered if she could survive the pain again without growing mad with hate and revenge?

Meryt could not surrender to the silence. "Why are you two so quiet? Is there something I should know? Did I do something wrong?" Meryt asked in an irritated manner.

In half of her scenarios either she had died or they all died trying to leave the coven. So she was elated to have survived with minimum bumps and bruises. Truly she thought of it as a reward to have Rene coming home. She knew the mission wasn't over until they were safely in the Falls, but it felt good to be out of the coven with Rene and Fritz.

Fritz answered, "Do you realize you killed a dark angel in hand-to-hand combat inside one of the oldest covens? No human in our history has accomplished such a feat."

Meryt began to feel a little defensive. "I came because you asked me to come. Did you really think I would go unprepared? I had no idea where you were taking me, but common sense should have told you it was most likely going be a hostile environment. The person you were saving your brother from tried to kill me the last time we met. What were you expecting, tea and biscuits?"

"Meryt, that's not the point, you killed a dark angel inside the coven."

"Exactly what is your point, Fritz? I asked your leader, Smenkhkara, how to free a vampire from his maker. This was your coven's rule, not mine. I don't recall, you standing up to Elizabeth. You knew what had to be done. Pleading with the brethren was not an option. Sometimes rules are rules. What other option was there to save your brother?"

Fritz agreed slowly, "You're right. I should have challenged Elizabeth myself."

Again, silence fell in the limo for a few moments, and then Fritz spoke. "Meryt, how did you defeat Elizabeth?"

"I've been working on the formula since Elizabeth left. I knew she and I would cross paths again, and I wanted to be prepared. You know exactly where I derived the formula.

"Meryt, that's not what I meant. I understand the concept of the formula, but how were you able to strike back? Elizabeth is a dark angel. With her speed and her age, you should not have been able to touch her," Fritz said.

"I used her strengths, her agility, and her temper to my advantage. This is basic Hindu karate. I assumed you knew my military background. I was trained in hand-to-hand combat."

Fritz would not leave the issue. "Meryt, I understand your background. As indepth as your combat skills are, you should not have been able to kill or even touch Elizabeth. Dark angels move faster than the human eye can track. That is the point; I don't think anyone in that room had ever seen a human fight a dark angel successfully." Fritz sat back recalling simple moments from their past, where he could have seen a clue or hint, that Meryt moved faster or was stronger than the average human. One moment came to mind. The image was muddled because at the time that was not his concern. It was the night at Meryt's house at the pool when she reached for the vodka bottle before Lolita could touch the bottle. He tried to think back further, trying to recall similar cases.

Fritz's words hung in the air. The silence remained in the limo until they arrived at the airport. A whirlwind of thoughts exploded as Meryt began to analyze the situation. *What am I missing? Are we not alive and heading home? Is there a thank-you? I did not make the rules. I simply followed their rules. Fritz asked me to help him return his brother home. And on top of it all, Rene has not said a single word.*

They did not fly home on the private jet. Instead, Fritz insisted they fly a commercial airline. Luckily, they were able to secure a flight leaving within two hours, just enough time to change and get through customs. Meryt had to leave certain items in the women's restroom trash, because she didn't plan on checking bags and she wanted to clear customs without a fuss. The flight flew directly into New York. From there, a small connection would take them to upstate.

They had only spoken a few words among the three of them. Meryt was enraged with Rene and Fritz. Meryt fell for the same foolishness all over again. The pain that was stored in a far corner of her heart was being pushed to the front.

Within the hour, they were sitting in first class. Meryt was sipping on Jack and ginger ale, trying to figure out the reason for the silent treatment. Rene sat next to her, and Fritz sat alone behind them in the next row.

One . . . two . . . three . . . breathe.

Meryt had to speak. "Why the silent treatment? Rene, what is going on? Why do you not seem happy to go home or even to see me?" At first Meryt could not look into Rene's eyes. She was afraid he would see the hurt and the anger in hers, but slowly she looked up into his eyes. Just at that moment his eyes flashed red momentarily, returning to their blue color.

Rene softly spoke. "I never thought that I would see you again. I was prepared to die. I wanted to die before I allowed anyone to hurt you, but I couldn't bring myself to do it. I wanted to see you even if it meant your death. When I first heard your voice, I thought it was a trick, but slowly I recognized the love and conviction in your voice. I wanted to live. You gave me the strength to live. I had no idea you first approached the brethren. When I heard your request, I was angry with Fritz and myself for placing you in danger. Meryt, no one in that room thought you would survive, not even me. Once you took the pledge to fight, I wanted to die all over again. I promised myself that night I would kill Elizabeth for killing you."

Meryt touched his hand. An electric shock took her back to their making love. The emotions hit her one after another causing her pulse to jump.

Rene pulled his hand away. "Meryt, I apologize for our silence, but we have put you in grave danger. The coven will not let you go free. They will not forget what they saw. You have caught their attention, and I have no idea how far they will take this issue." Rene placed her other hand in his, "Your life, my life, and my family's lives are all in danger. I've caused this mess. The very people I love, I'm putting at risk. And I have no idea how to fix this."

"Rene, are saying you love me?" Meryt never thought she would hear him say those words again. Her mind went off on its own. Rene loved her. She finally had her one true love. She didn't have to be alone any more. Meryt was complete.

Rene released her hands. "Don't you understand, Meryt? We will never have the relationship you deserve." Rene immediately stood up, turned to the row behind them, and sat with his brother.

The pain rained down over Meryt. It had returned in full strength. She felt her heart skip a beat, followed by a tight squeeze. It felt like her heart was in a steel box three sizes too small. With every breath, she felt the cold steel box pushing back growing smaller in size and, slowly suffocating her heart.

Her mind was spinning. The pain was mocking her, laughing and rejoicing in its return. She felt her body temperature drop a few degrees. Meryt had seven hours to be on the plane. Seven hours of the raw pain building in her chest and the cause of all this pain sitting two feet away.

She shook her head in denial. *Fool me once shame on you; fool me twice shame on me.* She knew twice the Danielses had fooled her.

Meryt caught the attention of the flight attendant and asked, "Please, may I have a double Jack and ginger ale? And don't stop them until I fall asleep."

Within moments, the flight attendant brought the first cocktail, followed by the second and then a third. The Jack finally kicked in on the fourth.

Meryt lay back, extending the footrest on her leather seat and allowing the torture to begin. Her only prayer was that the Jack would allow her to sleep before the pain stopped her heart, causing her to scream out loud.

The race began on the fifth drink.

Chapter 50

They landed in New York. The brothers were a little less stressed; maybe it was due to the fact they were so close to being home. Meryt still felt the same slow, suffocating pain in her chest. She decided that they had to depart company. If she stayed another moment in Rene's presence, she might take her own life. Meryt hurt that bad.

"Hey, guys, I need to freshen up. We've got two hours to get through customs. I just need ten minutes," Meryt said as she stretched and pulled out her back. The fight from earlier had her back and neck a little tight.

Rene came over and kissed her forehead and touched her lower back. Lightning ran through her body, starting from the location of his fingertips on her back. "Sure. We'll be over there looking at the flight times, my love," he said, pointing off to the monitor about twenty feet away.

Meryt went into the restroom. JFK airport used to be her playground. She knew there was another exit on the other side. The restroom sat between two terminals, F and E, which ran parallel to one another. From the other terminal Meryt could go to the US Air Club and purchase a ticket on the next flight moving. She walked into the restroom, and then straight out on the other side. Once exiting, she headed directly to the club. Meryt checked her watch fourteen seconds had passed. By the time she arrived to US Air Club, one minute four seconds had passed. She was in luck, no line.

"May I help you? Are you a member?" asked the female attendant.

"Yes, I'm curious. I need a flight to LaGuardia. When is the next flight?" Meryt said as she passed her Black American Express and her membership cards over the counter. She knew the two airports had shuttles that constantly ran back and forth. She would not need to go through customs to board. Since it was a commuter flight to LaGuardia, passengers cleared customs there. After a quick phone call while in the air, Meryt could pass it by all together. That was her plan.

"Ms. Brownstone, we have a flight leaving in twenty minutes. It's boarding now. Gate 4 F, right outside the door to the left. Take the escalator down for our local shuttle. The ticket will be $343 plus tax. Do you have bags or need a return flight?" the attendant requested.

"No, it's a day trip. I have no bags. Please book the ticket, so I can catch the flight." As the words were leaving her mouth, Meryt heard the printer burning the ticket. Within seconds she had the ticket in her hand. Four minutes thirty seconds.

"Thank you." Meryt turned and headed for the door. She opened the door hesitating then looking left and right, no Danielses in sight. Meryt quickly walked to Gate 4 F. Five minutes twenty seconds. As Meryt arrived at the gate, her stopwatch read six minutes flat. Her little angel, the attendant, was correct. They were boarding. She continued moving right into line. Moments later she took a seat on board. Meryt looked down at her watch seven minutes ten seconds. She had time to spare. After seven minutes and ten seconds she could breathe again. Meryt took her phone out made a quick call. Customs was clear and a car was waiting.

When she heard "Ladies and gentlemen, please turn off all electrical devices. We are now closing the cabin doors," it was music to her ears. She had made it. Meryt looked down at her watch: eight minutes twenty-seven seconds.

Now the pain started to creep its cold, icy fingers around her heart again, but this time the cause of the pain was not sitting two feet away.

Chapter 51

"Rene, do you think Meryt is okay? She didn't look well," Fritz said.

Rene looked back toward the women's restroom. "I was wondering the same. When I touched her, she felt a little cold. We are going to have to explain to her what's going on. It's better for her to stay at our house than for me to stay with her at her home. Plus, we need start making arrangements for our next move. We have a week at best to remain in Niagara Falls."

Fritz continued, "I'm hoping NeiNei will have some insight on this problem. She may still have connections to convince them to stay away." They both now looked back at the restroom. "Rene, I know this is not the right time, but have you thought about transforming her into a dark angel. As one of us, maybe the coven would not judge her so harshly?"

"Yes, I have thought about it, but I am not prepared to propose such a commitment, especially when she hasn't agreed to a long-term relationship to me. She does't seem interested in the concept of dark angels."

"It's been about ten minutes, and she still has not returned from the restroom." Fritz looked at his watch. "Do you think she's okay? It's been awhile since she's been in there. Do you think the coven followed us here?"

Rene's adrenaline picked up as he quickly scanned the area. "No, I don't feel any other dark angels present, but I don't feel Meryt either. I noticed at the coven that I didn't sense her; maybe it's the drug she had in her bloodstream." They walked closer to the restroom and waited a few more minutes.

Five more minutes passed by and no Meryt. "I can't take it anymore. Where is she?" Rene said as he reached out and touched the hand of a woman who was leaving the restroom.

"Have you seen an attractive African-American woman with long hair pinned into a ponytail dressed in black in there?"

The lady replied with a smile that was inviting more than a conversation. "No, but can I help you?"

"No."

"Fritz, you stand outside the door and ease the ladies as they come out. I'm going in." Rene walked directly into the restroom, searching up and down the two corridors of stalls, finally coming to the back entrance. He quickly returned to Fritz. "She's not in there. She's gone."

Fritz asked, "Can't you find her? Don't you feel her?"

"No! I can't find her, and I don't feel her. I barely felt her on the plane. I could hear her heartbeat on the plane, but not here. There are too many sounds, too many people," Rene said angrily. "We've got to decide what to do."

"How did she pass by us?" Fritz asked.

"There is another exit to another terminal on the other side."

"Let's head down the other terminal. She couldn't have gotten that far."

The two brothers moved quickly down the hall, looking at each loading gate. They had come to the end of the terminal, and they hadn't found Meryt.

"Where could she have gone?" Rene asked. They both went to the nearest monitor to see what flights were departing. There were too many to determine which gate Meryt could have taken. Rene brushed his hair back, thinking, *what's next?* His eye caught a camera scanning from left to right. Normally he tried to avoid being filmed, but this time it didn't matter.

"That's it. Let's go to security. They have to have her on film going somewhere. She just can't disappear into thin air."

Fritz agreed, but in the back of his mind he wondered if the brethren had made their first move. Fritz, without missing a beat, turned up his senses and followed closely behind Rene, looking for anyone he recognized.

Chapter 52

From LaGuardia it was only a matter of hours before Meryt was free to breathe again. From years of training, she had learned to keep cash stashed away in safety deposit boxes in key metropolitan cities. In New York, for its size, activity, and location, she had a total of four boxes. Meryt always saved a little something, something for rainy days, and today it was pouring. In truth, there was a slight overcast with light rain showers outside. It was the weather she liked the best during the day. It was the kind of weather that a person could easily hide behind and simply slip away and no one would ever notice. That was her cowardly plan. She planned to slip away and think through these past twenty-four hours, but more importantly, she planned to heal her aching heart.

Meryt planned to sail away into the Atlantic on a yacht she had won in a bet three years ago. It was one of her many secrets. No one could trace it to her name or any of her aliases. Not even Deacon knew she had it. Being on the water was her one simple, private pleasure that she kept to herself.

Next stop? Who cares?

Chapter 53

Rene and Fritz knew it was too late to follow after viewing the security tapes. They were a minimum of forty-five minutes behind Meryt's trail.

"Why did she leave?" snapped Rene. "What did you two talk about before you came to Naples?"

"Nothing out of the usual. I asked her to come and help me save your life. She initially was not enthused at the idea." Fritz was always so factual. "At first she seemed rather pleased with the idea of you in pain. She mumbled something about people die every day, and then she decided come. Meryt was packed in an hour." Fritz spoke with concern in his voice. "We must consider that perhaps the coven has already made their first move in retrieving her."

Rene quickly replied, "No, I think she left on her own accord. Why she left, I have no idea, but I know someone who may know where she's heading. Call home to inform the family on what has happened and warn NeiNei of the impending visit from the coven. I'll book us on the next flight to Virginia."

By late afternoon, Rene and Fritz had reached Deacon's office. Deacon did not seem surprised by the visit, nor did it seem that he cared. It was late in the day, and Deacon was preparing to close the office, even though it was barely 4:00 p.m. He was mentally exhausted; it had been a tough year. He still had loose ends from the kidnapping, but he had finally made a connection from Lord Atken to old money trail coming from Europe. He was getting close to something big.

Deacon sat behind his desk, typing on his computer, pissed at the day's events. He had more jobs than men to place in play. Since the president's breach in personnel security, Deacon had to open all files on the Secret Service. This had taken more time than he hoped and more of his personal agents to help reinvestigate the remaining staff. Not to mention starting a fresh investigation on the new recruits to replace the ones who were killed.

Without looking up, Deacon greeted the two brothers. "What brings you by this afternoon? Are we friends? So you think you can just drop by because you are in the neighborhood? Sorry if I left you that impression." Deacon never trusted a man who had holes in his background. With today's technology and his access, Deacon had the ability to write a biography with pictures and voice excerpts on every person walking the earth. When Deacon researched Dr. Daniels, he was barely able to compose a five-paragraph essay with no photos.

"I've lost her, she slipped away at JFK Airport and took a flight to—"

Before Rene could finish, Deacon finished his sentence. "LaGuardia. I know, she phoned a friend to clear customs." This time he stopped typing and walked over to his bar and poured his usual, a white Russian.

"Why would she want to give you the slip? When you and I last spoke, you two were in love. She told me, you might be the one. Three months later she was begging me for suicide missions," he said as he sipped on his drink, returning to his desk.

"I know you must be aware. I had to leave due to special unforeseen matters. Meryt came with my brother to visit." Rene stood back. "My apologies, I have not introduced you; Fritz is my brother and a dear friend of Meryt's." They exchanged glances and both sat down. "As I stated before, she came to Italy to help bring me home."

"'Unforeseen matters,' is that what they call a wife these days?" Deacon continued to drink his cocktail. "Meryt mentioned your brother, who interestingly has your same background. It must run in your family—no history."

"So she has spoken with you about this matter?"

Deacon nodded his head. "Yeah, you can say we spoke about that particular matter." Deacon sat his drink down, growing tired of the conversation. "Let's get to the bottom of this. Why did she leave you, and why should I help you find her?"

Rene felt disgusted having to share more about this trying event and exposing more family matters to a human. "My brother asked her to help bring me home. I agreed to leave, and on the way home we argued; then she slipped away. Look, I just want her back, to tell her how much I care."

Deacon turned to his computer again, picked up his reading glasses off the desk, placed them on, and began typing on the computer. He finally spoke a few minutes later. "Not good enough. Try again. I'm not into children's bedtime stories. I deal with truths."

Rene looked over to his brother, puzzled, giving Fritz a look, asking for help.

Fritz spoke. "Sorry to meet you under these circumstances; you seem to really care for Meryt."

"What circumstances? Your brother wants me to believe they had a lover's quarrel and she split. If that is the case, then she'll come back when she is ready. This hardly seems like circumstances, son. So tell me like a two-year-old: Why do you need my help?" Deacon put his glasses down again and rubbed his eyes and forehead. "Listen, I don't have time to play this game anymore, so spit it out!"

Rene, aware that his integrity was in question, blurted out, "Meryt killed the woman you call my wife. The three of us were returning home together. She asked to go to the restroom. While she was gone my brother and I were talking about the ramifications. Nothing illegal because the death was in self-defense; however, the family may want revenge, a life for a life. If I don't find her first . . ."

"Now we are talking. Why would you put her in that kind of jeopardy?"

"I didn't know she was coming, and I surely didn't think matters would go that far," Rene said. "Please help me find her before the family finds her first. I love her. I want to protect her with all of my life."

"That is the most truth you've spoken to me today. Now I will share some truth with you. I don't know where she is, but I do know she won't be found unless she wants to be found. I'll run searches, but I have a feeling they will come up dry. Give me a contact number. I'll call when I have information."

"That's it? You have no idea where she is? I would have been better off trying to pick up her trail at LaGuardia," Rene responded angrily.

"Son, what else do you want me to say? You were probably one of the closest people to her. You pissed her off. When she gets pissed, she leaves. She's left before. She usually comes back in a few weeks. The best lead I can give you is this: she likes the south, and she loves music."

"South where? South America, South Pole, South Carolina?"

"The South meaning New Orleans, Alabama, South Florida, the Keys. Go on the Internet and look for concerts coming to town. It's too soon for her to leave the country. Plus, we know she flew to LaGuardia. LaGuardia is known for its domestic flights. If she were planning to leave the States, she would have flown out of JFK on an international flight. Look in the Caribbean. It's easy to get in and out." Deacon took another sip of his drink. "She let you in; you have spent time with her. What type of people would she be around? What's her favorite mode of travel? Think. The best way to find her is to think like her. She's got cash stashed away and new identities everywhere, so don't trace her name, but trace her actions. She can't change her nature. And if she's really pissed, you won't be able to track her at all. The only thing I know to do is watch and wait." Deacon sat back in his chair with his fingers behind his neck, stretching, repeating again, "She can't change her nature. Something will happen and it will have her name all over it. That's the best I can do. If you were anyone else, I would have killed you at the door, brother and all. Go start your search, and I will contact you when I have information."

Chapter 54

It had been three days without a trace from Rene. Meryt couldn't believe she allowed herself to think of *Rene*. She needed to lay low for a while and get her head screwed on correctly.

Meryt should have never allowed Fritz and Lolita into her home that night. She should not have listened to their pleas for help.

"I'm nothing but a fool. Now look at me, thousands of miles from my home, on the run, sitting on a boat, drifting. Having a pity party, thinking about the ramifications of my actions." She wondered if the coven would come after her now. The brethren did not seem over pleased with her actions. Meryt couldn't shake the feeling of loathing. Whatever the case, she knew for sure her death was required payment for a debt unknown.

The brethren would easily find her home in the Falls. For all she knew the Danielses would give them her address and her personal cell phone number. Crap! Thank God she had thrown that thing in the trash before she left New York.

None of those things mattered. Meryt was going to take her time and enjoy the water and the assorted ports along the eastern coastline. She was going to live the simple life for a while. When she grew tired of boating, Meryt would dock the boat and get a little fast number and travel by land.

Meryt had forgotten how much she loved the ocean. The water helped put things in perspective. It made her realize she was just one living creature with a few problems compared to the world that surrounded her. She would continue to head south. Next stop Virginia Beach, get some fresh supplies and prepare *Warhorse*, her boat, for their summer trip. She shouldn't have called *Warhorse* a boat. True boatmen would call a seventy-five-foot Lazzara with her spacious cabin, a beautiful yacht.

For now, Meryt called it home as she launch off on a new adventure.

Chapter 55

Queen Hatshepsut started the rituals of the Lunar Enlightenment. She sent for the tribal leaders. As she waited for them, she knelt down in the moonlight, looking up to the heavens. "Creator, the Sun god, the only god I know, you have sent her again. This is her rebirth. I will not fail her twice." Queen Hatshepsut's faithful companion, Senunmut, stood in the background watching as she began chanting to all the spirits from the past to come forth to provide wisdom and strength for the war ahead.

All seven leaders appeared within the hour in her front chamber. The Queen's home had changed over the years. It had fallen beneath the sand creating underground passageways. It was no longer the pharaoh's palace, but a series of connecting tunnels and caves that varied in depth into the earth. It used to be Akhenaten's palace in Nubia for his Queen Nefertiti when she returned home. The Pharaoh of Egypt built new temples in Amarna and Nubia to promote the new one-God religion, the new religion of the people. Within two years there were more than twenty thousand people within the city walls. Now the city was nothing but a ghost town full of memories from the past. A few pieces of the once-great kingdoms were stored there in the caves. They were still beautiful, serving as proof to a lost union between two kingdoms. Paintings and gold statues celebrating Egypt and Nubia's union decorated Queen Hatshepsut home.

The front chamber was one of the highest levels in her home. The room itself was a cave with a huge opening in the center of the ceiling. At night, the stars and the new moon were so close; that it gave the impression they were in arms reach of the night sky. White linens that moved with the night desert breeze hung in all four corners of the room. Along the two parallel sidewalls were long fire pits that softly lit the room. The seven tribal leaders stood in silence, waiting for the Queen to finish her prayers.

The tribal leaders recognized this prayer, it was one, they had not heard in centuries. It was the prayer for war.

Queen Hatshepsut slowly rose from her knees; her long, curly, black hair was blowing in the wind, and she was dressed in traditional off-white linens draped around the front and a gold necklace with sapphire stones embedded in continuous rolls with matching cuffs on each arm. She moved with authority. Each step, each movement of her hand, and each glance from her eyes moved with a purpose. She looked as regal today as she had some three thousand years ago. She once ruled both kingdoms. During her short reign, they had prospered under her new trading laws versus warring. She was one of the few women in Egypt's history who attained the full titles and regalia as a pharaoh. Just as monotheistic religion was stripped away from Egypt and lost in history, so was her reign.

"Our warrior has returned. As the moon loses its full form and returns again to full power, she will return. And, as all great warriors do, she will fight. It is in her nature and she will need an army by her side. Go prepare your people for war. The time is near." As Queen Hatshepsut spoke these words, she threw fragrance and incense into the fire pit along the wall. All at once, red and purple flames grew higher and higher on the cave's wall.

There, a faint ghost of an illusion. Meryt lay in her sleep tossing and turning. Within moments the image was gone.

The tribal leaders cheered and broke into their own chants of war. Queen Hatshepsut continued, "We have waited long enough. It is our time to come out of hiding from the brethren! We will once again command the respect of our bloodline." Celebration continued on through the night.

After Queen Hatshepsut finished the rituals, she left the courtyard cave and retired to her private quarters with Senunmut. He had not spoken a word the whole night until now. "Do you think she will succeed? She has failed once. How can she succeed when she does not know her enemy? This is how she failed before. She is destined to fail again. Why would the Creator play this evil trick?"

"The evil trick was not played by the Creator, but rather by man. Smenkhkara is the evil one. I cannot tell you the future, but if we do not plan and prepare for the future we want, we are doomed to always follow someone else's."

Hatshepsut slowly walked closer to Senunmut and caressed his face, the caress that melted his heart the first time she touched his face three thousand years ago. His eyes flashed red with fever. His whole life was dedicated to the kingdom and to his one true love.

Queen Hatshepsut spoke softly. "Will she defeat the brethren? Yes. Will it be this time?" She held the words in the air for a moment. "I know this, if we do nothing to help, what are her chances?"

Chapter 56

Meryt picked up supplies in Virginia. *Warhorse* didn't need too many repairs. She stood true to her name. The Lazzara yacht was in perfect condition. Meryt started to feel like her old self. She wondered why she had ever left this life in the past. There was nothing like sailing from port to port, meeting new people, laughing, having a few drinks, and pushing back off to the ocean to be alone. No worries, no cares. She came and she went like the rolling tides, collecting sand, dropping off some shells, and returning back out to the deep.

There was something special about salty air over the ocean. It smelled sweeter than the air over land. It always felt like summer time. The ocean air left her feeling young and invincible. Her senses were open to the world. No negativity, no pollution from malcontents, only rolling waves. It was the fountain of youth. Meryt was ten years old again. She felt like fun. Meryt felt the way she did when Rene and her first . . . *never mind*. Meryt went back to pretending to feeling better while boating.

Next stop, Jacksonville. She couldn't wait to be back in her old stomping grounds. Meryt was surprised at how much things had changed over the years. She had some of her best summers as a child in Florida, riding up and down the interstate 95. Summer fireworks on the beach, frozen drinks before turning twenty-one, and she promised herself to never forget the wet-T-shirt contest. Being young was definitely fun.

She unhooked the lines, ran back to the captain's chair, and put *Warhorse* in slow full reverse. Meryt said, "Atlantic, here I come." She figured it should take nine hours from dock to dock.

By the time Meryt arrived in Jacksonville, she was beat down and ready to sleep for the night. She was thankful they had room in the port. Meryt contemplated long and hard about being adrift while she slept, but she wasn't ready for those types of boating complications.

Meryt did not leave the confines of her new home for two days while docked in Jacksonville. The fatigue led to depression and a painful pity party. She wasn't ready to be seen by the world. Meryt was not ready to answer questions from staring eyes. Meryt knew that no one knew her, but the mind can play powerful tricks when a person is depressed. Rene and his family occupied most of her daily thoughts. She constantly worried that Rene would be able to find her. She thought Rene could track her scent, since he tasted her blood. She still had the tiny twin scars to remind her of that night. As she prepared to step off the yacht on the second day, she changed her mind. Meryt's heart began pounding with pain. She knew she was not ready to leave familiarity of *Warhorse* and be exposed to to naked questions of the world. Meryt called the tower and started the process of plotting her next stop, Freeport. She was determined to make it in nine hours.

Chapter 57

Meryt sailed around the Caribbean for almost month. She spent the first two weeks in Freeport and the other one hopping ports. Now, it was time to explore new ports along the west coast of Florida, not to mention that *Warhorse* needed new parts that could only be found on the mainland back in the states. Meryt set up new coordinates for the Gulf of Mexico.

Meryt first arrived in Tampa. She was completely spent. She had to sleep. It was a full day before Meryt left the boat. She awoke early in the afternoon to boat chores like cleaning the salt water off *Warhorse*, pumping waste, and refilling fresh water into the tanks. By late afternoon, Meryt had completed her chores and was ready to explore the area. She wasn't ready to explore the city, but she was ready to find a little bar with decent music. It was her lucky day. She asked around and sure enough, there was a blues bar within walking distance of the dock.

The place was just as she had hoped. It was a small hole in the wall. It had about ten tables and a bar that ran from one end to the other. The name was simple, The Bar. The waitress came over and took her order. Meryt ordered the house special, catfish and chips. Since it was her lucky day, it happened to still be happy hour. There was only one thing better than a Jack and ginger. Two Jack and gingers for the price of one. Meryt closed the place down. She sat back and drank a little, ate a little, and did a ton of people watching. The waitress, Sara, came over from time to time to deliver new drinks. It had been three weeks since she had been around Americans while in the states.

Meryt had to admit it was nice being off of *Warhorse* getting her land legs back. Four hours slipped by, Sara did her usual by delivering another Jack and ginger, but this time she spoke. "Are you here alone?"

"Yes," Meryt replied. "Sometimes I find it best to be alone. No timelines, no one to disappoint, and no one to disappoint me." Meryt smiled and gave her a toast.

Sara returned the smiled and said, "Amen," while picking up an emptied glass and crumbled-up napkins on the small table.

Meryt had been watching her all night. She wondered, *what was her story?* She seemed to be little smarter than the average person. Waiting tables in a hole-in-the-wall bar didn't seem like a good fit. She possessed something more behind her pleasant smile. She appeared to be in her mid to late twenties. She still had life in her. Meryt could see the passion in her steps and the twinkle in her eyes. Maybe she was hiding from something as well. Meryt finished off her drink. She had a good feeling about this port. Meryt decided to stay a few days, as she walked back to docks.

Meryt came back the next night and two more nights that followed. Sara finally satisfied Meryt's curiosity and told her life story on the third night, after her less-than-polite boyfriend showed up at the bar and got drunk. Sara was feeling a little low and wanted conversation so she told her story. Sara had fallen in love with the star football player and had gotten pregnant right after graduation. They had always planned to move away, but something was always in the way, money, family issues, and timing. Finally time had run out, and her star player died in a tragic car accident. Sara was alone and grief stricken, she couldn't move on, so she stayed. She needed money and a job, hence, this place and her new boyfriend.

As Meryt listened to Sara unfold her life story, she contemplated, *what makes a woman stay, and what makes a woman leave after her heart is broken?* Meryt couldn't stand to be near Rene when he had broken her heart, yet Sara felt obligated to stay in the same town for her lost love.

It was Saturday, her fifth night in Tampa, Meryt was doing her usual, drinking and people watching as Sara did her nightly routine. Jim, her boyfriend, had come in earlier with his friends. They had just finished a baseball game. The boys had been drinking and laughing all night. Jim clearly had too much to drink by the late evening hour.

The Bar owner, Bob called out, "Last call!"

This triggered Jim to shout over to Sara for another round.

Sara walked over and said in her southern accent, "Jimmy, I'll get you another round, but I'm going to need your keys. You can't drive drunk as a skunk. I'll drive you home when I get off."

Without warning, Jim slapped Sara's face, causing her to fall backward over a nearby barstool. "You stupid cow, don't ever talk to me like that!"

Meryt knew he was a piece of work, but she wasn't expecting violence. Sara fell to the floor, dropping her tray and tip money. Sara looked up at him with her arms defensively over her head. Meryt knew the sign. Jim had hit her before. Sara was bracing herself for the next assault. Meryt saw blood dripping from her lip. Her lip was split, and she would have a nice cherry on her cheek tomorrow. Meryt went over to her slowly. She wanted to help Sara up off the floor. Before Meryt was able to help, Jim grabbed Sara's other arm and snatched her to her feet.

Meryt's anger management was ignited.

"Wait a minute, let's slow things down. Clearly, things have gotten off to a bad start," Meryt said while picking up the tip money off of the floor and handing it over to Sara. By this time, Jim's friends started to surround Meryt, and what few patrons were left had gotten up to exit the bar. One of Jim's friends went behind the bar to corner the owner.

Jim turned to Meryt and said, "You want to be a nosy, busy body? This is what happens when you stick your nose in were it doesn't belong." He released his grip on Sara and swung at Meryt. He was moving so slowly that Meryt could have gone to the bathroom and returned before his fist connected. Meryt jumped back from the swing, causing Jim to hit the side of the bar. As she stepped aside, his friend to the left caught Meryt's cheek. She tasted her own blood.

In a blink, Meryt was ready to kill. Before she knew it, she had broken the guy's leg in two places. Meryt blocked another swing in midaction, ducking from another guy's swing.

Jim's two friends ran out of the bar, one with a broken wrist and the other with fear. The one with the broken leg pulled himself across the floor, away from the fight. Jim tried to jump on Meryt's back, but he was still moving too slowly. Meryt sidestepped, reached over her head, and gripped his neck and flipped his body over using his own momentum. She finished him with a blow to the face. His nose broke instantly, and Meryt felt the snap beneath her palm. She stood up over his body as blood exploded everywhere, and surveyed the damages done to the bar.

"Let this be a lesson on who you decide to hit."

The two other guys came back in the bar when they heard Jim screaming. This time they had two baseball bats. Meryt pulled a 9mm from her side pocket and pointed directly at them. "Gentlemen, are you prepared to die over a bar fight tonight? If not, drop your bats and take your friends to the hospital." Like two lost, scared boys, they dropped the bats and began picking up their friends. Meryt turned to the owner and Sara. "Sara, where is your baby?"

"At my mama's," she replied. By this time the wannabe gang had dismantled and departed. Meryt gathered her belongings. She searched through her olive green dilapidated bag and pulled out seven thousand dollars in cash. "Here you go. Take this money. Get your baby and go. Take the next bus or train to any big city. Enroll your child in school, and promise me you will live your life for you and not look back."

"I can't take this. I can't pay you back."

"I'm not asking you to pay me back. I'm asking you to leave this town and start living your life." Sara hugged her.

The owner gave a nod. "Go, girl, get out of this town. I'll be all right. Just go."

Sara picked up the rest of her tip money and her keys and, prepared for her escape. She looked back one more time and whispered, "Thank you."

"You're welcome. Now, just go."

Meryt turned to the owner, trying to assess the damage. "Well, I gave her all the money I had on me. Can I help you clean this mess up? If you give me your address, I'll wire you some money for the damages." She was still evaluating the mess. "I don't think I'll be coming back anytime soon."

"Don't worry. You gave me two gifts tonight: getting Sara out of here and giving those punks a beating they won't soon forget," he said, smiling. "You should leave before the cops get here. I can handle it. No worries."

Meryt strolled over to the door, looked around, and said good-bye. She jogged back to *Warhorse*. "*Warhorse*, I've done it again. We gotta go," she thought aloud as she pulled the lines in from the dock. As if *Warhorse* knew instinctively, she pulled away from the slip while Meryt prepped the engines. Meryt didn't call the tower to notify them of her departure. She silently slipped away into the Gulf. The water looked like black sparkling mercury under the moonlight.

Chapter 58

In just a few hours out to sea, Meryt was comforted by loneliness while at the helm. She felt relieved to be away from all the excitement on land. As the serenity of the water wahed over her emotions, a lost thought began to emerge. Meryt remembered she still required a part. Fuck! Immediately, different options raced through her head. *What do I do? I need the part. I can't stay out at sea without it.* Finally it became clear Meryt had two choices. She could go to a new port in a new city and reorder the part and wait another week, or she could return and wait one more day for the part. She knew what she had to do.

Chapter 59

Rene got a call early Monday morning on his cell phone. He knew the name and wondered if he had a real lead. Over the past month, he had been to every concert south of the Mason-Dixon Line. And more high end car dealerships than he cared to recall. He staked out Meryt's mother's house, other family members, and old drinking pubs she used to frequent. It was all the same, no one had seen or heard from Meryt. It was as if she fell off the face of the earth.

Deacon started speaking without any greetings. "Rene, you may want to fly down to Tampa. I found a news report about a local bar fight involving a tourist."

"Do you really think it's her?"

"The article reads like her MO. It's in the south and it just fits. I pulled the police report separate from the local news article. Three men received injuries, a broken wrist, a leg fractured in two places, but most impressive, a broken nose that should have been fatal. In addition, the tourist was never found. This sounds like my girl's work."

Rene closed his eyes as Deacon described the injuries. He imagined Meryt causing the injuries from their joy ride in the woods with Mr. Smith. "I'll call you from Tampa to let you know what turns up."

"Rene, don't get your hopes up too much, because the police report came in Saturday night and the article appeared in today's local paper. So if it's her, she's gone. But we now have a location to fan out and start a new search area."

Rene knew Deacon was right. Being two days off her scent was better than any of their past leads. Within hours, Rene and his brother, Fritz, were in Tampa. They rented a car at the airport and plugged The Bar's address into the navigation system. The system calculated a forty-three-minute ride to destination.

As they got closer according to the land nav, only five miles before final destination, Rene had trouble believing his eyes. His Meryt would not have been in this town. The town impressed him as being too southern. Surely Meryt would stick out. People would take note of a fancy car and an African-American woman running the streets ordering Jack and ginger at the bars.

Rene studied the town's people laboring about with their daily chores in jeans and T-shirts that advertised either beer or candidates for the next elections.

"This can't be correct. Meryt would stick out like a sore thumb in this town," he told his brother.

The nav system confirmed the location of The Bar: "*Bing . . . Bing . . .* You have arrived. Your final destination is on your left, *Bing . . . Bing.*"

Fritz pulled the rental car into the parking lot of the bar. The establishment was an old, rundown wooden building about the size of a one-bedroom efficiency. Nothing special about the place, unless you count sand and dust that surrounded everything. They both got out of the car, slamming the doors, but the sound was instantly muffled in the heat and the humidity. The sand kicked up initially, but quickly settled down to the ground from the weight of the air.

Rene glanced over to Fritz. "This can't be right." They walked into the bar, and Rene knew instantly he was wrong. She had been there.

Rene walked over to the bar. The owner was standing behind the bar, wiping glasses, getting ready for the nightly crowd. Bob was short help since the fight two nights ago. He had spent the last two days playing handyman, and had repeated his favorite phrase to all who disturbed him while he was fixing his place up "Nope. No comment. It all happened too fast."

Jim and his boys had come around looking for Sara. When they weren't there, the police came by, wanting a full report. There was also the sweaty, pimpled-faced reporter who truly made the whole ordeal bigger than it needed to be.

"Excuse me, sir; have you seen this woman before?" Rene slid a picture of Meryt across the bar. It was a picture of them at the annual charity ball.

Bob looked over the picture, and pushed it back. "Nope."

Rene pushed it back. "Don't lie she's been here. Her blood is all over the front of your bar. I will ask this question one more time. You had better think carefully about your answer."

Bob contemplated long and hard. He was not a stool pigeon. He really liked Meryt, but he was not prepared to die over all of this either.

"Look," Bob said while tossing the dishrag into the mini sink behind the bar, "I don't want any trouble. Everybody keeps asking me questions about this girl. Making her out to be some crazy chick, but truth is, she seems like a real nice lady. What is it that you want from her?"

Rene breathed a sigh of relief finally a lead. "I just want to find her; she is a very close friend of mine. Her name is Meryt Brownstone. Can you please help? Every minute that goes by she gets farther away." Bob felt this man's words were true.

"She started coming around here about a week ago. She would come in around four or five in the afternoon and stay until I closed. She would sit over in that corner. She ordered the fish of the day, chips, and drank Jack Daniels and ginger ale. She wouldn't cause no troubles. She'd speak when spoken to, but mainly she was a watcher. She would watch people come and go. Over the week she started talking to my waitress, Sara. Sara was a pretty girl but always kept the wrong type of company, if you know what I mean. Two nights ago Sara's boyfriend, Jimmy, and his crew were drunk, and he started knocking Sara around. Your friend, Meryt, stepped in to break up the fight. One of Jimmy's boys caught your friend on her cheek. Blood rolled down from her lip. One of his friends came behind the bar for me, but before I knew it, she opened up a can of whoop ass on them. At some point, they all were trying to fight her, but none of them could get a lick in on her," he said with a smile. "When the boys had had enough, or either she had had enough, she told them go to the hospital." Bob stopped for a moment and leaned over the bar. "When the boys left, your friend gave Sara all of her money—it was seven thousand in cash and told Sara to leave town. She looked to me and apologized for the mess, but I didn't care about the mess; I was happy someone was able to help little Sara out."

Now all three men walked outside, into the midday sun.

Rene asked, "Did she say where she was going?"

"Nope."

"Did you ever see her car? Do you know the make and model?"

Bob replied, "Nope, she had no car. She always walked here and walked back to wherever she came from. At night she ran off, down this dark road. I'd sometimes ask if she needed a ride. She said, 'No, I'd rather jog. I got a lot to think about.' Off she was into the night. She took off in that direction. I assumed she was staying at one of the local hotels about two miles up the road."

Rene looked down the road, imaging Meryt jogging. He remembered the night he had seen her cutting across the parking lot running. He looked back to his brother and said, "You go check out the hotels and I'll walk down this road."

Rene turned back to the owner and passed him a card. "Thanks for all your help. If anyone else comes around, call me. Please answer their questions if you value your life." He hesitated. "Perhaps you should leave town for a while." He reached into his pocket and pulled out two thousand dollars and gave it to the owner.

"Wow, my wife will be excited. She's been on me to take her out. Not to mention, I needed to do some repairs on my boat. I can kill two birds with one stone. Thanks."

The owner walked back into the bar.

Rene faced the dusty, dirty road, imaging his Meryt walking up and down this path the last few nights. "What was she doing here?" It was obvious: hiding. Deacon had been right. She could change her name, but she couldn't change her nature. Now the question was, where did she go from here and how did she go? Deep in thought, he realized he was at the end of the long street. He didn't even hear Fritz drive by. The street bottomed out. Rene had to make either a left or right. Right led toward the hotels, the direction Fritz had gone in. Left led to where? Rene turned left and followed the road. The road was a little bigger, but still dusty and dirty.

Rene followed the road for another mile; it led to private homes on the left side of the street. Nothing special, homes on stilts, due to potential floods. To the right, there were shrubs. Some bearing flowers, most of them were bearing a full population of bugs. Could she have rented a home? That would explain why she walked to the bar because she lived so close. Rene studied each home, pondering the idea of ringing each doorbell to see who answered and if he could pick up her scent. Rene continued forward studing the homes and wondering. As he continued his stroll, he noticed a trail on the right side. The trail cut directly through the shrubs.

"What the hell, the homes aren't going anywhere. Let's see what's down here." As he walked closer, he knew. He could smell the water, and he could hear the gentle tide. Within twenty feet, the paths led to a half-wood and half-brick dock. Again, Rene had to make either a left or a right. Left led down to the beach, he calculated about a quarter of a mile. The right led to boats. It looked like slips for boat storage.

As he walked past the boats they got bigger in size. They went from little boats with single outboard engines to larger boats that required the engines to be stored underneath. Rene could only smell the salty water and an occasional dead fish. Rene flipped his phone open to dial Deacon.

Before the second ring Deacon answered. "Well, was it her?"

"Yes. The one witness believes she left town. I have a question. Can she drive a boat, or should I ask, was she ever into boating?"

"Rene, that woman can drive anything that can be driven. And you do know she lived in Florida."

"Thanks for the help." Rene flipped the phone shut.

By this time he started to approach a boathouse supply store. Well, that's what it appeared to be from the outside. It was the only building down on the docks. It had twin glass doors. Painted in black on the outside, it listed gas pricing, boat rental fees, and tour guide times. Rene walked in; he felt the cool breeze of the air-conditioner blowing. He didn't know if it was his mind playing tricks, because he wanted to smell her scent so badly, or if it truly was her scent. He stopped at the cash register counter in the back. Someone had to be here. The store was unlocked and it was still light outside. Rene causally looked over his shoulder up at the different aisles and rang the bell for service.

A potbellied man came from around back and said, "Hold on, I'm coming." He wobbled back and forth, like he had a bad back. He was average height, with a huge gray beard.

"Can I help you?"

"Yes, have you seen this woman?"

The old man took the picture and studied it for a moment. "Yeah, she was here for a week and just left a few days ago. But I assure you; she did not look like this pretty dame in the picture. Don't get me wrong. She is a pretty lady, but she did not carry herself like a dame that would fix up like this."

Rene let out a little growl, and the potbellied man turned around to see if an animal had snuck in. "Did she say where she was going when she left?"

"Naw, and I didn't ask. She seemed nice but not the type with a lot of words. I tried to make small talk, but after twenty minutes, I found myself talking to myself as she was slipping out the door."

"Did you see her boat?"

"Oh, she didn't no have a boat. She had a yacht. It was a beaut. We don't normally get that kind in here. You see, that's why that picture strikes me as funny. Any dame, traveling alone maneuvering that tub in the ocean isn't the type of dame getting all fixed up and smelling nice."

The old man felt a little uncomfortable calling Meryt a dame. He sensed Rene didn't like that word, so he laid the picture down. He always felt a little uncomfortable around rich landlubbers. He preferred oceans and the people who sailed them.

"Did she say anything?"

"Naw. Just small talk and ordered parts. You see, that's what I'm talking about. How does a dame, I mean a woman, like that" he picked up the picture, "know about boat parts?"

Rene took the picture from the old man. It was a nice picture, but it was the only picture he had. It was taken the night of ball, the very same night they had made love for the first time.

"Thanks for all of your help." Rene turned toward the door and took two steps. "Hey, do you know what type of yacht it was?"

"Sure, it was a seventy-five foot Lazzara. Matter of fact, come around back; I got cameras all over the place. I'm sure I've got her on film. I was a little worried about her, so from time to time, I took a little peek. I hope you don't mind. It was for safety reasons only."

Within a few moments, Meryt appeared on the camera's review screen. She was cleaning her yacht. Rene could see the color and style, but he couldn't quite make out the name on the back. There was a tarp or box covering the rear area. The old man was right the yacht was nice.

"Thanks," Rene said, and he left the old man alone still talking about the different types of yachts that had come through.

"Deacon, she's got a yacht. That's her mode of transportation. It's blue and white, a seventy-five foot Lazzara. Can you run a trace? See if any port is expecting her and run a trace on any parts being ordered?"

"Sure, I'll check. Understand that boaters are hard to trace. There is no official way to track them across the oceans, because there are no true boating plans, like for aircraft. Boating is meant to be a hobby or a means for food or getting lost." He took a deep breath. He knew this was his girl, always thinking five steps ahead. "Rene, I'll call you back with any news."

Rene called Fritz to pick him up. He started walking back to the main drag. Rene spotted Fritz and jumped in and immediately started briefing his brother.

"Fritz, she is traveling by boat. Now we have to figure out where she's going to dock."

They were riding up the main street. Rene was wondering about his next step. He needed to get to a computer and google yachts. He needed to know how much fuel could that type of yacht hold? How long could she possibly stay out to sea before returning to land? He was sitting in the passenger seat, staring out of the window but not really looking out of the window.

Suddenly, a ghost or glimpse of a ghost passed by his outter vision. It was Meryt.

"Stop the car! She's still here."

Chapter 60

Rene jumped out of the car before Fritz could bring it to a stop. Like the moving wind at dusk, he was there in the exact spot where he thought he'd seen Meryt. He was confused between his wishes and the reality of the situation. Was it really her standing there just moments ago? He wondered if his mind was still playing tricks because he thought he smelled her scent. Could this really be her scent? He quickly scanned up and down the street. Where did she go? Three steps from his ghost image of Meryt was a door to Dirty D's Bar.

Rene opened the door to the bar and stepped inside. It was dark. From its interior decorations, patrons would never guess it was still daylight outside once they entered and the door closed behind them. It was true. Meryt was in there. Rene spotted her at a table. In one blink of an eye, he was with her at the table.

Meryt jumped at his presence. They both stared in disbelief for a moment. "What are you doing here?" Meryt asked.

Rene replied, "Looking for you."

Meryt stammered as she collected her things, preparing to leave. Clearly it had been a bad idea to come off the yacht. No telling who else had come.

"Are you alone?" she asked.

"No, Fritz is here," Rene said softly. He could barely talk. He thought for the first time that there was something in the world he wanted more than blood. He wanted her. If it wouldn't draw too much attention, he would take her now on this table.

"Look, Rene, I don't know what the hell this is all about, but you are free. You owe me nothing. I don't want to be your maker. We have neither kinship nor any partnership. You are free to live as long as you want and go anywhere you want without me."

Rene touched her arm to motion her to stay seated. He couldn't stop the passion, the craving, or the yearning.

"What are you talking about?" he said aloud. Rene refused to believe that today was the day he would find Meryt. Mainly because he believed in those days for the first two weeks and great disappointment always followed at the stroke of midnight when it did not happen. It turned into another day passing with no signs of Meryt. Deep in his heart he started to consider Fritz's conclusion, that perhaps, the coven had Meryt. But his anger prevented it from existing as a possible truth.

Meryt contemplated long and hard on her word choice, while studying Rene's reaction. Her eyes were hungry for him. She only had her imagination to conjure up pictures of him in the past. Now she and Rene sat two feet apart, and her eyes would not look away. They wanted to behold as much as possible. Her eyes were constantly feeding information to her brain, comparing older images with the present image. Rene didn't seem the same, but one thing was for sure: her heart felt the same. Meryt's heart was quickly turning her over to enemy hands. *One . . . two . . . three . . . breathe.*

"Rene, I really don't have time to pretend anymore or play little girl games. You are killing me. I went to Naples for you. I didn't want you to die. I wanted us back. I wanted the three loving months we had this past spring. I wanted it so badly that I was prepared to die at the mere chance that we could have that life back."

Meryt withdrew her hand from his, as she was spilling her dignity. She no longer wanted to feel Rene's touch. That was a lie. Meryt wanted him to touch her, but she felt foolish wanting someone who did not return her love. Meryt had to turn her head in shame.

"When we left the underground cave, I thought it was our time to be together." She shook her head to stay focused and to hold back the tears. It felt therapeutic to release the words aloud in the air versus the little voice in her head recounting the story to her subconscious.

"When we were on the plane, I looked into your eyes and measured your body language. None of it said the same. You told me, 'We weren't going to have the relationship that I deserve.' I'm not stupid. It became quite evident; I had become another problem for you. It tore my heart out. It felt as if you were leaving me all over again back in the Falls. My heart broke then, so this time I left. I wasn't going to take your pity. I wasn't going to go back to the Falls and pretend to be your best friend. I just needed to move on and get past this," Meryt said with a little disgust in her voice.

Rene could no longer resist. "Meryt, I love you." He had no idea he had caused all of her pain. He reached for her from across the table. They kissed. She fell back in love, back in time, back to her house, on the carpet, in the bedroom, and in her dreams. For a brief moment, Meryt felt his love. She had no insecurities; only love filled her heart.

Rene pulled away. "Meryt, you have to run. It's not safe. They are here looking for you."

"Who's here?" Then Meryt saw a tall vampire in the left corner of the restaurant, by the restrooms, and two more at the bar. "Did you bring them here?"

"No, they must have followed me. Where's Fritz? Maybe they won't risk an open confrontation. Walk close to me; let's get to the car."

They started making their way toward the door. The vampire by the restroom pulled Rene off of Meryt's arm. She was now standing alone in the middle of the floor. "How do I always leave myself wide open when he is around?" Meryt rubbed her inner gum with her tongue and pushed open a cap full of the drug she had at the coven. At the same time, she pulled two knives from her sleeves. On key, the two vampires from the bar were next to her side.

"Ready?" Meryt asked her wannabe captors. Meryt swallowed some of the serum and spit the rest onto the vampire on her left. He fell to his knees, hiding his face in his hands as blood began to pour in between his fingers onto the floor. Meryt *thanked God it was a dark bar*. It was too much blood coming too fast for him to be considered human.

The other vampire took a split second to observe his partner's injuries or maybe it was the scent of the blood. Meryt took the opportunity and cut him beneath his throat. It was a clean cut from front to back. It all seemed in slow motion. She started running towards the door. The door flung open and two more came through. Meryt swapped the one knife for a gun she pulled from her bag. She shot one in the head spattering gray matter all over the door. When the other one snatched Meryt from the behind causing her to drop her gun from the pure force of the vampire's reach. Before he tightened his grasp, Meryt turned with her right hand, which still had the knife and cut him across his face. He fell back, dropping to the floor as blood poured out of his wound.

By now, the bar was filled with vampires. They were coming from all directions. The humans in the bar started to recognize this was not just a bar fight and were fleeing. Meryt heard someone scream, "Vampires!" It had come down to hand-to-hand combat and a feeding frenzy.

Again Meryt headed for the door. The bar had turned into a true hellhole. Blood and screams filled the air. At first she couldn't make it out, but in her peripheral view, she saw Rene was in the fight for his life, in the back by the restrooms. Meryt set forth in his direction. She couldn't leave him like this. No sooner had Meryt changed direction, when three vampires jumped down from out of nowhere. Meryt pulled another gun from her bag and began firing her weapon continuously clearing a path to Rene. She shot two as they landed. More blood spattered about the restaurant. Within her direct line of fire, she saw Rene pinned down on his knees with two vampires on both sides and another standing behind with knife coming down around Rene's neck. They were about to decapitate him.

"No!" she screamed. She didn't have time to breathe. Meryt pulled the trigger and fired three final rounds. Meryt felt her body being lifted and a blow to her hands, knocking the empty weapon free from her reach.

Meryt screamed, *"Rene!"* He didn't move. All four of the bodies lay in a pile.

Meryt was too late.

Chapter 61

When Meryt finally saw light, she was in the coven back in Italy. This time there were no finely dressed vampires in the room. It was Meryt in chains, bound by her hands and feet. She was soiled in dried vampire blood. She had no idea why they did not kill her while she was unconscious. Meryt assumed it would be safe to say that they planned for some other form of torture. What kind of torture would centuries-old vampires have in mind? Meryt guessed it should also be safe to say that nothing she'd learned in the army's POW training was going to hold a candle to what they had in mind. Crap!

Meryt noticed she was in the same room decorated in black and red tapestries. This time there was no gala spirit or even curiosity about who was the human. She knew from her last visit, she was not welcomed to return even though their words said differently. This time there were four vampires dressed all in black. It felt oddly familiar. She had a vampire on each side of her and the two brethren were seated on their thrones. They knew not to touch Meryt because the guards had on thick rubber gloves.

Smenkhkara spoke first. "I see you have a talent for killing vampires. I've never known a human to openly kill so many at one time. Who are you?"

Meryt responded, "You know who I am. I can't imagine you've gone through the trouble of bringing me back to ask me that silly question. You could have googled me and saved yourself the expense and the vampires' lives you've lost. And as far as killing vampires, I do possess a special talent for killing the undesirables." Meryt sensed he wanted to take her life right at that moment. To be honest, she thought it would have been a blessing versus being tortured to death.

"What do you want from me? I'm sure you didn't do all of this to ask me my name because you forgot it. You could have called me on the phone. I would have given it to you."

Smenkhkara stood up and walked toward Meryt. "Who are you really?" He looked closely into her eyes studying the details of her face, as if the answer was written in some dead language on her forehead.

"How do you manage to weasel your way into my plans every time? You killed Lord Atken." For a moment, Smenkhkara was lost in his thoughts trying to figure out how she always got tangled in his plots and suddenly he snapped back. "Well, it makes no difference. You are dead to me."

Atem finally stood up and walked toward Meryt. "Brother, remember you can't touch her."

Smenkhkara answered quickly: "Entomb her." Immediately, Meryt was being dragged backward by her chains onto the floor, out of the room through a matrix of corridors. It took all of her strength to hold her head up to keep it from being beaten by the uneven stone ground. Then Meryt began to wonder why? It would be quicker and less painful to die this way, compared to whatever plan was in store, but that was the coward's way out.

The two guards dragged Meryt for ten to fifteen minutes. They finally came to a halt. It was cool, dark, and damp in the narrow hall. They picked her up and shoved her into a little brick cove. She didn't think anything of it at first, other than thank God she was not being dragged anymore. Then Meryt began to focus and understand the situation; they were bricking her into the wall! Meryt went to stand up and one of the guards hit her in the head with a brick. Lights out.

She awoke in total darkness. As Meryt began to collect her bearings, she remembered the last thing. She was being bricked into a wall. She raced her hands over the walls. It all felt like cold bricks. She tried to stand up to feel higher along the walls, but her chains now popped back in her memory. "Fuck!" The weight of the chains caused her to fall forward, hitting her head on the far wall, which was three feet away. Meryt sat with her eyes open or were they closed? It was so dark it made no difference. She could hear no noise, at least not at first. But as she sat still in the darkness of her prison, she was able to make out a soft gentle breeze crossing her cheeks. Meryt couldn't tell the direction. She tried standing up to feel if it was coming from above. She allowed her fingers to be her Seeing Eye dog and searched along the walls, as far as the chains would permit. Meryt felt cold brick all around the small room. She stooped down to the ground searching along the floor. Within an hour, she touched every square inch of her cell. All information collected from her senses was the obvious. She was entombed in a two by three cave. The top of the cave was beyond her reach, which probably had some type of opening causing the breeze she felt across her face; no water, no food, no light, only darkness. Meryt slowly fell back down to a seated position, thinking what could be her next move, because at this moment she was feeling like checkmate.

Meryt sat in silence, rolling playback tapes from her memory. She played back every moment in the bar. She played back every moment in the coven. Meryt had to have missed a clue or a signal. Her life couldn't end in a cave deep in the cliffs of Naples. This did not feel right. Meryt pressed her head back against the cool brick wall, taking a deep breath, "I've got to figure out the missing link? What is it that I'm missing? All I've got is time, and it's running out."

After Meryt finished playing back her last memories, her fingers began to wonder along the chains connecting her hands and feet. Its entire length was three feet. She also discovered the chains were not fixed to the cave. Meryt thought if she could dig herself free, she could leave the tomb. She started poking her finger along the mortar line, hoping to find a weak spot between the bricks.

Chapter 62

Queen Hatshepsut was perched in the cave window admiring the nighttime desert she had grown to love. She had seen so many sunsets and so many dawns from this very window; she wondered if she could live any other place than here? Her prison had become the home that she cherished. She let the night air blow against her face. In an instant, Hatshepsut was bracing the wall. She had the sensation of falling off a cliff. Anxiety rushed through her body and there was sourness in her stomach. She continued falling and falling, finally resting within Meryt's imprisoned walls. Queen Hatshepsut was there in spirit. She saw Meryt's shallow breathing. She sensed Meryt's aura was dull, not vibrant as before when they first mind-melded in the Nubian Desert. She noticed Meryt's hands were bloody and swollen. Her eyes followed the trail of blood to a small hole in the wall. She realized Meryt was trying to escape.

"Nitocris, you will fight until there is nothing left of you." Queen Hatshepsut took a deep breath and sat down in Meryt's body. The two women were as one in the dream world.

Chapter 63

"My Queen, it was only his body we found. His soldiers were located further back, we assume where the initial battle had taken place. Believe me my Queen, there was nothing left of the soldiers to bring back."

Still looking at Atum in disbelief, Queen Nitocris spoke, "Clean him! Prepare his finest linen, now! I will free any slave and present riches, jewels, and their own slaves to anyone who has information on his last battle."

Queen Nitocris sat next to Atum as the nursemaids cleaned his body, which lay like a statue, never to move, never to speak her name, never to confess his love or receive hers. The Queen's stomach soured from the sweet berries she had eaten earlier. The berries were threatening to come back up.

"Why?" she whispered, with tears rolling down my cheeks. "Atem and Smenkhkara promised me your safe return."

Nitocris sat up recalling their last conversation. Atum promised to discover the truth about this proposed war. She closed her eyes and swallowed the bile inching up. This meant war with the Babylonian's, the filthy, lying cowards.

Queen Nitocris informed her second in command, Pliny, "Prepare my army and let the new pharaoh of Egypt know we launch in two days." Nitocris turned back to the nursemaids. They completed the task of cleaning Atum and dressing him in his finest linens.

"Get out!" she yelled, sending everyone from her chamber. She wanted to be alone to grieve over her lover. Nitocris lay naked next to his body, rubbing her fingers along his chest, expecting to see the simple rise and fall as he breathed. She wanted time to stand still while she lay by his side forever, but time continued to move forward. Nitocris longed to feel his touch. Her heart grew colder with each breath. The pain of missing him grew more intense with each heartbeat. She wished she would have known that the last time they had made love was the final time. "Oh, my love, come back to me. I will never love another until you return." The queen kissed his cold lips and cried next to his body. With each teardrop, a new Queen Nitocris was born, one who desired revenge.

She didn't know how long she lay next to Atum. Queen Nitocris gazed past the blowing linens that covered the windows; the sky shown red. She supposed it was sunset. The queen knew it would remain red from the blood she planned to spill and would continue to spill until she had her revenge.

Chapter 64

The air rumbled like thunder, and clouds billowed around her chariot racing through the battlefield. Queen Nitocris opened her eyes. Time had marched on, but her bitterness did not heal; rather, it grew colder and stronger. She wore the bitterness as armor and the hate for the Babylonians as a shield. She held the bridle in one hand and swung her long sword in the other. The queen stood in the midst of an active battlefield. All around her, soldiers were fighting, pressing forward to victory. The horses, her men, and the slaves were clanging swords against armor and flesh. Screams from intense agony and battle cries echoed all about. The Nubian army laid siege on the city of Edom. They had been fighting all day. The proof surrounded them in blood pouring in its streets in all directions. She smelled of blood, and death was in her eyes, but it only made her stronger.

It was another lesson from her father: "The only thing constant in war is chaos. So embrace it and allow it to make you stronger."

Queen Nitocris's sole focus was winning the war and finding the truth. She ordered her soldiers to gather the dying and wounded enemy for inspections and interrogations. The Babylonians wanted war; she was bringing them a quick, swift death. Before dusk, the Nubians had won the city of Edom.

She ordered the soldiers to take nothing. "Leave it for Smenkhkara and his army." She didn't want her soldiers to be tainted by any of Babylon's trinkets. The one thing she wanted from the Babylonians was the truth behind this war.

Chapter 65

Thunder crashed in the air. Clouds tumbled forward, and loud claps pulsated in her chest followed by a flash of lightning stirred in the air. Queen Nitocris was sitting on her horse, on a new battlefield, searching for a new battle cry to ignite her warriors. The soldiers fought hard for weeks during the campaign. She wanted to reignite their courage. She wanted to call on their killer instincts within them because today they would fight Moab, a stronghold for the Babylonians. Queen Nitocris sat back on her steed as he jumped, his two front hooves waving in the air from excitement. The queen was on her favorite horse, all dressed in black, with her black shield in one hand, the reigns in the other, and her khophesh swords hanging from her waist.

"You all know my father was a great leader and a fearless soldier. He taught me life is precious. Like anything precious, you must fight and you must kill to keep it. Our calling today is as it's always been: we will fight and we will kill for what is ours. We are warriors!"

The soldiers burst into screams.

The Queen spoke even louder to be heard over their cheers. "Today I'm asking you to fight for your Nubian brothers and for your new Egyptian brothers. We must free our precious land from Babylonians' tyranny. We must send a signal to our enemy. They must learn that we will press forward and we will kill again and again! We live to bring our enemy to his knees. Our enemy must be taught fear, so he will never return to our precious homeland again. As warriors, we live to see only victory because a dead man will never see defeat in his enemy's eyes. To victory!"

The soldiers were now warriors prepared to enter the battlefield demanding their victory. Their battle cry was the match and Queen Nitocris was the gas. She felt the flames grow higher as her soldiers stormed by. It was battlefield madness. She wore this madness; it covered her from head to toe. It would never die out, it would only continue to burn higher until the war was done and she found the truth about the war and the men who killed Atum. Yes, victory was close at hand and so was the truth. Queen Nitocris could see Babylon's colored flags on great walls of Moab. Her soldiers' cries would shake the walls down of Babylon, causing their colored flags to tumble down to the bloody ground.

"This war will soon be ours," Queen Nitocris swore.

This fight was the heaviest of all the fights, but her soldiers were no ordinary soldiers. They were born and raised as warriors. The Nubian warriors trained to collect every inch on the battlefield and turn it into feet. By midday, her words rang true. The walls of Moab that held the Babylon's flags fell. The city now lay in mercy to the Nubian warriors.

"Queen! Queen! We are being attacked from the rear," her second in command, Pliny reported as he pulled his chariot alongside Nitocris's horse.

"Who attack us from the rear? Smenkhkara, the new pharaoh, protects our rear."

"It is he who attacks us!"

"Pliny, carry on the attack to the front. I'll take a squad to the rear. I'll find the truth in this matter." Queen Nitocris pulled the reigns of the horse, turning him to the rear and rode with the same fury and speed. There would be more blood today.

Queen Nitocris rode to the rear. After riding for twenty minutes she found the new pharaoh's tent with his elite guard about one hundred yards away attacking her rear soldiers. Nitocris slid her khophesh sword from its cover and rode through the elite guards, killing all who touched the sword. As the queen and her black horse passed by, they left a trail of dead bodies in their wake. Queen Nitocris for the first time saw the truth. The pieces started falling into place as she came in contact with the pharaoh's elite guard. One by one they fell down dead onto the bloody ground from her lethal sword: the union of Nubia and Egypt, the death of the Atum, the death of the pharaoh, the separation of the armies, sending Atem into the sea and her into the mountains. It was Smenkhkara's plan from the beginning to become the pharaoh. Babylon was an excuse, a mere distraction from the main assault: killing the royal family and taking power.

As pieces fell together creating the master plan, Queen Nitocris saw a swarm of black arrows raining down from the sky. She jumped from her falling horse and lifted her shield for protection. Once the rainfall of arrows ceased, Nitocris slowly stood and removed her shield. Her horse was dead and so were her men. The elite guard surrounded the queen.

The guards escorted her to the pharaoh, Smenkhkara. As she entered the tent, she saw her sister Nefertiti beaten and lifeless on the floor. Nitocris held her head down thinking how much blood must be spilled today. She searched the room for Atem. She wondered if he was a part of the master plan. Or maybe he was already dead.

"Queen Nitocris, I'm so happy you could join us. As you see, I've already asked your beautiful sister for her hand in marriage. Sadly, she refused me. The strain of the refusal killed her." Smenkhkara spoke as if there was nothing wrong.

Raw instincts took over. Queen Nitocris tried to break free from the two guards. *One . . . two . . . three . . . breathe.* The queen bit the guard on her left, freeing one hand. She began the attack on the second guard using the first guard as shield. Quickly Nitocris pulled two small throwing knives from her inner thigh belt. She slit the second guard's throat and threw the other at an approaching guard. Five more guards entered the tent and joined in the fight. It wasn't long before Nitocris was wrestled down to the floor. Two remaining guards took turns kicking her in chest and ribs, while two guards tied her hands behind her back.

Once they finished their retribution beating, they sat Nitocris up on her knees. Smenkhkara spoke again. "Join with me. Be my queen. We can rule both Egypt and Nubia together."

One of the guards from the assault yanked Nitocris's head back, as to show respect to the pharaoh. The queen jerked her head away and spat blood at the pharaoh's feet.

"My answer is no. There will be no union."

Why is it when death is near, the weather is never good? Nitocris thought to herself. It was so hot that it gave the fear and anger in her mouth a sweet, raw flavor. She was tickled to feel any emotion. It had been a month since she had felt anything other than anger and revenge over Atum's death. She knew it was the end. It was only fitting her body matched her soul; she'd been dead on the inside for nearly four weeks. Nitocris was nothing more than an empty shell of hatred, the same hatred that had blinded her and allowed her to be used as a vessel to kill with no regard or mercy. Little did the pharaoh know, he was doing Queen Nitocris a favor by putting an end to her physical being. She was only disgusted with herself for not being able to see through the lies to find the truth earlier. Smenkhkara had laid a trap to gain the crown. Queen Nitocris only thoughts were *who will be left to kill him for all of his evil deeds?* If it were possible, if she could will it to be, she would gladly kill Smenkhkara. *He will die by my hand.*

Chapter 66

Queen Hatshepsut returned to her windowsill in the desert after reliving the events leading up to Queen Nitocris's death. She had always wondered how Queen Nitocris felt on that fateful day. Hatshepsut was left behind back in Nubia. She was still in training. Queen Hatshepsut heard the reports from that day, filtering back, stating the queen had shown no fear, but that never totally satisfied Queen Hatshepsut, since she knew there were lies surrounding Nitocris's death. The stories never quite answered the real question of what Queen Nitocris felt in her heart when the truth behind the war, and the one who caused the death of her lover and her sister and destroyed her family's dynasty erasing it from history, became known. What did Queen Nitocris feel when she was able to name the demon, the one who betrayed her, Smenkhkara?

Hatshepsut opened her eyes to find Senunmut holding her on the floor. She smiled, relieving his worried eyes.

"We must travel to the coven. They have her imprisoned in the walls. Her time is short. If she is to defeat Smenkhkara, we must help. The first battle begins now."

Senunmut lifted Hatshepsut up on her feet, his longtime lover and his queen, and said, "She has returned. We will not fail her again."

Chapter 67

Fritz quickly pulled the dead bodies off of Rene. He found his brother at the bottom of the heap.

Fritz saw a cut along Rene's neck. He immediately cut his own arm above his wrist and allowed the blood to drip into Rene's mouth. "Drink," he whispered to his brother.

In a few moments, Rene returned to his normal color, gasping for air. "Where is she?"

"Meryt is gone. I would assume back to the coven. By the time I got here, the battle was over, except for a few feeders I disposed. I only found you and this mess." The brothers looked around the disheveled bar. Dead bodies, both vampire and human, cluttered the room's floor.

Fritz spoke. "We must depart before the authorities come."

Fritz moved first. He appeared by the bar. He started throwing bottles of alcohol around the room; the room shook from the glass and alcohol scattering. Rene copied his brother. Once all the shelves were empty, Rene poured the last bottle over the countertop and lit a match. They escaped through the rear entrance, as the flames grew higher destroying any evidence of dark angels.

Once in the car, the gravity of the situation settled over Rene. He had found Meryt and had lost her again.

"Fuck," he said to himself, gritting down on his jaw.

What happened next surprised even Fritz: Rene smiled. The smile was followed by a little spark of hope. *Fuck* had now become his go-to word. Rene knew in his heart that Meryt would always be a part of him, and therefore, she still lived. If the brethren wanted war, then death they would receive.

"Fritz, let's gather the family. I'm going back to the coven."

CPSIA information can be obtained at www.ICGtesting.com
Printed in the USA
BVOW042031191211

278753BV00003B/16/P